PAMELA HANSFORD JOHNSON was born in London in 1912. She was educated at Clapham County Secondary School and the Société Européenne de Culture, and then took up teaching appointments at a number of universities abroad, including Wesleyan and Yale.

In 1950 she married C. P. Snow.

Her first novel, *This Bed Thy Centre*, was published in 1935, inaugurating a long and varied career as a published author of fiction, essays, and plays. Her books include the 'Dorothy Merlin' trilogy (*The Unspeakable Skipton*, 1959; *Night and Silence, Who is Here*, 1962; and *Cork Street, Next to the Hatter's*, 1965), *The Humbler Creation* (1959), and *The Good Listener* (1975), and her works of criticism on Thomas Wolfe and Ivy Compton-Burnett.

In 1975 she received the CBE.

A. S. BYATT was born in 1936 in Sheffield and graduated from Cambridge. She is the author of four novels, *Shadow of the Sun*, *The Game*, *The Virgin in the Garden*, and *Still Life*, and of a forthcoming book of short stories, *Sugar and other stories*. She has published critical work on Iris Murdoch, Wordsworth and Coleridge, Ford, Willa Cather, and Wallace Stevens. She reviews for the *TLS*, *Encounter*, and other papers, and is a regular broadcaster on BBC radio.

She was Senior Lecturer at University College, London, until 1983, when she became a full-time writer. She is married with three daughters.

ALSO AVAILABLE IN
# TWENTIETH-CENTURY CLASSICS

PAMELA HANSFORD JOHNSON

*An Error of Judgement*

◄◄◄◇►►►

INTRODUCED BY
A. S. BYATT

Oxford   New York
OXFORD UNIVERSITY PRESS
1987

Oxford University Press, Walton Street, Oxford OX2 6DP

Oxford New York Toronto
Delhi Bombay Calcutta Madras Karachi
Petaling Jaya Singapore Hong Kong Tokyo
Nairobi Dar es Salaam Cape Town
Melbourne Auckland

and associated companies in
Beirut Berlin Ibadan Nicosia

Oxford is a trade mark of Oxford University Press

First published by Macmillan & Co. Ltd. 1962
First issued, with an Introduction by A. S. Byatt, as an Oxford
University Press paperback 1987

British Library Cataloguing in Publication Data
Johnson, Pamela Hansford
An error of judgement.—(Twentieth-
century classics)
I. Title   II. Series
823'.912 [F]   PR6019.O3938
ISBN 0–19–282058–3

Library of Congress Cataloging in Publication Data
Johnson, Pamela Hansford, 1912–
An error of judgement.
(Twentieth-century classics)
I. Title   II. Series
PR6019.O3938E7   1987   823'.912   87–1599
ISBN 0–19–282058–3 (pbk.)

Printed in Great Britain by
The Guernsey Press Co. Ltd.
Guernsey, Channel Islands

# INTRODUCTION

## BY A. S. BYATT

Pamela Hansford Johnson might be called a transparent realist. She does not speak with an insistent voice of her own, and there is no element of caricature or distortion in her best work, though there is much intrinsic comedy, both black and brilliant. She believed in realism, and she associated realism with moral truthfulness. 'In the time that remains to me I hope to tell, in my writing, the absolute truth.' she wrote, with alarming ambition, in 1974, conscious that she was defending her kind of realism against a rising public preoccupation with the fabled and the fantastic. 'Of course, since I write novels, they must of necessity be largely fabrications: but I want to tell the psychological truth as stringently and clearly as I can see it.' She shared with her husband, C. P. Snow, an often irritable impatience with experiment in art which 'has all too often meant pure stylistic experiment and no experiment at all in the extension of human understanding.' She believed in clarity and lucidity; she admired Stevenson, that great and recently underrated stylist, for his perfect simplicity; she was prepared to call Trollope a stylist, condoning certain clumsinesses, because of his human truthfulness. She did not condone what she considered the unnecessary obfuscations of the late Henry James. Her own best novels appear to speak, in the tradition she admired, almost for themselves, showing twists and turns of human behaviour with moral precision and persistence. She was also a remarkable craftswoman, arranging her scenes and images with an unassertive wit and economy.

## Introduction

I think the peculiar force of *An Error of Judgement* (and also of those other excellent novels, *The Humbler Creation* and *The Last Resort*) derives from the fact that the truths she wants to tell are not only psychological but in some sense religious. All three titles have resonances from the banal and the conversational to the desperate and ultimate, and their strength lies in the way they weave the one into the other. *An Error of Judgement* is partly a wry social comedy and partly a study in good and evil, creation and destruction, paradise and the pit. Its central character, Setter, is a surgeon who knows that his virtue covers in him a desire to maim and damage, which he characterizes as evil. His name, besides suggesting the setting of bones and setting to rights of what is wrong, makes him a kind of Hound of Heaven, and he is placed comically in this context, elaborating on it himself with his descriptions of psychiatrists as 'dog-faces' whose analysis of motives is useless to remedy the ills that flesh is heir to. (Dog is of course God in reverse which can be taken in all sorts of ways.)

Graham Greene remarked in 1945 that with the death of James the religious sense was lost to the English novel. 'And with the religious sense went the sense of the importance of the human act' he continued, claiming that the characters of Woolf and Forster were only cardboard symbols in a world that was paper-thin. Some such loss of moral authority and moral weight along with the sanctions of religious belief has been diagnosed by Iris Murdoch, whose characters typically disentangle the importance of the human act from a muddled world in which God's absence is a painful void. The power of Hansford Johnson's novels seem to me directly connected to what she called 'the streak of emotional Calvinism in my make-up' and associated with the grim vision that drove Cowper mad. 'The doctrine of the Damned and the Elect is one of the most dreadful ever formulated, but, though I don't believe it, I cannot forget it.' she wrote. It went, in her case, with a sense of pervasive guilt and with bouts of depression, which she has analysed in herself and in many of her characters. It went also with an interest in crime and punishment which was almost too much for her when she voluntarily involved herself in the reporting of the trial of the Moors Murderers, out of which grew her disturbed, disturbing and painful tract, *On Iniquity*. She believed in evil, in the stink of the pit, in Judgement. *On Iniquity* was published in 1967, five years later than *An Error of Judgement*; it blamed the permissive society, the sense that there were no absolute moral sanctions, the giddy sense, demonically mocked in Dostoevski's murderers, that 'all is permitted', for the horrors she had seen. And it is this haunted awareness of horror, of the difficulty of virtue, that gives her characters a reality and an absorbing importance that we don't find in much contemporary realistic depiction of social discomforts or fine emotional distinctions.

'Vengeance is mine saith the Lord: I will repay.' Two of the characters in this novel make errors of judgement, of very different kinds. Jenny misjudges her mother's behaviour and state of health — a 'colloquial' error of judgement, one might say. Setter takes upon himself a judicial function; he presumes to judge delinquent Sammy as a judge might, or even as God, in whom he doesn't believe, but whose watching presence troubles him. Jenny pays with racking guilt and nightly dreams of the pit which are brilliantly imagined and written. Setter's relation to payment is altogether more complex.

If the novel nevertheless strikes us as civilized rather than terrible this is because of the choice of Victor, gently fussy and hypochondriacal as a narrator. He is a curiously fluctuating presence, half innocent, half naturally wise. Malpass, the clergyman, praises him:

Victor thinks he is an ass, it is comforting to him to think so, but he is a

vii

very wise man . . . Also he has pity. He is really sorry for people which most of us are not.

A good realist novel is not only judicious, it is also full of curiosity about the workings of people and things, and Victor is the instrument of the reader's curiosity, mediating for us the physical world of gardens and aeroplane flights, and the curiously comforting mental world of vividly coloured pre-dreams, for instance, a form of experience at which Pamela Hansford Johnson is particularly good. His life may occasion-ally more resemble that of a peripatetic novelist than a personnel officer. (He discusses his narrative problems and choices with us with a pleasant candour — and what is he doing hob-nobbing with Russian poets?) But in some curious way this doesn't detract from his reality. And he mediates judgement, in both senses, for us. For instance:

To me, all hells are better in retrospect if I can make them seem funny. And pretty well any horror can be made amusing in the telling if it is not a physical one. Only the most appalling of human creatures is able to guffaw at flesh tortured by disease or by design: but some of our best men make their lives tolerable by the fantasy that the spiritual torments they have lived through, the cruelty of friends, of parents, or of children, the sickening loss of love, have really been quite funny at the time. Be fond of the man who jests at his scars, if you like: but never believe he is being on the level with you.

This begins with a comfortable social cliché about the saving grace of a sense of humour. But it ends as something quite different; an uncompromising judgement. It is akin in tone to Victor's comment that 'Virtue is fine, but it's not, and never has been, an awakener of affection. About virtue (as about vice too) there is nothing cuddlesome.'

*An Error of Judgement* takes place in an ordinary world, the world Hansford Johnson grew up in, the world quite literally of the man on the Clapham omnibus, travelling to the South London suburbs, dealing with an encroaching mother-in-law, discontent in the workforce, dressing for dinner, household detail of bills, broken fences and begonias. 'London enclosed me like the womb' Victor tells us, 'liver-coloured, restrictive, gentle in its deplorable suction.' But this little world is shot through with intimations of the other world, the world of the Clapham Sect at their most uncompromising, the smell of flesh eternally burning, the fastidious shrinking from eternal pain. The dreams of hell in this novel are real dreams and contain elements of both worlds. The novel opens and closes with a natural miracle and these are uncomfortably and yet hopefully comic, framing the darker things.

# Chapter 1

SUSPECTING myself of a cardiac disease, I went one morning to Harley Street to see Setter, who had been recommended to me by my doctor.

I am not, I think, hypochondriacal, though I am made anxious by pains which appear in places to which no concept of 'symptoms' is normally attached; and when I began to suffer discomfort at night from my right shoulder-blade and the back of my left knee simultaneously, it did occur to me that this might be a precursor of serious trouble, known to, but deliberately concealed by physicians, and in conspiracy kept out of the text-books of popular medicine.

I am forty-two, and my life has been a jerky one, an odd-job life — advertising, the B.B.C., the navy (war-time), political agent, management consultant, and finally, personnel officer to Hancock Motors. It is not that I cannot stick at any one thing. It is simply that I have not yet found a congenial thing to stick to.

The foregoing, I see, re-reading it, makes it clear that I am indulging in irony at my own expense: which means that I *am* hypochondriacal and, though not a failure in life, have not yet had the dizzying success for which I hoped when I came down from Cambridge with a good Second in Modern Languages. I am also physically vain, and if my parting is not quite straight, or if there is so much as a phantom spot on my tie, it irks me as much as though I had a pebble in my shoe. All these things I know. And I can do nothing whatsoever about them.

I have dark hair and eyes, my height is five feet seven and three quarter inches. Thank God I shall never run to fat. I am married and have no children.

Setter sat in a big impersonal room with thin green curtains pulled against the pouring sunshine. I had a flashback to childhood, sitting with Lucy in a tent on a hot day, Lucy green all over with the light, green hair, green face, green frock, and the smell of the grass so hot and intoxicating that one could have fainted dead away. In fact, Lucy did, for she was having her giddy spells at that time, and she never recovered from the last one.

He was a big grey man in a grey suit, and his hands, locked on the blotter like crabs in combat, were enormous. Later on, I found that his hair was blond and grey, and that he was only forty-five. He had a dull voice.

The year before, when I was in Moscow on business, I met at a reception their, as it were, poet-laureate, Alexander Tvardovsky. Setter looked like him. He had the same bulk, the same broad, Slavic face, flat nose, small, Cambridge-blue eyes with a downward pull at the outer corners. He lacked the charm, and the brightness of eye. He asked me the usual questions, gave me the usual examination.

Then he said, 'Well, I can't see anything the matter with you.'

I am not one of those who react with anger when their doctor says this, so perhaps I am not a hypochondriac in the deepest sense. I was filled with peace, and a deep feeling of gratitude to Setter for making me quite well again. I saw myself putting the key in the door of our little dark house, which had taken layers of white paint with the sullenness of brick-built basement-areas treated hopefully in the same fashion. I saw Jenny running towards me, her face alight with hope and fear. I saw her transformed into Maenad joy when she heard my good news, clutching at me, clawing at me, in the force of her delight nearly spilling us on to the linoleum.

He added that I could have a cardiograph done if I chose, but his voice implied that this would be a waste of everybody's time.

'I'll take your word for it,' I said. I began to consider how I could broach the matter of payment, speculating at the same time why, to consultants, who are enriched by their great fees, it is always necessary to broach.

He said, pulling the curtains back a little, so that broad rainbow flashes flushed the bevel of the mirror over the fireplace, 'I'm not a dog-face, thank God, but I must say I'd like to know your reason for connecting up your right shoulderblade and left knee.'

I learned later, for I did not like to ask him at the time, that 'dog-face' was his word for psychologist. And indeed, I did not wonder at the time what he meant, for I was only too eager to explain to him something which seemed to me of importance, both to him as a consultant, and to the medical profession as a whole.

I said eagerly, 'But that is the point. I was worried because my symptoms——'

I saw him smile faintly: it made him look a steadier, a sounder man even than he had looked before.

'— *were* incomprehensible. Now if I had been bleeding from my rectum, I shouldn't have worried nearly so much. I might have felt fatalistic, but I should have known. It is the unknown which disturbs me.'

'What would you have known?'

I smiled in my turn: I was a knowledgeable layman.

'Much more likely to be piles,' said Setter. Suddenly he thrust out one of his huge hands, palm upwards, and indicated a brown blotch, fish-shaped, or like a map of Venice, extending

3

from the ball of his thumb halfway down his wrist. 'If you'd got that, now, you'd worry, wouldn't you?'

I was shocked into silence. It seemed to me so petty, so mean that I should have bothered, on account of a mere, putative heart ailment, a man who was probably doomed.

'Yes, you'd worry all right,' he said, nodding his big head. His eyes closed.

I dared to do it. 'What is it?' I said, in much the same brave rasp as a great, but baffled specialist might use, in exposing evidence of an obscure disease, to another great but baffled specialist.

'Burned my hand on the oven,' said Setter.

He rose. 'My wife's in Italy, the cook's quit. So I cook.' A hungry look came into his face. 'Is your wife a good cook?'

I said she was; magnificent. I spoke very brightly, because he had made a fool of me, and I did not wish him to think I minded.

'I like food. That will be four guineas.'

'Do you mind my cheque?'

'Why should I? Does it bounce?'

We grinned at each other. I sat down again and wrote it out. Extending his hand to me, he rang for the receptionist. 'Have a good weekend.'

I had a horrible feeling that when the front door had closed behind me, he and that girl would laugh together at my expense.

I put my key in the lock. Jenny came walking towards me.

'Darling,' I cried, 'I'm all right! I'm all right!'

'I never thought you were anything else,' she said, replacing my constant image of her by the equally constant reality. 'And what did all that cost us?'

# Chapter 2

THAT was Saturday. In the evening, Malpass came to dinner.

Malpass was an Anglican priest, who had been with me at Cambridge. He was a tiny, tattered-looking, sparrow-like man, with a shock of silky dark hair and a thin, sly, comic, rueful face. Whether he had acquired a cockney accent from the daily rub of his East End parish or had cultivated one deliberately, so as to narrow the distance between himself and his flock, I do not know: but he was a bishop's son, and at the university had spoken standard English varied by a few fancies such as 'crorss' for 'cross' and 'poyt' for 'poet'. He had married Jenny and me, and was fond of us both: Jenny liked him in his presence and was irritated by him in retrospect. Yet for his sake she would dress up with more than her usual care, put on a brighter lipstick than usual, use eyeshadow, wear her highest heels and all her jewellery at once. This was, I think, an infantile reaction to all clergy, whom she suspected of a hidden Cromwellian zeal in spoiling everybody's fun. This zeal, as I always told her, must have been deeply concealed by Malpass, whose manner was worldly in the extreme.

'Hi, me duck!' he said, kissing her. 'Does me good to see you. And for God's sake, I could use a drink!'

Jenny told him in her little-girl way that she rather hated to hear him swear. She was looking more infantile than ever that evening. I wondered whether, like M. Valdemar, she would ever age at all, but liquefy suddenly at the age

5

of eighty. The thought was displeasing and smacked of treachery.

'And *I* hate to hear it!' he retorted energetically, swinging round on his toes. 'It's a hell of a habit! I know, Jenny, I know, I ought not to do it, you horrible prig, you. Now give me some whiskey, I've had a day of it.'

When we were seated in our very white, very dark drawing-room, which looked onto a shed and a fence, I told him I too had had a day of it, but with a happy outcome.

'There was *nothing* the matter with him,' said Jenny, holding my hand, 'there never is, and it cost us four guineas.'

What I felt, I told Malpass, was that Setter had actually performed a miracle. By telling me I was perfectly all right, he had made me so.

'Could be.' He closed his eyes, drank deeply.

'What do you mean, "could be"?' Jenny cried.

'Well, I believe in miracles, you don't. Victor could have had *angina pectoris* at ten-fortyfive, no *angina pectoris* at eleven.'

'But you seriously don't believe he had?' Her eyes were lustrous with indignation, and she held me tighter.

'No. But it could be.'

'Cancer? One minute, not the next?'

'Could be.'

She suggested several other organic diseases. Malpass was quite imperturbable.

'A broken leg?' said Jenny triumphantly.

This made him pause.

'Aha!'

'No "aha",' he said, 'but I have to think. No. Not a broken leg. That's different.'

'Why?'

'I don't know. It is.'

Letting go of my hand, she sat back on her heels and threw her head back so that her pretty red hair dangled on her shoulder-blades. 'Take something else. Suppose war had broken out at eleven and the first H-bomb had fallen. Could a miracle make it *not have been so* at eleven-fifteen?'

'Ah yes,' said Malpass, with a return of confidence. 'That's easy.'

She jumped to her feet. 'Oh, I can't, I really can't! And I must see to food.'

She went out into the kitchen to fetch a risotto which, I knew, would be the disagreeable yellow of a *sanbenito* and reek of garlic. When I had told Setter she was a magnificent cook I was lying, but out of love for her and pride for myself. She could not, or would not, cook simply; every horrible recipe from a country with no good cooks, such as Greece or Spain or North America, found its way into Jenny's *repertoire*. And because in the early days of my love I had told her I liked the stuff I could never bring myself to repudiate it now. On such petty repudiations, love can be wrecked. I loved Jenny with all my heart. Even now, I still do.

She brought the mess triumphantly to table, where it looked even more sinister by candlelight, and gave us all too much.

'Well,' she said, harking back, 'I really cannot, after all that, bring myself to believe in God!"

'More fool you,' said Malpass.

Though Malpass did not despise those who had not the Christian experience, he always felt they could have it if they tried. To him, they were simply like children who would make no effort to learn arithmetic. He was sorry for them: for the lack of a bit of trying, they missed so much.

While Jenny was out in the kitchen washing up, he asked me about her mother. 'I don't see her,' he said, peering round

7

as if to discover the old lady in some unlikely place, crouched behind the sofa, on all fours behind the television set.

I explained that she was spending a few days, reluctantly, in Sussex, with one of her old friends in whom she had completely lost interest. She had, in fact, lost interest in all of them and had centred herself entirely upon Jenny and me.

'Is she any better?'

I said no, and she wouldn't be. Partially crippled by arthritis, her spirits lowered by eight aspirins a day, she seemed to be getting, if anything, worse.

'I shall never understand why you did it,' Malpass said, putting bird-boned fingers through his feathery hair. 'She is an appalling drag on you both. And it isn't as if she had no other children to go to. You had no moral obligation to take her to live with you——'

'We discovered it soon enough when we got married.'

'Seven years of that,' said Malpass.

'—— after I decided that it was no good trying to build happiness on the unhappiness of other people. She would have hated it anywhere but with Jenny.'

'So now the three of you are unhappy.'

'A bit strained,' I said.

He did not look at me, but I felt, with a touch of resentment, his condemnation. Malpass was a believer in happiness. He felt that, through giving Jenny what she desired, I had deprived her of it. He was fond of her, knowing that she did not much like him: this struck me as an attitude rare in Christians, and, come to that, in anybody else. In order to love, most of us have to be loved in return. This was a consideration which had never seemed to worry Malpass in the slightest.

'But it is surprising how used one can get to being strained.'

It made me feel better to say this, more courageous, even gallant. Even to tell Malpass that what can't be cured must be endured, gave me the spirit to find endurance (in Stephanie's absence, at least) more easy. This was one of those moments when one seems to jerk from one plateau of human understanding to another: when life seems like a progression of moral improvement that never stops till life itself stops.

Malpass, now sitting somewhat affectedly on the hearthrug, arms clasped around his knees, said nothing till Jenny came back with coffee.

We started talking about the state of the world, and the conception of face-losing. 'If every one of these repellent statesmen was prepared to lose face, even to the extent of pushing peas twenty miles with his nose, we might get somewhere,' he said. 'I can never escape the feeling that all statesmen are mad. Being mad is a prerequisite for the job. What can "losing face" matter, metaphorically, if the alternative is losing it in a perfectly literal sense?'

'One can't be humble,' Jenny said thoughtfully. 'It is just not in people.'

I was by no means sure that she wasn't right: if she was, it was a tragedy. Our tragedy. I tried to give her support, while at the same time attempting to jolt her into a little more spirit.

'Sticks and stones may break their bones,' I said, with, as I thought, some wit, 'but names hurt them like hell. This is such a peculiarly *silly* world. It would be easier if it were merely wicked.'

At that moment I felt a very odd pain, situated in the upper part of my right arm, a kind of numbness. Since seeing Setter, I had had no more trouble from my knee or shoulder-blade.

'Now what?' said Jenny.

I did not reply directly. Instead, I remarked how different an angle on the world's ultimate fate must be held by people who knew they were going to die before their time. 'Say, disseminated sclerosis.'

Jenny jumped up. 'Oh, God! You're not going to get *that* now?'

Not looking sheepish is quite easy if you use your will, and I used mine. 'What on earth are you talking about?'

'You were rubbing your arm with a significant look on your face.'

I told her the action was meaningless and that she had misread my expression.

For some reason, she flew into a temper. Turning from me she addressed herself to Malpass, face flushed, eyes furious.

'You know, he is such an ass, such an ass! He takes nothing seriously, absolutely nothing. He can't. He's too busy waiting for fresh aches and pains. Can't you make him be more serious? I love him, he knows I do, but he clowns so. He is an ass, Mal, isn't he?'

She was appealing for his support in some private war she had just begun with me. It may have been the four guineas which rankled, but I don't think that was more than a contributory factor. From time to time she raged at me, feeling a deep dissatisfaction in herself which she knew I would never be the man to alleviate. With her, it was like that sudden uneasiness of the whole epidermis, the whole internal organism, which dislocates us suddenly when we are recovering from the effects of a major disappointment or a dose of benzedrine.

Then something surprising happened, which was Malpass's praise, given on so curious a count that he might have been referring to somebody else.

'Oh no, you're not fair. Victor thinks he is an ass, it is comforting to him to think so, but he is a very wise man. And he has far more in sight than anyone I know. Also, he has pity. He is really sorry for people, which most of us are not.'

At this she smiled dubiously, patted his knee, apologised for her bad temper (which was not bad temper, but a plea to God through the intermediary of a priest that he should alter me really radically), and changed the subject.

I sat in a warm glow in which guilt was strongly mixed. I had, I felt, no right to accept this at its face value: yet why shouldn't I? I did feel I had some insight, in any case more than Jenny had, though that wasn't saying much. I was sorry for people, though not in the way Malpass supposed. That is, I could never resist the notion that all maddening persons could be less so if they tried, and all sick ones get up from their beds and walk if they really made an effort. But when they were maddening — in the case of Jenny's mother, being *menacingly brave* — or when they were ill, I was usually driven to try to do something about it. This action on my part was, I know, a compensation for guilt-feelings about not being really compassionate: but it was a kind of being sorry, wasn't it?

He said, 'I want you to try to sort someone out.'

He mentioned a young draughtsman at Hancock's, whose mother was one of his parishioners, a man who was so hating his job that he talked at home about nothing else, and was causing his family the greatest anxiety. It was pure coincidence that Malpass knew him at all, and something of a coincidence that I did, for Hancock's is a big organization. But I had had bad reports of this man, who was coming late day after day, and doing as little work as was consonant with Hancock's retaining him.

'I shall have to see him anyhow,' I said.

# Chapter 3

HIS name was Ulick Purdue. He was a big thin man with sharp downward lines, eyes, nose, mouth, shoulders, and his hands hung down over his knees. He looked at me miserably across my desk and said nobody could work with Lawson. I agreed that it was generally considered difficult, but that Lawson was unique and quite unlikely to be removed from the range of problems common to everybody.

'So that won't do,' I said. 'What else is wrong?'

He replied vaguely that he didn't sleep, he had headaches, his girl had left him, he had an obsessive suspicion that his breath smelled in the morning. 'So that's what makes me late, Mr. Hendrey. I brush my teeth when I get up, then after breakfast, and then, just as I'm leaving the house, I feel I have to do them again, so I rush upstairs and do it, then I miss the bus.'

Also, he added, he was worried about the state of the world. Not that he believed it — that is, he believed no more than anyone else, really, that we were going to be blown up, but all the same he got a sick feeling in his stomach whenever there was any sort of crisis on. If he listened to the news it was awful: if he didn't, he was afraid he might get to the works and find war had been declared, everyone knowing it but him, and then what a fool he'd look! Not that he believed in war coming, not really; only Americans really did. But you never knew, and it gave him acidity. He looked at me with that peculiarly hopeless kind of optimism I had seen so many times on the faces of men like him.

There are men with so little faith in themselves that they will credit anybody with the power to work miracles. For them the world is a place of disobliging fakirs, who could do so much, and won't. You will see them in the tobacconist's, listening to the old lady behind the counter, see them in the pub, hanging with passion on to every one of the barman's golden words. They are filled with hope that somebody, somewhere, will speak the single word to put all things right. If they had not been so, they would have cut their throats years ago.

'And I can't seem to get up much interest in the work, if you get me.' His vocabulary was limited.

I thought of a miracle-worker who, I believed, could do all things. I asked Purdue if he'd got four guineas and explained why.

'Can't I have him on the N.H.S.?' he enquired cagily, but he looked eager.

I said I thought probably not.

'Any port in a storm.'

He rose and went to the door, walking as if he were upheld by invisible wires, his movements were so uncoordinated. He said, 'Setter's a name for a sort of dog, sort of. Irish, Red, and there's one other sort.'

I didn't see him again for a fortnight, but the reports were, even from Lawson, that he seemed much more cheerful and was getting on with his work again. He now brought his toothbrush to the works, doing on the premises what had once been the cause of his shaky time-keeping. He said to me, without looking up from his drawing-board, 'I went.' But that was all.

I did, however, telephone Setter, feeling it was part of my responsibility to our work-people. His voice on the wire appeared to be more inflected, more various, more lively, than it was in actuality: or possibly, while contemplating his heaviness, I had heard a heavier voice than he possessed. I apologised for taking up his time.

'You're not interrupting me,' he said, 'I've nothing much doing today.' I respected and marvelled at a consultant who would cheerfully admit as much.

I told him Purdue seemed much better, and was pulling his weight again.

'Quite a weight to pull,' said Setter. 'Big bones. Must be heavier than I am.'

I asked how he had accomplished the feat. 'Did you tell him you couldn't see anything the matter with him?'

'Well, no, because I could. He's anaemic, and his blood pressure's low. I've sent him back to his own man for treatment. I expect it's working.'

'Did he tell you about his toothbrush?'

'About what?'

So I told him instead.

'That's work for dog-faces,' said Setter, sounding cheerful, as people do when they have washed their hands of some aspect of the human condition. 'Well, let me know if you have any more trouble with him, but you won't.'

I was quite sure I would not. Setter had become for me the final arbiter of everyone's destiny, mine included. Even to hear him on the telephone made me feel a fitter man; as I hung up the receiver, I noticed that the numbness in my arm had disappeared. I was glad I had sent Purdue along, even though I was faintly disappointed that Setter did not propose to make his cures entirely by suggestion.

It was always pleasing to me when I could actually do some good in my job. Most of the time I had an absurd image of myself chuntering wisely away for hours to respectful hearers and not having the smallest effect on any of them. Purdue seemed to have responded to my treatment. Any success, however trivial, took my mind from the problem of Jenny's mother, and how I was going to get Jenny to New York with me for a business trip in the autumn.

For she was, I thought, more rooted in childhood than I had ever been. Ever since her father's tragedy, sixteen years ago, when Stephanie had flown to her for comfort, and later, when we married, for a roof, Jenny had been torn between us. I had told her time and time again that 'forsaking all others' didn't merely mean forsaking all other young men: it meant that I came first. Intellectually, she agreed with this, but she simply could not feel it was so. Sometimes I tried to make her recognise that the pressures Stephanie exerted upon her were monstrous. She simply looked at me in amazement and said, 'She has never asked me for a single thing.'

Stephanie did not have to ask, only to suffer.

Only the unsubtle find it necessary to ask for things they want — that is, if these are things people don't want to give them. The really skilled demanders would choke rather than make a direct request. How does the dog get a piece of cake from the tea-table? Does he ask? No. For one thing, he can't. But even if he had the gift of tongues, he wouldn't. He sits there, patience on a hearthrug, very slightly palpitating. He is not an alarming sight, and nobody imagines that his palpitations are likely to kill him: but he is a disquieting one. Give him his cake, and he will go away. So Stephanie had palpitated. She had merely waited, oppressively, for what she wanted.

The sad thing was, that I had been fond of her. I had felt myself lucky in having such a humorous, understanding, approving mother-in-law. She had been fun: I had never wanted to leave her out of things, had beaten down her perfectly genuine offers to have a tray upstairs when we had parties downstairs. Now I was coming to dislike her because of a change she could not help. Only damned fools say that suffering ennobles. The most noble characters I have ever met have been fit as fleas. They have also got from life precisely what they wanted: worldly success is ennobling, too.

As Stephanie's arthritis grew worse, so she changed in herself, or allowed to come to the surface a bitterness, a jealousy and a greed which had lain dormant. She hated Jenny to be out of her sight. She hated us to go up to bed early. She so much hated us leaving her, even for short holidays, that I always had a last-minute fight with Jenny to make her go at all. And on the return journey we were both ridden by such travel-*angst* that it hardly seemed to us worth while having gone in the first place.

Yet people who knew Stephanie only casually, or who had renewed some youthful contact with her, found her 'fun', and often envied us. She was a small, young-looking woman of sixty-eight, with a schoolgirl's face now drying up under the flakes of pain. Her hair was still almost dark, her figure still neat, though her shoulders were beginning to hunch, and her knees and knuckles had swollen. She had very light, clear blue eyes, like small aquamarines; and when something went her way, she would flash them up with an air of such pleasure that she made me feel beastly with shame down to the pit of my stomach. Surely Jenny and I ought to make any damned sacrifice just to see her look like that?

Surely we ought not, I said to myself, when the fit had passed. Yet the guilt never left me. She made me seem ugly to myself. And indeed, so I was, so long as I could not desire through her eyes, through her kind of suffering.

Now, I could manage to take Jenny to New York on my expense account: and Stephanie could perfectly well go to either of her other daughters. Jenny passionately wanted the trip. She loved to be with me, to see new things with me; but she dreaded the inevitable punishment of her mother's grief. She was terribly torn: and the tearing was worse because she knew where her duty really lay, all right. It lay with me.

If Stephanie had been a good actress, she would have fallen ill every time we wanted to leave her; but apart from her arthritis she was healthy, and our doctor, though no good at understanding my physical make-up, was far too much on my side to condone pretence on Stephanie's part. 'Do you good to have a change yourself,' he would say breezily, when she protested that she was in no state to move elsewhere, even for a week, that she hated putting a burden on Fay or Joanna, who had their children to care for. I wished Jenny and I had the excuse of six children, all under the age of nine.

Coming home rather early one evening, while the New York decision was still in abeyance, I heard them talking together in the kitchen.

'. . . always remember,' Stephanie was saying, in that pious tone of hers which was faintly salted with mischief, 'that your father was a very gallant gentleman.'

Jenny's father had been a mild, cultivated, pathologically dishonest solicitor who, unable to face a fourth term in jail, had jumped out of a fifth floor window in Holborn, on a May morning, during the rush hour.

I heard Jenny's reply, seething with exasperation. She knew Stephanie was acting, knew she dared not admit the knowledge. She particularly hated being jockeyed into this kind of farce. 'Oh, how *can* you!'

'How can I find anything good to say of him, you mean?' (Very stiff, this.)

'Use such awful phrases.'

'Well, he was,' said Stephanie, with umbrage, 'and I don't see the words matter if the heart is right.'

17

'You do see.' A clatter of crockery. Jenny washed, Stephanie dried, sitting on a chair by the sink. 'You know perfectly well how awful it is.'

' "A very gallant gentleman",' Stephanie repeated, knowing it also. 'Must we be too cowardly to use the good old phrases just because they're out of fashion?'

Joining them, I said, 'Ah, talking about me!'

Jenny gave me one of the fierce, defiant kisses with which she tried to imply to her mother that I did come first with her, despite all appearances.

'Of course about you!' Stephanie gave a radiant grin. 'Who else could it have been?' She asked me if I had had a good day, to which I replied, 'Much as usual.'

'Take a pew,' she said, using her occasional obsolete slang, and she patted a chair. 'Now why don't you tell us something interesting about it? Here are we two poor women, bored to death with our own trivial gossip, and longing for a breath of news from the great world.'

'You know,' said Jenny, 'that he is not going to tell us anything.'

She meant — 'tell *you* anything'. In fact, I used to give Jenny every grain of news there was when we were in bed at night. This was one of the very few things I was able to withhold from her mother.

Stephanie gave a long sigh, a quizzical smile. Thunder overhung the kitchen. Then, with one of her lightning changes of mood, she picked up the passing cat, and sitting him upon her knee, made him beat time with his paws. 'Pussy is a gentleman, a Very Gallant Gentleman, he *says* he is a gentleman, a V.G.G.!'

Jenny dissolved into laughter. 'Oh, you are absurd!'

We all improved upon the song for the cat, feeling like a happy family.

18

When the meal was ready, Stephanie limped to the table, the animal still in her arms.

'Put him down, Mother,' Jenny said, 'he will only try to get at the food.'

'No, Puss,' Stephanie replied, not addressing Jenny directly, 'I am not going to let them turn you off my knee, am I? Because when they've gone to the far-flung Amerikeys, you're going to be all I have in the world. You're going to be my little companion.'

I said rather sharply that when we did go, there would be no question of leaving her alone in the house, whether or not the cat could provide her with an adequate social life. 'You'll go to Fay. The children will be at school, anyway.'

She complimented Jenny upon the tinned soup, and asked for some more. Then she sat up straight, wincing as she did so, and beamed upon us like the speaker at a prize-giving. She had, she said, quite made up her mind. Jenny would, of course, accompany me, it was right that she should see something of the world, but she herself would stay put. 'I may be an old crock, but I am quite capable of doing all the necessary things for myself. I expect it will be good for me. Limber me up. Who knows, when you come back you may find me hopping about the house like a two-year-old!'

It was a direct declaration of war.

I met it directly. Cutting across Jenny, who was bursting out — 'Oh, you *know* you can't!' — I said: 'You'll have to go to Fay's. Because we're flying on September 1st.'

# Chapter 4

ON my last evening in New York I ran into Setter, of all people, again.

I had gone to a party given by Ted Allen, an old friend of mine who lived on the third floor of a walk-up in the Village. He was a Rolls-Royce agent with intellectual interests, so his party was a boozy bohemian one, crammed with persons who were all very proud of who they were, though as I didn't know who they were even when I caught their names, they did not make me happy. It was a very hot night, and the air conditioning was on. I had been flirting with a witch-like girl who seemed to me perfectly hideous, and wishing I could go home. The conversation generally was extremely depressing. I had made some small success earlier by talking with enthusiasm about my Moscow trip, at the mention of which they all blanched but were wildly curious. 'What we notice about you,' one of them said, 'is that when you talk about Russia you don't *alter your tone of voice.*'

I could not, however, catch the general attention for long, and my girl was eager to get back to discussion of her psychological problems and mine, preferably hers. She talked about 'seeing my analyst' as an English woman might say, 'seeing my solicitor', and when I asked her why she went to one in the first place, looked at me with a smile as if I were the beloved fool.

The air-conditioning apparatus broke down. The windows were opened again, and the wet, dark, hot night clambered in over the sill, all over Ted's pot plants and all over me, so that I felt myself struggling as in the grip of a succubus, the sweat springing out all over my head and face. Excusing myself, I went out to find the lavatory, but being in a muddled state, instead of walking down, began to walk up.

I met with an obstacle.

Sitting half way up the flight, one arm round the banisters, his head on his breast, was Setter, in tears.

For a moment I could not believe it. The stairway light was dim, I could have made a mistake. I looked again. It was Setter, all right.

I did not know what to do. I couldn't just step over him and go on. He had seen me, so I couldn't retreat. I just stood there.

He recognised me, but did not stop crying. I had never seen a man cry like that, so organically, as if crying were like breathing. He nodded to me, said, 'God Almighty, you,' and cried on.

So I sat down on the step beside him and waited for something to happen.

Above us the house was silent. From below rose the castanet noise of Ted's party. A girl who must have lived at the top came up the stairs, looked at us with fleeting curiosity, stepped over us like a well-trained palfrey, and went on.

He said at last, in a hoarse, mumbling voice, 'What are you doing here?'

'I know the chap downstairs.'

'Ted Allen?'

'Yes.'

'So do I.' He took out a large stiff handkerchief and very thoroughly wiped his face, like an actor removing make-up. For a little while he stared in front of him, occasionally moving his mouth and throat as if trying to speak but unable to manage it.

It struck me that he was perfectly sober. He did not smell of drink, he sat with his normal steadiness, not the contrived and cautious steadiness of the drunk. I began to wonder whether anything more would ever happen to either of us, ever again.

Then, suddenly, he leaned over on to the banisters again and put his face in his hands. The movement had a childlike spontaneity, touching and maddening at the same time.

I said, 'Can I help at all?' It sounded utterly idiotic.

He could not answer at once. I made a tactful gesture as if to rise and go, but he put a hand out and kept me there.

He managed to say, 'How would you like it if you.' There was a full stop.

'If I?'

'If you. My wife — you don't know her — she just writes like that.'

'She's gone off?' I said, thinking this the most likely cause for grief.

'No. How would you answer *if*.' Tears threatened to overwhelm him again, and again he polished himself with the handkerchief.

'Well, what did she say?'

'Oh, she'll be back.'

'Then——?'

'How, if your wife just told you she didn't give a damn any more. How.'

'How would I like it?' I said briskly, helping him by a question mark. 'I wouldn't. I'd want to strangle her.'

'Don't be a damn fool. I love her. And I've got to live with her.'

He was speaking more easily now.

I was getting confused. I asked if he didn't want to live with her.

'Yes,' he said, 'but not like that.' He rose to his feet with such violence, such an effort of will, that it was as if a water spout had sprung up to the ceiling.

22

'Then why does she want to live with you?' I asked feeling silly.

'All right, all right,' he said, 'some other time. Got to get to that bloody party now. Where's the lavatory?'

We found it together. I waited till he was through. We went into the party, Setter ahead of me, bland, smiling, at ease. If I had not known myself the last man to have hallucinations, I should have found it impossible to believe in those past ten minutes on the stairs.

'Well, Ted, you old horse-thief,' he said, 'which is, I believe, the way Americans greet one another.'

Ted told him that was the exception rather than the rule, introduced him all round, and my girl took him over. I found myself in another group. Now and then I looked surreptitiously around to see how Setter was doing: he was sitting back as restfully as in his consulting-room, drinking whiskey in little sips.

I asked Ted, when I got the opportunity, how he came to know him.

'His wife's a Boston girl, used to be in college with Sue.' (Ted's former wife.) 'How did you?'

I explained.

'They say he's good. If he ever gets to treat the Queen, they'll make him Swilliam, one of these days.'

This was put in to exhibit, for my benefit, Ted's pleasure in knowing the best English usage. His friends might say '*Sir* William' when the time came: he would say Swilliam.

'What's she like?'

'Who? Emily? Big blonde, more British than the British. She never comes over here now. Sue couldn't stand her at any price.'

Setter was spooning up red caviare in cream cheese.

The girl was looking anxious, her forehead cross-hatched, her too large eyes reproachful. I heard her say, 'I don't get it,'

23

heard him reply, 'Because they look like noble dogs and their ears hang down.'

Ted Allen switched his attention, and his group's. 'Who do?'

'Psychologists,' said Setter, dully, but with conviction.

'But doctor,' the girl squealed, 'how can you, of all people——'

'Oh, I can.'

'— Now, of all the sciences——'

'Not a science,' said Setter firmly, 'not yet. If ever.'

'Greatest influence on twentieth century literature——' put in a young man with a beard.

'Nothing any dog-face could have told Balzac that he didn't know already.'

I was surprised, unfairly so, to know that Setter went in for serious reading.

Then he smiled at disconcerted faces and said, 'Don't mind me. Give me another drink and ask me about your ulcers. I'm sounder on those.' He shook his head at the bearded man who had commented on the psychosomatic element. 'I don't care how they got there, you know. I'm only interested in making them go away.'

And he did, in fact, encourage them to seek free medical advice, offering it as his party turn, as if he had been a conjurer or a fortune-teller. He was a great success. He looked braced and cheerful.

Just as the party was breaking up, he came across to me. 'When are you going home?' He meant England.

I told him I was flying back tomorrow.

'Comet? So am I. See you then.'

I slept badly that night. I was a little drunk, overexcited by the scene with Setter, and missing Jenny, who was not, of course, with me.

That was a war I had lost.

# Chapter 5

WE left Idlewild a little after nine. I hate flying; when people ask me why, I tell them I am either scared or bored, nothing between. This is not the truth. I am scared all the time, too much so to be bored. Yet if I have to fly, I would rather do it the quickest way and by night.

The plane was not full, the seat next to me unoccupied. Setter came and sat in it, and we had dinner and drank a great deal.

'That's what I like,' he said, 'looking down and seeing the stars underneath as well as on top. It's like a goldfish bowl.'

He said nothing about himself then, but encouraged me to talk about Jenny, which I did with a freedom of confidence one can offer only to comparative strangers.

'But why didn't you make her come?'

I told him, I could have done it, if her mother had not gone down with influenza the day before. 'I'd believe she did it on purpose, except that she obviously caught it from our charwoman.'

'I don't suppose she did do it on purpose. One of the other daughters could have nursed her, though.'

I said I had tried that: against Jenny's wishes, pleading over the telephone with Fay first, then with Joanna, my wife making tearful faces and hissing at me all the time. 'And they both had water-tight excuses, the bitches. I couldn't fault them.'

'Oh well,' he said tiredly, 'I expect it will go on like that. These things do.'

I told him he was not encouraging. He said no, he wasn't. He had seen too much of it.

The stewardess came to tuck us uncomfortably down, and switch off most of the lights.

I could not sleep, and did not much want to; the only pleasure I had ever got out of a flight was watching the dawn come up. First the sky trembled all over, turning from indigo to a deep peacock blue, fragile and luminous. The stars faded: still the sky throbbed and trembled. Then a ring of crimson light appeared all around us, glowing like red hot iron, carving the globe of sky into two hemispheres. From points along this ring, sparks lit up, gradually expanding into searchlight beams flushed from crimson to flamingo, each one combining with the other, fanning open, until all around was spangled and sparkling rose, no longer trembling but grand and steady.

'Fine, isn't it?' said Setter, whom I had taken to be dead asleep.

'You awake?'

'Of course, after all that coffee. And anyway, I hate it when the girl wakes me up and makes me have my breakfast.'

We gave up any pretence of repose, rolled over on to our backs and let the blankets slide. Sleepers all around us lay like Henry Moore's bomb-shelterers, amorphous, helpless, sad. A few reading lights were on: for someone, the stewardess was hushedly pouring Scotch.

'I regret the fine performance on the stairs,' said Setter.

'You made a good recovery.'

'Oh yes. I realised I was only getting my deserts. It was all perfectly fair.'

I wanted to know more, but couldn't ask him. Anyway, I knew that he would tell me. He wanted to talk, and it would be easy. Neither of us had anything to do with the earth below or the people upon it, only, for the moment, with each other.

26

## An Error of Judgement

He said in a steady mumble that his wife had not cared about him for years. She took platonic lovers, she went for soulful trips with them, always under the chaperonage of women friends who felt humanitarian when they acted as panders. She slept only with him and appeared to enjoy it at the time — 'but by herself. She has always enjoyed it all by herself. I know, all right. One does.' He had even hoped, once or twice, that she would leave him, and put him out of his agony; but that wasn't at all her idea. 'She thinks I may get a K. in the long run,' he said, staring without a blink at the racks overhead, 'and she'd stay on for that. She says so. She is very honest. She says she'd rather live with me than anyone else, but sees no point in pretending we're in love with each other. You see, she is trying to hypnotise me into believing the failure is mutual.'

'Any children?' I asked.

'One, poor bastard. At Winchester. Her idea. He's fifteen, he dislikes us both.'

Then I said, 'Why do you think you're getting your deserts? What have you done?'

'Oh, nothing much,' said Setter, 'but it is what I could do. I'd as soon be punished in this life as elsewhere.'

'What could you do?'

I was beginning to feel like the straight man, the feed, Mr. Interlocutor.

He turned his head very slowly towards me, and his small blue eyes widened out and out, as if they would split at the corners and turn into big ones. 'Do you look into yourself much?'

'Quite a bit.'

'And like what you see there?'

I considered this. 'I come to terms with it.'

It seems to me that although no decent person does like himself much, or rather, admire himself much, most of us manage to achieve quite good relations with the man within.

27

After all, I have a good many friends of whom I am fond, whose admirable qualities seem to me practically non-existent. We do not love for virtue's sake. Virtue is fine, but it is not, and has never been, an awakener of affection. About virtue (as about vice, too) there is nothing cuddlesome.

'Everything that happens to me, everything bad that happens,' said Setter, 'helps somewhat. I am paying off the things I could be and won't, or could do and don't.'

I thought that was that. He turned away again and closed his eyes.

(From three rows behind — 'Scotch on the rocks, please.'

'Now, Mr. Newbiggin, it's almost time for breakfast! Are you quite sure you——?'

'Scotch, I said.')

It was growing light inside the plane, pearly and clear, the last rose fading. Below me now was a great bank of clouds looking like detergents, domesticated, May-morningish, six-pence-in-her-shoeish.

'When I chose to become a doctor, it was because I was too fond of pain. I had to discipline myself not to give it. A good many of us are like that, we choose medicine because we can stop pain and enjoy giving it at the same time.'

'But you,' I said, 'everyone knows——'

'Only I know,' said Setter.

Then up came the sun, hitting us across the eyes, and the breakfast trays came rattling along, and it was all over.

The customs took a long time, and I lost him there, H. being too far from S. I was stupefied with tiredness, longing only to get my necessary greetings over at home and slump straight into bed. I tried to puzzle Setter out, but it was too much of an effort. My final thought, as I lumped myself into the firm's car and settled to a doze, was that I didn't think I'd throw any more Purdues his way. To be quite honest, I thought he was just a little dotty; which disappointed me. You think you've found a place to stand in this life, or rather, a rock to which to cling, and it goes sliding away under you as though some fool has pulled the rug away. A mad world, my masters, I said to myself in a silly sort of mumble. Nothing but mad doctors, mad politicians, mad income-tax inspectors, mad grocers, mad personnel officers. Mad, mad, *wahn*, *wahn*!

'What's that, sir?' said my driver.

I said, 'A bit on the nippy side today.'

# Chapter 6

MY mind was bursting with the struggle not to be angry with Jenny. I smiled and smiled, and tried not to be a villain. It was always like this when we had been parted, not at my wish. None of it was her fault, or her mother's (apparently), or Fay's or Joanna's, with their irrefutable excuses. Nobody was bad, everybody was good. But I could not help formulating denunciations in my mind. *You could have let them all rot! What would it have mattered if your mother was sneezing her head off and the girls had their plans ruined? Who the bloody hell do you belong to, them or me?*

'What's the matter, don't you like your egg?' said Jenny.

I gave her another smile, of such sweetness that I almost got stuck like it. 'It's a beautiful egg.'

'I only wondered.'

Fortunately, Stephanie did not share our breakfasts.

It was one of those clear, sharp autumn days that look like spring. Saturday morning. Jenny was wearing a bright green housecoat which she had bought to win me back to her. She would not realise that I could never go away.

'Good God,' she said, 'there's an elephant.'

'Where?'

'Just behind you. Look out of the window.'

Not only did I refuse to be caught by this tomfoolery, but it destroyed my good resolutions. 'Oh, shut up,' I said. 'I don't feel like it!'

She stared. 'Now what? And there *is* an elephant, I tell you!'

'You know damned well you ought to have come, whatever the damned cost!'

She was tugging at me, trying to turn me in my chair. She could think of only one thing at a time. 'Victor, I tell you there *is* an——'

And so there was, receding now along our suburban square, its small and touching tail swaying on the patient enormity of its rump. The animal appeared to have streamers, or placards, or something of the kind hanging down over its sides. I suppose it was advertising a circus.

'There you are,' said Jenny triumphantly. 'I told you so!'

'I don't care if the place is crawling with elephants! What do you suppose they mean to me? All I care about is that you let her get away with it again, you left me lonely as hell and sick to the guts in New York. That damned plane might have crashed with me on it, you didn't care, and all you can talk about is elephants!'

If I had not been a man, I would have cried; what I had said was a cue for luxurious, uninterruptable weeping.

'Really,' she said, 'I think you must be quite mad.' She sat down most placidly on my lap, and gave me a succession of little popping kisses. 'Yes, Victor, you are off your head.' (That was what I thought.) 'Oh, how nice it is to have you home again!'

Stephanie came in. Jenny jumped up as if she had been caught in adultery. Furious, I pulled her back again and stared defiantly at my mother-in-law.

'That,' said Stephanie, 'is what I call a nice thing to see. It warms the cockles of my heart, which need warming this morning because my tea was luke-warm. Darling, you *must* make it with boiling water.' She took a cup from our pot, twinkled at us and retreated again upstairs.

When she had gone, Jenny withdrew from me, sat down again at the table and put her chin sombrely in her cupped hands. She did not speak.

I demanded, what had I done now?

Silence.

'Do you mean to tell me you care if your mother sees us ——?'

She shook her head.

'And you know perfectly well you ought to have come with me.'

She shook her head again.

'For pity's sake, make yourself clear! Do you mean you don't know it perfectly well, or that you think you ought not to have come? Speak, can't you?'

She dissolved into tears, lucky Jenny, who could do so. 'It was the elephant,' she said. 'You wouldn't believe me.'

I told her this was the hell of a homecoming, that our weekend was ruined already, that everything was spoiled for me, that she was a destroyer of my pleasure, that she was *unfair*.

'Unfair to Victor,' said Jenny, brightening faintly. 'You should picket the house.'

Which was the end of that quarrel. My total defeat.

It is quite easy to write about this kind of upset in farcical terms: at least, it is for me. But the fact is that these upsets were becoming dangerously frequent. Most ominously, our quarrels were now tending to end not with a grand upsurge and a deep, gorgeous, visceral reconciliation, but with a mutual fatigued impulse to let them drop. There is no point in married people quarrelling if they don't give themselves a prize afterwards; once quarrels cease to end in bed they get a bad smell to them. They are simply little steps down to the Avernus of married tedium.

To me, all hells are better in retrospect if I can make them seem funny. And pretty well any horror can be made amusing

in the telling if it is not a physical one. Only the most appalling
of human creatures is able to guffaw at flesh tortured by disease
or by design: but some of the best of men make their lives
tolerable by the fantasy that the spiritual torments they have
lived through, the cruelty of friends, of parents, or of children,
the sickening loss of love, had really been quite funny at the
time. Be fond of the man who jests at his scars, if you like: but
never believe he is being on the level with you.

I was afraid for my life with Jenny, so I had to laugh at it.
But I also laughed because I was too much of a coward to set
things right. I ought to have gone to her two bloody sisters,
and . . . And. Done what? What good would it have done?
But all the same, I should have tried.

I was shaving in the bathroom, after this trying breakfast
interlude, when the telephone rang. Jenny called up, 'It's for
you.'

'Who is it?'

'I didn't ask.'

She had never learned to ask, despite my efforts to teach her.
She let me in for some awful people.

I came downstairs.

A light, blonde voice, edged and assured, replied to me.
'This is Emily Setter. You know my husband. We were
wondering if you and your wife would care to dine with us on
Tuesday, if you're free. I should just love it.'

How, I thought, could she know she'd just love it? But it
was what people said.

I pretended I had to look at my engagement book. In the
meantime, I whispered to Jenny.

She sparkled up, as always, at the idea of any new develop-
ment in our social lives. She loved a really watertight excuse for
getting out of the house with me.

'Black tie?' said Mrs. Setter. 'Seven-thirty for eight?'

I accepted. When I told Jenny, she hugged me, and said she would have to have a new dress. 'But it is odd,' she added, 'especially as she seems to be so awful, and so unkind to him. And why on earth should she want to know you?'

Anyone, I said, would want to know me. That presented no problem.

'All the same, it is odd. It sounds like a party, doesn't it?' Now she looked despondent. 'I expect some other couple let them down at the last minute.'

Yet when we arrived, we found we were the only guests. Setter, bulging out of his dinner jacket like a teddy-bear stuffed into the shrunken vest of a doll two sizes smaller, apologised for his wife. She would be down soon. She really wouldn't be long. What would we have to drink?

Jenny, who had expected some vast dinner of candlelight, white shirt fronts, glitter, tiaras, and a noise like the parrot-house at the Zoo, looked down at herself and twitched nervously at her skirt. I knew what the matter was. Suddenly, she had felt over-dressed.

She could not have done so when Emily Setter appeared upon the scene.

Emily was a very tall woman; she must have stood five foot eleven in her stockinged feet, and in high heels she could give Setter an inch. She had a bland, pale, smiling face, dimpled at the corners of the mouth, wide blue eyes set so far apart that the effect was vaguely uncomfortable, very light hair, biscuit-coloured, swept into an elegant kind of bun. She was the kind of woman whose nationality would never be apparent in any Anglo-Saxon country — she could have been English, Dutch, German, Scandinavian. Because she was big and moved rapidly, she brought a sort of wind with her, a refreshing disturbance of the room's flowery, elegant softness. With Emily's coming, windows shot open. She wore a blue dress with silver threads in it and a whole kit of sapphires — earrings, necklace, brooch, ring, the lot.

She paused as if in surprise before Jenny. 'Why, you're so little!' To Setter, 'Isn't she *darling*?' I only heard her being American again once, during all the time I knew her.

Then she welcomed us both with great cosy handclasps, telling us how wonderful we were to come and take pity on two lonely people. 'Don't sit on that one,' she said to Jenny, 'it's all over cats' hairs. Anyway, it's as hard as iron.'

Setter sat among the cats' hairs instead.

Despite what he had said of her, I could not help responding to Emily. Her warmth might have been bogus, but at least it threw out heat. She had the clever hostess's trick of seeming to sit as she would among old friends, confidentially, not gracefully, her legs tucked under her. At any moment, one felt, she would remember to take off an imaginary apron and toss it behind the coal-scuttle.

'Bill so much enjoyed coming back with you on the plane,' she said to me, 'that I was dying to meet you. I bet you were both stinking.'

Jenny looked a bit huffy. Even in jest, this was a painful idea to her. Not that she minded me getting drunk on occasion, so long as she was there. But when she deserted me, when she left me on my own, she became a dog-in-the-manger. She could not bear to think I might be enjoying myself.

Setter smiled. 'Rolling, of course,' he said. 'Victor —' he had not used my first name before — 'had to be put in irons in the fuselage.'

'*Were* you drunk?' Jenny burst out uncontrollably.

'No, no,' said Setter, 'we just talked. There was only one chap who drank all night.'

'We ought to be drinking some more now, anyway,' said Emily. She uncoiled, and served us. '*I've* been in Italy.'

35

We said, Oh, had she? At conversational openings she was excellent.

'It was sinfully cold. A friend who was with me was so frozen one night that he sat out in the Piazza San Marco in an eiderdown.' She looked at Setter under her lashes. 'A mad Englishman. That's what they all thought. They are fantastically considerate of the mad, so no one commented.'

'If I know Bernard,' said Setter, 'that must have disappointed him.'

She patted Jenny's hand. 'Have you ever noticed, have you ever happened to observe, that all men are cats?'

Jenny, who was simple enough to regard this comment as original, eagerly agreed, and the conversation became silly until dinner-time.

It was a splendid dinner, served by a sad, pasty, pedagogic looking houseman called Ferenc. I noticed that Emily ate enormously, with an air of schoolgirl enjoyment. Stuffing herself, one might have said. Setter ate moderately. Jenny, allured by dainties that didn't often come our way, ate till she began to look both mournful and scared, which meant that she felt sick. But after a while her colour came back.

The talk was general: politics, the theatre, new painters, new books. Emily was knowledgeable about the painters and the theatre, but never seemed to read at all, or to consider politics her business. Setter knew nothing about the theatre, and apparently never went; nothing about painters: but read a great deal. He liked music, too. Politically, he seemed to be a fair way to the left; anyhow, sufficiently so to make one feel at home. He would have talked longer on the subject, I think, if he had not been checked by Emily's air of affectionate but stop-watch patience, as of a mother who has drawn the bath ten minutes ago and is waiting for her snail-like infant to put his toys away.

She said, at last, 'We won't separate the sexes tonight. I adore port, and I shall have it here. Besides, they must have unloaded their pitiful store of filthy stories on to each other on the way over.'

Setter began to talk to Jenny about her mother. I had told him about her, he said. He was sorry: it was a wretched complaint. There was nothing much one could do.

Jenny said dolefully, 'And it makes them so trying. I love my mother, but she used to be such fun and now she often hates me.'

'Of course she doesn't!' Emily bounced in her chair. 'I bet she's jolly proud of you and boasts of you to all the world.'

'Yes, of course, when she sees the world. But she's boasting about me as I used to be, and not about me now.'

Setter, who had, I think, been regarding Jenny as attractive but quite commonplace, looked interested. 'Do you think that?'

'If she does think so, she must be wrong,' Emily said decisively, cracking a walnut and skilfully extracting it whole. 'Bless you, you're so pretty!'

This made Jenny look with a nervous smile in the other direction, as if rejecting a Sapphic advance.

Later, when we were having a final drink before our departure (which Emily only permitted with reluctance) Setter said, 'Would you like to send your mother along to me? It's not my field, but I might think of something. One never knows. Fix it with her own doc.'

Jenny hesitated.

'No money passes,' he added, 'because I don't expect to be useful to her. It's simply that the thing interests me.'

'Oh, but we couldn't——'

'For my benefit,' said Setter. 'And it might take her out of herself, to talk about herself. I don't imagine she's allowed to much, at home.' Jenny began to look indignant. He said

37

quickly, 'I mean, she has said it all to you two too often. She could make a fresh start with me.'

'Dear old William!' Emily took his hand and shook it lovingly up and down.

'Not dear. Cheap old William. Trying to cadge my friends' mothers for guinea pigs.'

On our way home in the taxi Jenny burst out, 'He cannot *possibly* be interested in her arthritis! He's a big man, everyone knows about him. There's no sense in it!'

I said I thought he was trying to be good.

'Well, it will give us a rest, anyhow.'

She brooded for a little on Setter and his motives, then forgot about him. In the light from a passing car she smoothed her dress down, looked pleased with it. She came close to me, as she always did in taxis, putting her arm through mine, kissing my cheek. I told her she had looked nice that evening, never nicer. She smiled with satisfaction. She said, 'Did you like Emily? I think she's false. Nice, but that, too.'

I said, Yes, I liked her.

# Chapter 7

'YOU must thank your friend,' said Stephanie, with her deadly gentleness, 'but I will not see another doctor. I haven't your faith in them, Victor. And besides, I am not well enough.' She smiled, and set her feet firmly together side by side.

Jenny flushed up, and said she must. To refuse would be to reject a kindness. Besides, she owed it to us to try to help herself. It wouldn't cost anything, either.

'Not charity, I think.' Stephanie's smile widened. 'I *don't* think so. With all my faults, I haven't come to that, yet. And if I am a burden on you and Victor, at least I try not to be. You must ring Mr. Setter, and tell him very nicely that I am afraid I should only waste his time.'

She moved, and winced. It hurt her to move: she was nagged by pain morning, noon and night. But she always winced with her face turned towards us. She smiled again. 'No, I haven't come down to the charity of strangers yet.'

'Mother,' Jenny said thickly, 'there are times when I could choke you.'

'I don't doubt it, dear. You make that quite plain. Please ring your friend.'

Jenny wouldn't, so I had to. Setter didn't seem surprised. 'Well,' he said, 'make it social, then. Tell your mother I should be very pleased if she would have lunch with me on Friday. I'll bring her back myself.'

When the substance of this was conveyed to Stephanie (my hand over the mouthpiece) she was startled, as well she might have been: but she rallied. 'Certainly not,' she said. I accepted for her and hung up.

'What's this for?' she demanded. 'To get me out of the house? I hate meeting strangers! I don't want to see this man!' She added that he must be pretty poor at his job if he had so much time to waste on jaunts.

It was tragic, when you came to think of it, a man like that being forced to tout for patients. What did we suppose had happened? Was his reputation bad? It must be, or he would never have the time to pester people to come to him, which was obviously what he was trying to do. He might be a doctor of a certain *type* — she had heard of doctors whose foot had slipped, who had a bad name throughout the profession. She was certainly not going to lay herself open to criticism. She wasn't so old that she couldn't smell danger. She advised us to think about our new *friend* very carefully, before we let the acquaintance go further.

In the end she worked herself up into such a state of distress, trembling and tearful, that I had to promise her I would cancel the appointment when Friday came, if she still didn't wish to go. It was true that she clung to us now as if the rest of the world were in league to kill her. It was an agony for her to meet new people. Jenny had told me how, after her husband's ignominious death, she had put a brave face on it, had gone about boldly, smartened herself, accepted all invitations, held her head high. She had done so for three or four years. Then, with the onset of arthritis, she had begun to change, as if suddenly realising the depths of her humiliation. Even when she went for short walks, little shopping expeditions, she would come bolting in the front gate again with a harried, high-strung look, like a fox to its earth. Here she was safe. I believe she would even have kept the blinds down if she could. She never sat near windows, never cared to look out.

Yet she had once been a lively and amusing woman, much loving. She had lost her love for her husband even before things began to go wrong with him, but she had been devoted to her daughters. These were her jewels, all right. In the beginning she had even been prepared to think of me as a jewel, since I had married one of them; but that was years ago. Now, a jewel was about the last thing I was.

On Friday morning, I found her dressed in her best, miserable, her face set: all this at 7.30 a.m. Jenny, filled with compunction, said that of course we would put it off.

'I don't think so,' said Stephanie. 'These things are cooked up behind my back and I have to go through with them. Jenny will take me in a taxi.'

I was about to continue the absurd argument — that she would like Setter very much, that she always did have a good time once she could bring herself to the point of going out, etc. — and then decided not to. I went to the office, where I had to discuss some staff matters with Lawson.

Into an ashtray squalid with butts (ashtrays become squalid after about the eighth) Lawson dropped another. It was one of those curiously stuffy days one gets sometimes in early December, still, grey, with a dense pulpy sky. The radiators were too hot, as usual: the draughtsmen loved to swelter. It must have been over seventy. Outside, the geometric lawns round the office block, our pitiful attempt at beautifying industry, shone stagily green. There were still a few spots of colour in the horrible concrete rockery.

Lawson was big and square, with a craggy Red Indian face and hair *en brosse*. Tweeds that would have looked hairy on most people looked like a pelt on Lawson, despite an attempt to domesticate them with a pale yellow shirt and agate cufflinks. Thirty-seven years old, with a First Class Honours degree from Cambridge, Lawson was a pioneer: and one of the best people we'd got. Bickerton, my immediate boss, had cursed this pioneer up hill and down dale. 'The men don't like it, but what can you do? And it makes us look progressive to employ Lawson — sort of show piece. You have to say, fair's fair: and so far as the actual work goes, I never need have a moment's worry.'

'Is it Purdue again?' I asked.

'Oh, he's better,' Lawson said, 'all things said and done. He takes his iron pills.' An air of contempt here for pusillanimity. 'But these new young ones, Grey and Parker, they want a boot up their backsides, I can tell you, Mr. Hendrey.'

She offered me a cigarette.

I ought to have said before that Lawson was a woman. Gruff, ugly, eccentric, strangling with masculine protest, she was one of the ablest engineers I have ever met. We had taken her on out of the desire to publicise our sexual egalitarianism: as the Chief said, it was no good hollering out for scientists and then rejecting half the human race. We had taken her on eight years ago in quite a lowly capacity, but once we had got her we couldn't keep her down. She was simply too good for us. Her work was impeccable and the place ran like a dream, except for the fact that the men couldn't stick her. The more sophisticated thought, and said, that she was a bloody old Lesbian. They were entirely wrong. Lawson was all woman and longed to be loved. She would have liked to wear pretty clothes, make up, high heels and go on the town. (She had told me as much once, in a burst of confidence.) But if she had done so, she would have looked like a female impersonator. As it was, she had to put in an appearance at the annual dance. Muscular in black velvet with a little row of pearls, grimly foxtrotting in reluctant arms, she looked terrible and she felt it. On Lawson, life had played a singularly tasteless and tragic joke. Because she looked like a man, except for her heavy breasts, she had to pretend to be one.

So both the men and women thought her a fool and made fun of her behind her back. It can't have been any sort of life for her.

That day she went on and on about her subordinates, who peeped at us apprehensively from behind their drawing-boards. 'A boot up their backsides,' she repeated, pitiably. It had always been an article of faith with her that if she talked like the men, they would accept her more gladly: she had never discovered her error. I listened to the details of complaint, said I would talk to Bickerton about transferring Grey and chewing up Parker. Lawson nodded and gulped. I saw to my astonishment and alarm that she was near to tears. I said, Why didn't we take ten minutes off in the canteen? I could do with a coffee.

'When the bloody cat's away . . .' she said, but she rose.

The canteen was almost empty at that hour. We helped ourselves and sat at a table by the window.

'Excuse me,' said Lawson, and went to the lavatory.

When she came back she had powdered around her eyes.

Stupidly, I asked her what the matter was. There came a gust of tears; she turned her Minotaur head violently from one side to the other, as if to heave off her misery. She said thickly, 'Nothing.'

'Sorry.'

'A personal matter.'

She drank her coffee very hot, in great gulps. There was steam round her mouth. It was a kind of Homeric performance, most disconcerting. I did not know what to say next.

In a moment or two, she calmed down. 'You've always been very kind, Mr. Hendrey. I shouldn't have treated you to that.'

I assured her that though it had scarcely been a treat, I thought it might have helped her to let go a bit.

'My fiancé's dead,' said Lawson.

I was so staggered that I could not at once control my face, which, I knew, had twitched, then dissolved. I managed to murmur condolences. Lawson got up and bought herself another coffee. She looked at her watch. 'I'd better be getting back.'

She did not look in a fit state to go back; and as a matter of fact, she did not attempt to. She told me all about it.

She had met, six months ago, at a church whist drive (for Lawson was religious) a widower in his late fifties, a newsagent in a decent small way of business. 'For some reason, we just got on together. I don't know how it was. He was a quiet little chap.' They went to the cinema twice. On their third outing they dined together in Soho, and he asked Lawson to marry him. 'In the old days one would have said he wasn't my class, but that doesn't matter now. And he was bloody lonely, his daughter had just got married herself, his place was in a mess, he was eating out of tins. I'm good at domestic things,' Lawson added, 'though you might not believe it.' She had not worn her engagement ring at the works, fearing people would laugh at her. Then, ten days ago, he had complained of feeling unwell. Aches and pains, 'flu coming on, he supposed. Next morning, his roundsman came to the shop and found him dead. The funeral had taken place on Saturday, so Lawson hadn't needed to ask for time off.

She bowed her head, her big, grotesque head, and drew a face in some spilled sugar. 'Funny, you think you can stand up to it, then you can't.'

'Go on home now,' I said.

'No bloody fear. There's no one there, I'll be worse by myself. I dread it when the whistle blows, I can tell you. Well!' She shot to her feet. 'This won't do, will it? Thanks for the friendly ear. I must be pushing along.'

Half the human race in tears, I thought. I was depressed.

When I got home, I found my mother-in-law in such brilliant spirits that for one hallucinatory moment I thought she must be drunk. Still in her town hat, her painful but smart town shoes, she was drinking tea with Jenny, who had that look of relief, of all-my-troubles-are-now-over which I had come to dread, because of the consequential let-down when she found that they were not.

Stephanie began by acknowledging handsomely, with sweeping gestures, that I had been quite right to make her go to Setter. He was a charming man, he had teased her as if she were a girl. Though he had only confirmed her own doctor's treatment, he had given her quite a new outlook on life. He had taken her to lunch at the˙Athenaeum Annexe and introduced her to the Queen's doctor. She had had potted shrimps, Dover sole, coffee ice-cream, and had shared half a bottle of white wine. 'He drew me out,' she said, rather mysteriously. 'I found myself telling him things I had never told a living soul. Not even you two.' We found this hard to believe, but made no comment. 'I should say he was essentially a *well-adjusted man*,' she finished, proud of having hit not only upon the right judgement, but upon the right phrase.

Half the human race in tears. And the other half off its rocker.

# Chapter 8

I CAN never be quite sure at what point our acquaintance with the Setters fell into intimacy. I think it began from the day Emily rang up to suggest that she and Jenny went shopping together. Jenny was not keen on the idea at first. She hadn't, obviously, so much money as Emily; also, Emily made her feel *petit-bourgeoise* (which Jenny is, and a good thing too, if I may say so). But from the first trip, things went well. Emily, a realist if ever there was one, did not restrain herself from buying at Finnegan's and Asprey's if she felt like it: indeed, she took the view, quite correctly, that Jenny would enjoy watching the process; but she also showed Jenny a multiplicity of ways in which a small amount of money could be spent for a startlingly large result. She knew London shops as some people know the London Zoo, that is, knew all the best animals and the best keepers. She had even made a remarkable topological map, like an underground map, of the central shopping districts, with notes appended as to what one should buy where, and arrows leading from one shop to the other, indicating the quickest way to get around for various specific purposes.

Jenny never really came to like her, but they became great friends. Dislike and friendship are not mutually exclusive; I have found this out for myself time and time again. And in the course of this friendship, Jenny learned something of what was going on.

For some time past, Setter had been keeping up his strange relationship with Stephanie, taking her out sometimes or, when he visited us (which was usually without Emily, who preferred to spend the evenings with her Platonics), talking earnestly with her after dinner while Jenny and I retired to do the washing-up, as if we were parents rather showily leaving a courting couple alone.

I wish I could say that these attentions had changed the whole course of Stephanie's life, but they hadn't: they changed her only when they were actually in process. In his presence pain seemed to leave her; her body straightened, her face grew clear, young and sunny, her voice rose a couple of tones. The moment he left she was back in the dumps, or in one of her moods of half-derisive, sub-acid self-pity.

Then, about February of that year, he started to visit us rather less.

'Do you know what he's up to?' Emily said to Jenny, over morning coffee at Fortnum's. 'It is most peculiar. He is giving little social evenings for strange lame ducks at a strange little club in Soho. He won't let me come. I sometimes think he is dotty.'

But, Jenny told me, Emily had not much seemed to mind if he were as dotty as King Lear. She had spoken of him as of a big, foolish youth having fun.

Looking smart and unsmart, her hat pushed to the back of her head because she felt hot, sitting slightly askew at the table, fine large legs crossed at the knee, she had beamed comically at Jenny as though they were both together in a great joke.

'Do try to find out what he's up to, darling. I'm sure Victor could.'

I found out soon enough, because one morning a card arrived for Stephanie.

# An Error of Judgement

William Setter
at Home
Phryne Club, 24 Soho Passage,
(off Old Compton Street), W.1.
Wednesday,
February 18th, 1959, 9 p.m.
(No reply needed.)

He had scrawled across one corner, 'Victor too if he likes.'

'Well,' said Stephanie, 'it will be a sight for my old eyes to see a night-club. Do you know, I have never seen one? Your father saw rather too many,' she added to Jenny, with a little pursy smile of the kind the French call *douce-amère*.

'I'm not asked,' Jenny said unreasonably, since she knew, and Setter knew, that on Wednesdays she usually went to see a friend of hers at Richmond. 'He might think of me. Left out of the gaiety!' she cried dramatically. 'Poor Cinderella without even a bloody pumpkin or mouse!'

'There will be mice, dear,' said Stephanie, 'if you don't do out the larder rather more often than you do at present.'

Meanwhile, I was all curiosity.

The night of February 18th was chilly and damp, and Stephanie had had one of her worst days. By 8 p.m. she had dragged off her best clothes (it had taken her an hour to dress), shrugged back into her old ones and announced that she wasn't going. So by the time Jenny had dressed her for the third time, we were well on the way to being late.

I don't quite know how to describe what we found at the Phryne Club. To begin with, we had difficulty finding it at all, and in any case no taxi could get down Soho Passage, which meant a painful journey for Stephanie over slippery cobbles. The club itself, in the basement below a coffee-bar, was belching forth an appalling din of bongo drums and a sour trumpet.

48

There were the usual cheesecake posters on the wall, signed photographs of persons unknown to me, Chianti-bottle lamps. The man on the door took our card and ushered us into the din. The usual thing: grubby tables, bar, small dance floor, not much light.

'If this is what it's like,' Stephanie whispered, with a wince, 'I wonder my late husband thought the game worth the candle.'

But then, quite suddenly, we were shunted through a curtain, through a baize door, into a dusty-looking, sitting-room-type cellar, half-full of people who were making almost no noise at all. There were men and women of varying ages, some with drinks, some with coffee, some smoking, others not. They sat on sofas and grimy pouffes. They looked rather like a Labour Party branch meeting of the 1930's, in a strongly Conservative constituency. Setter was drinking whiskey, on an object not unlike a church hassock, his great knees sticking up into the air, his flat face animated; he was talking about gardening. He did not see us at once, so Stephanie and I dawdled awkwardly just inside the door. The room was smoky. I didn't see anyone I knew. Then I did. I saw my friend Malpass, and, of all people, Ulick Purdue.

Setter spotted us, and rose. 'Take a pew,' he said, which seemed appropriate. He planted us on one of the sofas, pushing two pallid youngsters aside in order to make way for us, exactly as if he were pushing a couple of dogs off the best cushions. 'I shan't introduce all round. You'll find out. Oh — you know Father Malpass, and Mr. Purdue, I think. We were just talking.'

Purdue looked at me and flinched. Yet he was not put out by my superior presence: he expected me, quite rightly, to be put out by his. Malpass grinned and tossed his parrot-like beak. Like Setter, he had a whiskey in his hand.

'Well, we haven't a clay soil,' said a girl with a clayey countenance, 'but *we* grow roses. Our rose-garden — you ought to see it!'

'Ulick,' Setter said, 'you be barman, get them something to drink. Rheumatics playing up tonight, Stephanie?'

My mother-in-law told him all about them, in her voice a touch of vituperation due to sheer disappointment. She had expected glitter that evening, perhaps even naughtiness.

He nodded gloomily. 'Yes,' he said, 'it's a brute.' Suddenly he told a funny story. It had no relevance to what had been said, and he did not tell it particularly well, but it *was* funny and people laughed. As the atmosphere brightened, he did too, relief spreading across his face and intensifying the colour of his small eyes.

'I can beat that one,' said an unshaven boy in a very good suit, and did.

Setter considered. 'Too dirty,' he said at last.

The others agreed. It was all very odd: they appeared to me more and more like a committee sitting on something or other: but what was it? Purdue, to my surprise, told a shaggy-dog story, and then the conversation veered irrationally (or perhaps not so, dogs being in mind) to vivisection. Setter gave a brief, sensible lecture on this, while they all sat respectfully silent, their faces turned towards him. One of the girls was almost blind. 'Couldn't do much for you, Lena — which we will do — if we hadn't had a go on the animals once,' Setter said to her. She was sitting near him. She put out her hand. He gave it a gentle little shake and returned it to her.

The talk swung off again: to plays, films, sport. There was no coherence in it. There were frequent long pauses of the kind that terrify me, and usually drive me into the kind of idiotic chatter which only serves to make people stare at me with cold distaste; but nobody else seemed awkward and no one got up to go. Setter, now in a Buddha-like squat, made no attempt to dominate it. Later, when drinks were renewed, people stood up and began to form groups. Malpass hopped over to Stephanie and me. 'Well, well,' he said. He smiled with his eyes only.

I asked him what he was doing there.

'Your young friend Purdue brought me. Setter asked *him*. This has been going on for about five weeks.'

'What's it all about?'

He said he had never found out. With anyone else but Setter in the chair, you would have thought it was a kind of Lonelyhearts Club: but they didn't seem to bring him their problems, and he didn't seem to want them. One or two had, indeed, attempted to raise some personal trouble: if it were physical, Setter had listened carefully and made suggestions: if psychological, he had smiled it off, gently, but with the firm air of one ungifted in mathematics who is asked to make some complex calculation. No, they just liked to come, he liked to be there. I asked if there were any common denominator, besides a general air of ill-health and dinginess. 'I think they've all been patients of his, or acquaintances of some kind. Ulick nearly had a fit when he was asked; he'd only seen Setter once before. He never misses now, though.'

They were starting to sit down again, for Session II. When I looked at Stephanie I was surprised to see that, far from wanting to leave, far from showing irritation at the general aimlessness, she now seemed rooted and relaxed. For some reason, she was enjoying herself.

The talk was about war, or, precisely, about being blown up and charred to bits. 'I don't believe it will happen,' said the girl with the rose-garden, 'perhaps it's because I don't want to.'

'Most of the things we do believe we don't want to believe,' Setter said. 'It's fallacious to assume that we're all wishful thinkers.'

'I say to myself in the night,' the girl said, 'shall I ever die? That way, or any other?'

She was sallow and plain, she looked sick: but when she asked her question something seemed to sweep from her face, like dust, the troubles and the years; so that colours came up, and a kind of newness.

'You will, some way. But I don't expect you'll mind. You'd be surprised how many don't, when it comes to it.'

Stephanie said, in a wistful, false voice, 'If you know you are a burden to others, you don't mind nearly so much, I assure you.'

'Come off it,' said Setter. 'You're one of the ones who would. You enjoy yourself so much in the good times.'

'Good times?' (*Douce-amère* again.)

'Five per cent of your times aren't bad. Perhaps ten per cent.'

This made Purdue laugh. He bounced up and down on his pouffe, looking like a gleeful ape.

'But burning?' The girl again. 'To die like that?'

The light had fallen from her. She felt the fear of the flesh. A beaded evening bag, inappropriate to her jumper and skirt, slid to the floor and she fumbled it up again.

Malpass said, 'Quite. Cheerful subject. Still, I hope the Lord would see me through it, whatever it was.'

Setter was gloomy.

'Ah,' said Stephanie, with a touch of archness, 'but Mr. Setter doesn't believe in God.'

He looked at her, moving his head slowly. She flushed. He said, 'No,' and his hands hung between his knees like bunches of bananas. He turned back to the rose-garden. 'I expect something would see us through it, whatever it was. We should see ourselves through.'

'This conversation,' said the smart boy with the two-day beard, 'has taken a highly intellectual turn, has it not?' This was sarcasm.

'We're not all as clever as you, Duncan,' Setter said mildly' 'You mustn't point the finger of scorn at us.'

They all began to laugh. It appeared to be their custom to give and accept mild rebukes of this milk-and-water kind, without any trace of resentment.

I noticed that while several people drank rather a lot and others stuck to coffee, the general temperature was changeless. It seemed a dull sort of evening to me, but the rest must obviously have enjoyed it, or it wouldn't have had so many forerunners.

Only one thing happened which was remotely like an incident. They had been talking in their relaxed, contented, desultory fashion about social security, socialised medicine, pensions, the rest. An elderly woman with hair dyed coal-black and scooped-out eye-sockets, said suddenly, 'If we all had healthy bodies, perfectly healthy, would we be all right?'

Setter pondered this, as if nobody had ever asked such a question before. 'Probably. But they wouldn't stay healthy long if the mind grew sick. And it does. To paraphrase the old chestnut, "at least one can be miserable in comfort" — at least one can be mentally unbalanced in the greatest physical comfort achievable. I'm interested in bodies. That's all I know about.'

He sounded harsh, far more so than he could have intended. He added, 'That's *all* I know about.'

She came pushing towards him then, from her place at the end of the room, dropped down beside him in a curiously girlish way, flexible and neat. 'But you know more? Don't you? Don't you?'

'Only about myself,' said Setter, 'not about you.'

'Nothing? Nothing?' She turned up her face to him. 'Of course you know.' For a moment, it looked as if she would break into violent tears.

The strange thing was that nobody but myself appeared to be watching them. The others had fallen into private conversations, their eyes averted.

'Not one single damned thing,' said Setter, very clearly.

It was not said conclusively: it was not the kind of remark which breaks up parties: yet at that point the party did break up, with promises of reunion scattering all over the place like thistledown. People got into coats and scarves. Setter simply went away. Purdue vanished, after giving me an embarrassed, lop-sided grin.

I found myself with Stephanie and Malpass in the satiny drizzle of the street.

'Well,' I said confidently to the latter, 'now you can expound.'

'No, I can't. I've told you all I know.'

'Well, I think it was all very restful,' said Stephanie, who was walking more easily than usual, bearing down only lightly on my arm. 'I must say I enjoyed it.'

I asked her what she had enjoyed.

She replied vaguely, in the secret as I was not, though I don't think she knew what the secret was, 'It makes a change in a long, dull day.'

Malpass asked if he could look in on Friday night. He had a problem. He wanted to talk to me about some ex-parishioners of his, a family called Underwood. 'Great moral problem,' he added. 'Why do people think priests never want advice? I think I could do with yours.'

# Chapter 9

RATHER more than a couple of months ago (Malpass told me) some youths had set upon an old woman, pretty soused, who was making her way back along the edge of the common to her home behind Clapham South tube station. It was a dark, drizzly night, and the side streets were deserted.

The attack seemed to be motiveless, since she had spent nearly all of her money in the pub, and when her body was found, had only two shillings and sevenpence halfpenny, a doorkey, a swastika charm and three aspirin tablets in her purse. She had apparently clung fiercely to her worthless bag, thus driving the youths into such a frenzy of competitive desire for it that they had knocked her down and then, seeing her flopping about in the gutter, had systematically kicked her to death. They had kicked her eyes in, among other things: the injuries were too multiple to retail, and wouldn't get us anywhere even if I tried to. (Malpass retailed the lot, in a kind of gluttonous white rage.)

The body was found a few seconds after death by a policeman on the beat, who had seen three boys running away, but was too late to do anything about it.

Hunting for louts in that part of the world is no easy thing, as the police found. There are a good many of them, though only a vestigial proportion would be murderous. Hundreds of people were interrogated, but there wasn't the smell of an arrest.

Malpass, who had worked in the parish up to a couple of

years ago, when he had transferred to East London, was called in to see if he could help. No kind of contribution occurred to him at once; if your parishioners are parishioners at all, it is fairly unlikely that they will be homicidal. He told the police what he knew about the youth clubs, the broken and disorganised families, the strips of remaining slum. It was all too generalised to be of any use, and he would never have thought about the business again if, when he was just about to catch the tube home, he had not been accosted by a former choir-boy, Sammy Underwood, now aged seventeen and a half.

Sammy, whose fancy it was to turn himself out like an American high-school senior, in jeans and a bulky sweater with cabbalistic letters over the chest, had said, 'Well, Padre, fancy seeing you!' and had asked him to come and have a cup of char with his family.

Now Malpass was puzzled by this, for Sammy, as he remembered him, had been the last boy to bother himself with domestic life, with parson or church. He had been forced to go to church, had mildly liked (before his voice broke) to sing, had liked to muck around with the lads after morning service. But he had not been devout, and was by no means filial.

Sammy's father was a boot repairer in a fairly decent way of business, his mother was a nice little woman who took in dressmaking, his sister was sporadically on the stage. She was married and had a baby. Sammy himself, though a little undersized, was a decent-looking boy of the treacly variety, studying mechanical engineering at a technical school. The previous generation of Underwoods had been proletarian: this one had gone up a bit in the world and now voted Conservative, which would have been unthinkable to any of their forebears. They had a poky but scrupulously tidy house in the back streets a few hundred yards behind the Plough, which is one of those pubs conspicuous enough to be both a landmark and a bus stop.

## An Error of Judgement

If Malpass had not been puzzled he would have refused the invitation. It was late, he had had a long day, he wanted to hear Schoenberg on the Third Programme. Still, he went, and Sammy brought him home like a headhunter returning in triumph with the trophy.

The two senior Underwoods, both churchgoers, greeted Malpass with complimentary fluster. 'Well, look who's here!' Mrs. Underwood had cried. She prided herself on keeping up with the times, being a pal to her children.

'I saw the Father trying to creep away, Ma,' Sammy said exuberantly, 'but I caught him on the hop.'

'Well,' said Mr. Underwood, 'do you miss your old haunts?'

There was tea, ham, eggs, peaches, ice-cream. The family had supped earlier, but Malpass hadn't. They watched him with satisfaction as he ate. They were flattered to have a priest in the house, delighted to do him honour. Sandra, the daughter, brought down the sleeping baby for admiration. Her husband worked nights: he would be mad he'd missed Father Malpass. She herself had just finished a pantomime engagement, she had been the Fairy Queen — 'Fancy me!'

'And she weren't half bad,' said Sammy with pride.

Of course they wanted to know what Malpass had been doing in Clapham, and when he told them they looked glum.

'Poor old thing!' Mrs. Underwood cried. 'She was over seventy, too!'

None of them had known her really, they said, though she was a famous old drunk. But she had often had a sixpence to spare for the kids, always a friendly word, when it wasn't too slurred for you to hear it. She wasn't the sort you'd ask into your own home, exactly; still there was no harm in her.

'Addie Engbeck,' said Underwood, 'funny name. Doesn't sound English.'

'If a boy of mine had done that,' said his wife, 'done that, to an old woman, I wouldn't care if they hung him.'

'That's right, Ma, you wouldn't,' said Sammy, encouragingly. He seemed to be admiring her spirit.

'And I'd kick him around a bit before I gave him the rope,' said Sandra, 'just so he'd know what it was like.'

Good bosoms heaved. Mrs. Underwood actually cried a little. Malpass finished his peaches.

'My God, I hope they catch them!' Underwood shouted suddenly, after an interval of silence, which ended that part of the conversation.

After they had talked for a while of changes in the neighbourhood, the new bowling craze, the disappearance of the Teds, Malpass took his leave. 'I'll walk with you to the tube,' Sammy said, 'it can be mucky just round here at this time of night.'

The two small men, the apprentice, the priest, went out into the dingy night. Both were smoking. Sammy looked as if he were pleased, as if he hoped his friends would see him.

Under the lamps his new-cut head glittered. He talked openly to Malpass of his immediate interests, his job, his girl.

He was much changed from the choir-boy; easy now, jaunty, he had a place on which to stand.

Only his mouth seemed wary.

No, he didn't go around much with the gang; not nowadays. In fact, he'd practically given all that up. His girl didn't like it. His girl was a secretary, she earned nine pounds a week, she was something. 'You ought to see her, Father! She's class.' She lived on the west side of the common, her father had been in the Ministry of Pensions. Her name was Hilde; both her parents had been killed in the blitz. She lived with a grandmother — 'regular old vampire,' said Sammy — who had her at her beck and call all hours she was at home.

'She's eating her away,' he added fiercely, his voice changing, his eyes changing, 'bloody old cannibal. Excuse me, Father, ought not to have put it that way. But they get me down, these old vampires, I tell you they do.'

Malpass, well-fed but exhausted, was glad to get home. It was not until two days later that it occurred to him to telephone the incumbent of the church which had been his, and ask for news of the Underwoods.

'The old people still attend,' was the answer, 'and Sandra and spouse come at Easter and Harvest Festival. Sammy's no good, of course. He's always out with some gang or other.'

I don't think any man but Malpass (assuming that man as hard-driven as he was) would have given the contradiction a thought. But just as some small birds seem to burn with energy, so that their breast-bones pulsate, so did he. He had only one free night a week, on which he was accustomed to visit us or the highbrow cinemas, but this he now began to devote to the study of Sammy Underwood.

Sammy seemed only too eager to be studied. With a fawning air, he chatted hour by hour to Malpass in the pubs; and hour by hour, Malpass had become more convinced that he knew something, to put it at the lowest, about the death of Addie Engbeck.

'What does one do?' Malpass said to me. 'I don't know. This is fly-away *nous* on my part, probably not *nous* at all. But Sammy hangs on to me like a fruit bat to the vine. He wants to talk. But what does he want to talk about?'

He added, 'I might try him on Setter. He has ducks quite as lame as Sammy. And I'm at my wit's end.'

There are some things which it is impossible for the well adjusted English *bourgeois* — which I suppose I am — to believe: and one is that any acquaintance of any friend of one's own could conceivably have committed brutal murder (or even murder of the most soft-pedalled, gentlemanly variety).

'You've nothing to go on,' I said.

'A bit of a lie, me duck,' said Malpass.

'He wanted to get in good with you.'

'That I doubt. I have listened to his masturbatory fancies, which are on the literary side, but not calculated to inspire respect for his desire to charm.'

'What do you think, then?'

'I'm afraid to think. But I believe he wants me to.'

'So?'

'So let Setter think. He does it for fun, for nothing.'

My reading has always been serious; indeed, Jenny says we haven't got anything decent to read in the house. Joyce, Proust, Kafka, James, Amiel, Kierkegaard, Melville, Faulkner, I have been through the lot, with varying degrees of appreciation. But when I am dead tired I take to bed either literate detective stories, or Roughead's *Famous Trials*; and through them I have learned not only something of the laws of evidence, but of probabilities. I did not think commonsense was on Malpass's side. I did not believe Sammy Underwood had kicked out an old woman's eyes.

Let us be sensible: what had Malpass got? (a) The boy belonged to the district, (b) he had lied about his social amusements — i.e. he had claimed not to go about with other youths when in fact he did, (c) he had pursued Malpass around the place with conversation and greenstick confessions, (d) he had proffered an entirely irrelevant invitation.

What did it add up to? Damn all, except that Sammy, with his choral'past, found it alluring to suck up to parsons and to engage their attention.

'Yet at least he knows,' Malpass said, with his wild gleam, 'at any rate he knows something.' His clerical trousers, frayed a bit at the knees, let the bone glimmer through the cloth. He gnawed at his lips, which were always dried and purpled by this particular exercise.

'But what do you *know* of him?' Jenny asked. She had been listening to us. She wanted to make her presence felt. She spoke with that air of politeness which, because it is an act of bravery, always falters away into the silence of self-doubt. A display of confidence is the least successful of all displays, when it is a fake.

'I don't know anything,' Malpass answered, 'except what I've told you. And what he was like as a kid. He didn't care for anybody. He didn't love anyone, Sammy didn't. Not his pa or his ma, or his sister, or even the cat. He was as insulated as the mercury in a thermometer, was Sammy. He rose up hot, he sank down cold, but it was all on his own account.'

I suggested that, so far as I had been able to observe, Setter wasn't playing either diagnostician or detective. What he was playing, I didn't know. But neither of those things.

Jenny burst out suddenly, 'I don't like Setter! I never did.'

When I was incautious enough to ask her why not, she stormed at me that he was obviously self-indulgent, gathering his absurd group together in an absurd *milieu* simply for his private amusement. How people could bear to go, to be condescended to like that, she couldn't begin to imagine. For it was, of course, condescension. Setter was of quite a different — she hesitated — *kind* from the rest, from all she'd heard of them. Hadn't her mother any self-respect, hadn't that man Purdue, hadn't Malpass himself, that they had to go running whenever Setter called them? She looked so upset that I didn't argue, and nor did Malpass.

But when I was seeing him out, Jenny having withdrawn with the stately announcement that we must forgive her, since she was half dead with sleep, he said to me: 'Anyway, he will be a singular addition to Setter's menagerie. And Victor, I have to *know.*'

# Chapter 10

THE Setters were dining with us. Emily said in her soft, gleeful voice, 'I tell you, it goes from bad to worse. Doesn't it, darling?' she demanded of her husband.

He said nothing.

'Do you know what he's added to his collection now? A teddy-boy!'

'Not a Ted,' said Setter. 'They're out.'

'Well, whatever you call him. Have *you* seen him, Stephanie?'

My mother-in-law said she had seen him once, a nice quiet youngster; a little awkward socially, she added, in her best Emily Post fashion. In fact, Stephanie had begun to give up the Phryne Club, out of sheer bafflement, and preferred to lunch with Setter on occasion. She never seemed to see that these luncheons were at least as mysterious as the club evenings.

'Here we are all together, all friends,' said Emily, the tips of her fair hair taking sparks from the candlelight, 'no secrets between us.' She put her hands tip to tip, in praying style, all rings glittering. '*I* am the bold one, I am his wife.'

Setter smiled faintly. Jenny looked apprehensive.

Emily did not continue with her boldness till she had stuffed down some more of a dreadful salad, which Jenny had found in the recipe column of a Californian magazine: this consisted of lettuce, cream cheese, sliced peaches, a dollop of marshmallow and mayonnaise. Then she said, 'And now Bill will tell us his motives.'

'I haven't a motive,' said Setter, 'except to let people talk.'

'But what people!' Emily's smiling scorn had something imperial about it.

'Someone else from your organisation has joined us,' he said to me, 'a Miss Lawson. Poor Ulick told me about her — he can't stick her, but no matter — so I sent her a card. Also, she came to consult me professionally.'

'I'm afraid I don't know Miss Lawson,' said Stephanie.

'Why "poor Ulick"?' I enquired.

'Oh, he's fitter in himself. But he's an unhappy man. Nobody likes him much.'

'Ah!' cried Emily, almost dancing in her chair, 'now we have it! Bill has established a clinic for people whom nobody likes much.'

Stephanie sat up straight, bristling with offended dignity. 'I hope that isn't Mr. Setter's motive so far as I am——' (She could never bring herself to call him by his first name.)

'Or so far as I am concerned,' I put in quickly, and Jenny gave me an almost imperceptible nod of approval. 'After all, I belong, don't I?'

Setter shook his head.

'You mean,' Emily pressed him, 'that Victor doesn't belong, or that I'm wrong about your motives?'

'I haven't any motives.'

'Oh come, come, come, you must have. Do explain. We're all agog, aren't we, Victor?'

Then he took a bite at her. It was so unexpected, seemed so out of character, that for the moment we were all struck silent.

He said, 'I see no motives for your own amusements, my girl. Not even the crudest.'

She stared at him, flushing deeply. Stephanie began to hum a little tune under her breath, a trick of hers when she felt distraction was needed, though it had never distracted anybody.

Jenny, who could be firm when she liked, was the first to speak.

'I have a motive for asking you to eat up rather quickly, because there is a soufflé in the oven which is going to spoil.'

Any soufflé of Jenny's was spoilt from its inception, as it were, but that didn't matter. The trick worked, the moment passed off.

The Setters appeared, for the rest of the evening, to be upon the most amiable terms.

Next week, out of curiosity, I went to the club, and there I met Sammy Underwood. As it happened, there was a twenty-four-hour bus strike, so not many people were there; and at ten, Setter got a hospital call, and had to leave.

Malpass suggested that he and Sammy and I should snatch a sandwich in a pub. He knew just how curious I was.

Sammy Underwood struck me as an even odder young man than I had been led to think. If I had met him in the United States, I should certainly have taken him for a high-school student with good grades, that is, until he spoke. He attempted a touch of Americanism in his speech; but what he did speak was sub-Cockney. He looked, in his way, extremely smart: new blue jeans, a sky-blue sweater with collar turned out over the rounded neck, rather expensive brown suede shoes. He had a hare-like, but by no means unhandsome face, forehead high, eyes dark, brilliant and evasive, teeth slightly protruding. His hair was black and silky, cut short to his head, more like a cap than hair: but it was meagre right on top, as if he had once been tonsured. By twenty-six, Sammy would be going bald. His attitude to Malpass was something I can only describe as lover-like. It is a bad term, since there was nothing homosexual about Sammy; yet he seemed to yearn for a shoulder, yearn for rebuke, yearn for love. Towards me, he was at once slightly on the defensive. He hadn't wanted me to join them: something had been spoiled for him.

In the sour light of an undistinguished pub, he drank tonic water and wolfed down scotch eggs and potato salad. He listened while Malpass and I talked politics, about the coming Summit Conference, about the anti-bomb marches. He made only one comment. 'Silly bastards — beg your pardon, Father — they do it to show off, that's what.'

I began to feel drowsy. I can always sleep, given half the chance. Indeed, I almost lost Jenny, in the early days of our engagement, by falling into a doze when we were dining together, at the Savoy, of all places. She was bitterly offended. 'Why you have to spend so much money just to go to sleep, I can't imagine. You could sleep in a Rowton House for sixpence.'

I was jolted to attention by something Malpass said.

While my mind was wandering, he had led Sammy to the Engbeck murder.

'I suppose some people,' said Malpass, 'would have said the old lady wasn't good for much, not even to herself.'

The boy brightened, and so did I. He replied in a pious tone, 'Still, that's for a higher authority to judge, isn't it, Father?'

(You see why I suggested that he would have made good grades.)

'Certainly,' said Malpass, very prompt. 'But aren't there human beings who would make such a judgement?'

'Look,' said Sammy, 'I'm not excusing anyone, but some of those old birds do ask for trouble. The lads go out for the evening, see? And they have a few drinks inside them, see? And maybe there's nothing else to do, and they wish there was, and so they see a drunken old bag weaving all over the place, and they think, bit of a lark to make a snatch, and then she gets wild, and so do they, and they go pretty crazy, see? Mind you, I'm not excusing them. But it's the way it *works*, Father, that's what we don't know, you and me. We can't see into the minds of people like them.'

It was a long speech; he seemed excited to have said so much.

'You don't know chaps like that yourself, do you, Sammy?' asked Malpass.

'Me? Not likely. I go out with my girl, all the free time I get. I've got a lot of study, I can tell you, takes me up to midnight sometimes.' He launched into details of his work, of his aspirations; he seemed a fine young student, Sammy did, he had a future.

'All the same,' said Malpass, 'you must know the locals pretty well. Have you no idea who it could have been?'

Sammy looked wily. 'Could have been me, come to that. The cops interviewed some fellows I know. Got no change out of them, though. They just thought it was a lark, being asked things, I mean.'

I said, 'My imagination is lively. But it boggles at the thought of a chap who can get a good night's sleep after he's kicked an old woman's eyes out.'

'Well,' said Sammy, 'but aren't we all just assuming he gets a good night's sleep?'

He shot bright glances round at us, like a moderator in a panel discussion.

Malpass said cheerfully, 'I'm not. I don't think that sort of murderer has a conscience at all. That's a romantic conception. Good God, you kick a woman to death, and then you cry all night! You kick out her eyes and her eardrums, you rupture her bowels, and then you exhibit an excess of sensibility!'

'*Sense and Sensibility*,' said Sammy. 'We had to read that at school. Silly damn book.'

He drew a face in the beer slops on the table, added fuzzy hair to it. 'Jane Austen,' he added scornfully, 'silly old maid. What did she ever know about things? You've got to know about things to write books.' Turning, he looked hopefully at the snack counter. 'Those things aren't half bad.'

'Have another scotch egg?' I suggested.

Sammy was pleased. 'Sorry, folks, but I missed my tea.'

I asked him what his girl's name was.

He replied, not looking up, 'Hilde, spelt the German way, with an *e*.'

'Hilde what?'

He paused, grinned. 'Never mention a lady's name in the mess. Coo, what a mess, too!' He waved a hand to the barmaid. 'Got a cloth, Lil?' She took no notice.

Malpass said, 'You're a shrewd chap, Sammy. What does Mr. Setter give those evenings for?'

He answered without hesitation, 'Oh, I expect he's queer. Beg pardon, Father.'

Malpass laughed at this. 'What about the girls? And those elderly ladies?'

'That's a front, see?'

This was such nonsense that I said something pretty sharp, at which Sammy wilted. He didn't really know, he said, he hadn't thought. He hadn't the faintest, anyhow. Mr. Setter was a queer sort of bird, that was all, you couldn't get away from that. Then he added narcissistically, 'Well, I thought he had an eye for me.'

'Perhaps he has. But not the sort you think,' said Malpass.

'What sort?' For a second Sammy looked more hare-like than ever.

'How should I know?'

'Well,' the boy said sulkily, 'how should I?' He pushed the rest of the egg and sausage into his mouth, drained his tonic water. 'I've got to be pushing. Thanks a lot, both. See you soon.'

We watched him go, saw the strut of his Ted days moderate (as he remembered) into a transatlantic roll. He did not look back. The glass doors swung behind him, letting in a gasp of fog.

# Chapter 11

IN the spring, something both touching and exciting happens to the scrawny hedge which holds us off from the square. It has been rusty black all the winter, like old clothes dragged out for an unimportant funeral; now it spurts little ellipses of yellow all over. The yellow comes before the green. When the green sets in it will be like any other suburban hedge, a strong, flat colour carrying dust again: but in spring it looks lively and surprisingly personal, amorous, as if it had dressed up to please a girl. Jenny and I are more than fond of it: ours is a square in one of those semi-slum, once stately districts south of the river which in ten years' time will become smart. It is people like us who, by buying up unenticing leases, will have made it so: and the moment it is truly smart, our leases will fall in, and we shan't have the money to renew them. Jenny and I, starved of greenery, have gone out to *water* that hedge, to keep it looking sprightly, ravishing, lover-like, just a few days longer: but it's no good. A week, and it has gone. I have never loved even a cat (and I love cats) as I have loved that hedge.

What I do not expect to see, above the sparkle of those spring leaves, is an unfamiliar face. For, though we are only a couple of tube stations away from Clapham South, we are a kind of village. People like ourselves, a bright but not socially-dazzling 'young-middle-age set', people with incomes around the £2,000 mark, have come to set up house in these squares, sinking packets of money (far more than any of us can afford) into extra bathrooms, central heating, stainless steel kitchen units, Swedish furniture and curtains printed from designs by Dufy, or imitating *Toile de Jouy*. We are up to the minute in all things. Round about 7 p.m., the squares are full of the smell of garlic, enough to deter a wilderness of vampires, for all the wives cook very much like Jenny. We know pretty well everyone by sight: the actors at No. 10, the ballet-dancer at No. 20, the gossip-writer at No. 8, the handsome civil servant (Treasury) at No. 5, the B.B.C. producer at No. 23. We all earn much about the same, the youngest of us is thirty, the oldest in the middle forties. Problems of the world in general are discussed all right: some of us even go on Ban-the-Bomb marches, which is a morally excellent but politically euphoric thing to do, since when Father (the U.S.A.) says turn, of course we all have to turn: but we don't really believe in a wholesale burning one fine morning, after some big bloody ass or admiral has pressed a button. We live, and we talk, as if we expected our world of squares to go on for ever. If there is any health in the world, I think a bit of it is with us. Anyway, the older among us used to do a bit of marching too, in the Thirties, when you were dead from the waist up if you didn't sicken at the amount of hunger lying around, and vomit at the thought of Hitler. So much for us: the young middle-aged, cultivating our gardens not in resignation, but in unquenchable optimism. To prove we are hopeful, most of us (not Jenny and I) have two or three children. Jenny and I have had no luck, and it has left something of a mark on us. It was hard, once, to know that you were going to hope frantically for about three days in every month, and then be let down again.

So, as I say, living in our small ambience, we don't expect to see unfamiliar faces stationary over the hedge.

March was mildish, and the Saturday bright, when our face appeared. It was the face of a young woman who wore no make-up at all, but nevertheless gave an undefined impression o the theatrical. Actresses in the advanced theatres, these days, make a point of appearing off-stage in as mucky a condition as humanly possible: all the same, you can spot them a mile off.

Jenny and I were watering that hedge at the time, not professionally, as we had no hose, no proper watering-can, but with milk jugs.

The face said, 'I'm so sorry to trouble you, but I wonder if you know Father Malpass?'

Of course, we opened the gate, and in she came. She was wheeling a baby (we hadn't seen it before, because of the hedge between) in a pram more grandiose than any commonly seen in our neighbourhood.

She introduced herself as Sandra Hickey, the sister of a friend of the Father's. She wanted to get hold of the Father, but didn't know which his church was and his name wasn't in the telephone book.

The baby was eating bits of angora from the rim of an un-hygienic bonnet.

Jenny was about to rush in with a response, when I stopped her. I asked Mrs. Hickey how she had come to hear of us.

A change came over her face. It was an atavistic change, and you see it only in the faces of the once-poor, whose parents were poor, liable to hounding (or so they thought), and averse to the police. Averse, in fact, to any kind of questioning.

'My brother mentioned you, that's all,' she said, her lips buttoning immediately after she had spoken.

I said, 'Sammy.'

'That's right,' she said, 'Newsam. He's my brother.'

I do not know why these quite minor things are so shocking. I had always assumed (who wouldn't?) that his name was Samuel. But it wasn't.

'Oh,' I said, as if light had dawned, 'Newsam, of course. Newsam Underwood. It's an uncommon name.'

'It was Mum's father's. He talked about you. I just thought you might know.'

At that Jenny, eaten by curiosity, asked her in.

The girl hesitated.

'And the baby, too.'

'Oh, him. He'll be all right out here. He's placid.'

He was indeed a placid child, with pink voluptuous cheeks; he slept in the light, happy as a cat on a sunny doorstep.

So she came in, catlike herself, walking on her points.

We were alone that afternoon: Stephanie had gone upstairs for her nap.

'I didn't mean to disturb you,' said Sandra, 'it was only for an address. I shan't keep you half a tick.'

Now she was in a moderated light, out of the strong sun, I could see her clearly. She had a fierce, cat-like face, wide pale eyes, fine bones, a coarse pink mouth, the corners slightly upturned in repose. Her fair hair was chopped short any old how, and was none too clean. On the stage she might have looked splendid, though when I remembered that she had played the Fairy Queen, I confess I wondered what our pantomimes were coming to. She sat gingerly on a chair, refused a cigarette. 'No cancer for me,' she said in a self-righteous tone, 'I'm keeping my lungs clean.'

Jenny offered her a peppermint, and she refused that too.

It was hard to imagine at what point, from what point, conversation could begin. Sandra began it.

'Do you know this Father well?' she said.

I replied that he was one of my oldest friends.

'Is he *all right*?'

'What do you mean, all right?' Jenny put in, with the kind of fervour she used inevitably in defence of those of whom she did not approve.

'Oh, nothing *sinister*.' Sandra brought the word out in a fashion bordering between self-scorn and a sneer at us. Her gaze lit upon a rather commonplace Chagall print, and she sneered at that too. 'Only he's always around my brother. And it makes Sammy fidgety.'

My own impression was that Sammy, far from being fidgety, had persistently sought Malpass out. I said so.

'And what's this club?'

'It's a social club,' said Jenny, with an air of do-gooding superiority. She had hated Sandra at sight. 'That's all.'

'Do you go there?'

'I haven't time,' Jenny said.

'And I don't get asked. What is all this?'

I told her I had known Malpass since my undergraduate days, and that he was not only a decent man, but an exceptionally decent one. Needled by her tone, I added that Sammy was lucky to know him, irrespective of which sought out the other.

'I wanted to get hold of him,' Sandra said.

I gave her the name and district of his church. She wrote it down on the back of an envelope which she had found in her crammed bag, but made no attempt to go.

'Do have a peppermint,' Jenny pressed her.

She did not seem to hear.

I asked her how Sammy was doing in his work, what his prospects were, what his girl was like.

'What girl?' said Sandra. Her eyes opened to the full.

Hilde, her name was, I said. That was it.

She laughed. 'Is that what he tells you? Hilde Fredcricks? I can just see her giving him half a look! Not that he doesn't hang around sometimes. But she's years older than he is, and she's got scads of boy friends, anyway. Sammy and Hilde! Did he *tell* you that?'

Defending Sammy, I said I thought I might have got the idea

wrong. He had certainly seemed to admire the girl, but I didn't fancy he'd claimed her.

'I should think not! I can see her being claimed by Sammy and his lot. And what a lot they are!'

Her voice was sisterly and bitter, holding in it all the love of a guardian tried beyond endurance who is just about to administer a clip on the ear.

'Who are his friends?' I asked.

But it was too much. At the bare idea of her brother squiring this much-sought girl, she had been momentarily gay: now she was wary again, and whatever burden she carried was back on her shoulders.

'Oh, I don't know. They change and change about.' She got up and thanked us. I never saw anyone leave a house quite so fast, or with less ceremony.

We saw her wheel the pram out of the gate, and her face was thoughtful.

# Chapter 12

NEXT week I had the day off, so I went up to Oxford Street to see if I could buy something for Jenny's birthday. Here I ran slap into Emily Setter and a youngish man, whom she introduced as Bernard Greaves. He had one of those bare-looking faces which don't, like Chinese faces, seem to grow hair; his small moustache might have been stuck on. He was tall, well-dressed, looked peach-fed. A little trill of greyness was stroked back from each side of his parting, a discreet sort of curl, the merest hint of dandyism, like the almost imperceptible spot in the tie of the Baron de Charlus. At first, he seemed to me a fatuous type; then I noticed that his eyes were quick and keen between fleshy upper and lower lids.

One thing I was certain of, and at once: if Setter thought this affair platonic, then Setter was wrong. There is something unmistakeable between lovers, if you know what to look for: a sort of grin behind the eyes, a tendency to touch at elbow and hip, a secret shared, masking itself behind a somewhat excessive all-embracement of the rest of mankind.

'I've heard of you,' said Bernard, in his clipped voice. 'I hoped I'd meet you some time.'

'We're going to the pictures,' Emily said, 'believe it or not, at this hour in the morning. We're going to see a highbrow horror film at the Academy. Come and have a drink first, we've just got time.'

I went with them into a pub, and we sat in a dark brown corner.

'Bill was meaning to ring you,' Emily said. 'We're going down to the country next weekend, and we thought you and Jenny might like to come.'

I asked what country, and learned for the first time that the Setters had a house in Suffolk. It was odd, I thought, how really little I knew of either of them.

I said we'd very much like to come, but I didn't know if we could manage it.

'Oh do! We never seem to see you much these days, and if you come, it might drag Bill away from that demented lame duck craze of his. Do you still go to his evenings?'

'I'm never invited,' said Bernard with a faint air of genuine complaint. 'Though I tell him I'm lame enough.' He spoke as if he and Setter were the best of friends.

'Victor,' Emily said, leaning over the table towards me, her hands clasped, 'do use your influence with him to try to stop all this nonsense. It's getting around, you know, and people are beginning to think he's losing his grip.'

I suggested that in his position Setter might afford to lose a bit of grip, if it gave him any pleasure. She brushed this aside.

'I don't even know what he's after. "What do you *do* for all these people?" I say to him, and he says — "Damn all. I'm not trying to do anything".'

'After all,' said Bernard reasonably, 'there are still the big prizes ahead of him, and if the idea once gets round that he's odd in any way, those prizes are going to go elsewhere.'

'He's got a terrible huge Lizzie now, too, she looks like a pantomime dame. I saw her in the waiting-room one morning. She seems to have been sent by somebody you sent to him, if you see what I mean. Apparently she goes to his awful club, too. I think it's mad.'

I recognised Lawson, and thought I might possibly get something out of her.

Bernard took out a very fine pigskin cigarette case and began to bounce it up and down between his long, arty fingers. (He was, I knew already, general manager of an estate agent's in South Audley Street, but that didn't alter the shape of his fingers.) 'He's a wonderful chap,' he said, 'but he does worry Emily, you know.'

'He does,' she said, 'terribly. We're honestly upset about him.'

They were united in anxiety for Setter. They might have been his mother and father.

'But do come to Long Melford,' she pressed. 'I'll write details, or call you. Do come! It will be like old times.'

I wondered, like what old times, and for whom?

'Bill and Bernard will spend all their time mucking around the garden,' Emily continued, 'but the rest of us can sit round the fire and gossip. That is, unless you're mad keen on mud, too.'

I said we would try. They went off, then, to their cinema.

Sure enough, Setter telephoned that night and got Jenny. She had jumped at the idea, when I told her about it, but was absurdly anxious about leaving Stephanie, who had been complaining about pains in her back. 'There's Mother——' I heard her say. I was on the other line.

'Not your mother this time,' said Setter, 'just you two. It does you both good to get a rest.'

So we accepted, and Stephanie, with very bad grace, agreed to go to Fay.

On the night before the visit, however, she seemed in considerable pain: so much so that I got our doctor. He could find nothing wrong, gave her some pills, and told her it would ease up in a day or so. He thought it was a muscular strain: he asked her if she had given herself a wrench of any sort, had a fall, etc. She said no.

When he had gone she sat very quietly in her bed.

'Well, dears,' she said, 'I'm afraid going to Fay is out of the question. I cannot face any sort of move. I'll just stay quietly here and fend for myself — there's no need to worry.'

'You can't fend for yourself,' Jenny said with equal quietness, a turbulent note beneath it all. 'I'll get Fay to come to you.'

But Fay could not, because there was no one she could leave the children with.

'Do you suppose Joanna could come here?' Jenny asked her. 'It's only for a couple of days.'

But Joanna was in Manchester, accompanying her beastly husband on a business trip.

'Oh God,' said Jenny, 'it's just our luck, it's always like that!'

'Well,' said Fay, 'just wrap her up, put her in a taxi and bring her round here.'

'We could do that,' Jenny said to me eagerly, 'couldn't we?' She was longing for her weekend, for Suffolk fires, for the fields just greening over, for the smell of moist earth, the smell of roasting food which she hadn't cooked for herself.

We put it to Stephanie.

'Now listen,' she said, 'I really am in pain and I don't want to be moved. Mrs. Peel' (our twice a week charwoman) 'will look after me, I'm sure.'

So we contacted Mrs. Peel, who said the weekend was out: her son was getting married.

'Then I'll just fend for myself,' Stephanie repeated. Her jaw trembled. She was looking curiously waxy, but I thought nothing of it at the time.

Jenny began to argue, her anger rising. Stephanie remained obstinate and calm. She would not eat her dinner.

'Listen,' said Jenny, 'you have *got* to go to Fay. It's only ten minutes in a cab, as well you know, and there's nothing wrong with you but a pulled muscle. The doctor says so.'

'Does he, dear?' Stephanie enquired, with patient tenderness. 'But you see, it is my pain, and not his.'

That touched Jenny off. Her cheeks blazed up, her eyes glittered with tears of rage and longing and bad conscience. 'Mother, Victor and I hardly ever get away for a change! We never get away together! All I'm asking you to do is to let us wrap you up, like a bug in a rug, and take you to Fay's. Is that very much to ask?'

'I am a great burden to you both, and I know it.'

'Then don't be a burden this time, please!'

Stephanie asked her not to chop logic like a child.

'No,' said Jenny, 'because I am not a child.' She added, absurdly, I thought, 'I am a middle-aged woman!'

Stephanie smiled. 'Are you, dear? Be sensible, then. I'm not asking you to stay home. It's the very last thing I should ask.'

'You know we can't leave you by yourself.'

'Oh no, dear, I don't know that. You two run away, and have a nice time, and when you get back, you'll find me blithe and chirrupy.'

'What sort of nice time can we have worrying about you?'

'There's not the least need to worry about me. I shall be all right.'

Stephanie lay back on the pillows, groaned a little, moved her shoulders as if to throw the pain off.

'Mother,' Jenny said, 'you are going to Fay's tomorrow.'

She was gripping her hands hard together, so that the knuckles were like little billiard balls.

There was a long silence.

Then Stephanie said, 'Very well, darling. I will do anything to please you, as you know.'

Next morning she had her breakfast in bed, as usual, and said little to either of us, except to ask what time the cab would be coming.

Jenny cried, 'Oh don't go, if you can't bear it! Victor and I will stay. We don't mind all that much, honestly we don't.'

Stephanie said nothing at all, and kept us on tenterhooks for half an hour. But by nine o'clock she was downstairs. She had dressed herself in a heavy old coat which she had not worn for ages, and over her head, wound about her shoulders, was a black woollen stole with silver threads in it, which Jenny had once worn to parties. In all this blackness, Stephanie's face looked waxier than ever. Her lips were set. She looked like someone out of Greek tragedy. She tried to smile, saw to it that we knew it was only a try.

'Well,' she said, in a strange, faraway, jocular voice, 'here we go. *The Transit of Venus*.'

Jenny flung her arms around her, though she was torn with both pity and anger. She was sure Stephanie was acting, yet terrified by the idea that perhaps she oughtn't to be so sure. She said, meaning it, but sounding quite false, 'You don't have to go. Vic and I will stay with you.'

'Oh no. You want to go. I want you to go. I shall have quite a nice time with Fay. And the journey won't take long.'

She gave us a peculiar, stony smile, kissed us both.

'Oh, it's *no* good——' Jenny began.

Stephanie told her to call the cab.

When it came, she seemed to totter across the pavement, her back bunched under that horrible stole.

'*She is doing it on purpose*,' Jenny whispered to me, her teeth chattering.

I thought she was, too.

'Have a good time!' Stephanie cried gaily to me, as Jenny got in beside her. But when the cab started, I saw she was sitting motionless and that she did not wave her hand.

In half an hour or so, Jenny was back in the house. She looked more cheerful.

'Well?' I said.

'Oh, it's the usual thing. The moment she got into the house and saw Fay, she brightened up. I left them drinking cocoa. But she does put one through it, doesn't she?'

I agreed.

'How wonderful it is,' Jenny cried. 'We're all on our own, and we're going for a weekend in the country with nice rich people! Isn't it wonderful?'

For a while we were exultant. We debated whether I should take her to bed for half an hour, but she said no, that could wait for Suffolk. There might even be a fire in the bedroom, and we could watch the flames on the wall.

She did not mention Stephanie again until we were safely in the train.

'I do love her, you know. You do know that?'

I did know it. That was what made it so hard for her later.

# Chapter 13

THE Suffolk house had that kind of extreme comfort which can only be produced by the rich working on the antiquated. It had been built about 1640, on foundations much older, so that the carved staircase sprang away from a big stone-flagged hall, now soft with rugs and firelight, and just hot enough to make one sweat in a pleasurable way. It cost over four hundred a year just to heat: even so, a few small draughts lurked in the gallery out of range of the radiators and along the passages hazardous with different levels.

Here, Emily became a rustic housewife in blue cotton overall and fetching pink headscarf, squatting on the long stool before the hearth in a jolly peasanty way no less engaging because it was histrionic. She and Jenny and I luxuriously talked and drank whiskey at 11 a.m. (This was, and I know I sound Biblical, the morning of the second day.) Outside in the half-tamed, half-wild garden, Setter and Bernard were grubbing up weeds. I saw their figures distorted by the window glass. It had been impossible for me to tell just how friendly they really were — or rather, whether they liked each other or not. Setter lumbered peaceably through the hours, not talking much, but grinning when Bernard, who was something of a *raconteur*, told stories against himself and his job. The Phryne Club had been mentioned by no one: Emily was on her best behaviour.

Few things are more pleasant than doing nothing but eat and drink in the company of apparently amicable persons who make no demands on one. Jenny, as a rule rather feverishly vivacious when finding herself in new surroundings, was relaxed here, and enjoying herself. She had forgotten that she did not really like the Setters: she was not showing off to them or compensating for the guilt of dislike by behaviour exaggeratedly affectionate. She was just Jenny at her nicest, and very nice too.

The day was chilly and grey. The church bells sounding across the vasts of sugar-beet made one grateful to be both agnostic and indoors. I was happy. I thought we all were.

Just before lunch, something happened.

Emily had brought a game pie down from Fortnum & Mason's, so there had been nothing to cook. Jenny helped her to lay the table, and called the men in.

'Ten minutes to clean up,' Emily said, 'and it's all yours. I must go and pretty myself, too.' She went upstairs, followed by Bernard. Setter went to the kitchen sink, sluiced his hands and face, and came to join Jenny and me for a drink. We were doing the *Observer* crossword together, with Setter reading out the clues and numbers of lights, when something fell heavily above, and Emily cried out, between a screech and a laugh.

Bernard's voice: 'All right, I've got you. O.K.?' He called down to us, 'She fell over one of those damned steps.'

It sounds nothing in the telling, indeed, there can't be anything. But the tone of Bernard's voice, when he first spoke, was unmistakeable. It was the tone of a lover who has had a shock.

Setter, who had risen, sat down again. His colour was high.

It is a terrible thing to hear, in the note of a voice, something so disastrous (yet, it now seems, something which must have been obvious to anybody else months ago) that it makes nonsense out of a lifetime. In any discovery of this sort we are tormented doubly: first, because our trust has been laid in ruins, second, because we are made utterly ridiculous. We stand alone: and the one who stood, we believed, at our side, is now apart from us, across a great river, laughing at us with her friend behind her hand. Our side is laid naked from shoulder to knee. We were clothed by the body who stood at our right hand. Now we are horribly cold, and the wind goes through us, and everyone is laughing like hell, all the wise people who know, who knew, who have always known. When we see them next time they will be very, very nice to us, and modestly lower their eyelids.

'I'm all right, Bill,' Emily called out. 'Only a graze. Just coming.'

'Twenty-two down,' said Setter, '"nap points", in six letters. D blank blank E blank S.'

'Dozens!' Jenny shouted joyfully. She was very good at crosswords. 'Doze — N —S. See?'

He entered the word, laid his pencil down. He was looking up towards the stairs. Jenny glanced at me, having missed all this. Her mouth opened.

They came down, Emily limping and laughing, Bernard respectfully supporting her. Setter simply stared.

'What's the matter, silly?' she said to him. 'I'm not dead!'

'I think you ought to know something,' Setter said in a heavy voice.

I was stricken with nervousness: I did not want to witness a scene. I was sure there was going to be a scene.

'Yes, dear. What?' She was on the flagstones now, pushing Bernard aside. 'Do you know, I've laddered *both* damned stockings. My God, I loathe Tudor, or whatever it is, no, it's Caroline. Let's all go and eat, shall we?'

'In a minute,' said Setter, 'I haven't finished my drink.'

He drank slowly and deliberately, making them wait.

Even Emily had realised by now that some sort of trouble was in the air, but hadn't the slightest idea what it was, since she, poor girl, had been doing nothing on this occasion that she hadn't done before — in fact, had been doing considerably less. 'Darling——' she began.

'The food's cold. It can wait.'

Jenny raised her eyebrows at me frantically. Only Bernard seemed at ease, pouring a drink for himself.

Setter said, 'I think I'd better tell you that I'm giving up my work.'

I was stupefied. I think I had expected some embarrassing denunciation of wife and lover. Emily wasn't merely stupefied: she burst out laughing.

'Darling, you're going off your head! And what times you do pick for it! *Giving up your*——'

'Giving up my work. I'm finished. The rest's up to you . . . two.'

She laughed again: she could think of nothing else.

Bernard said, 'I can't see that it's up to me, of all people. But you're not serious.'

'I am serious. You won't starve, Emmy. Nor shall I. But no more medicine. All right, lunch.'

He got up, leading the way to the dining-room. He looked terribly heavy, as if he were in armour, and his walk was not quite steady.

We went in after him, Emily still with that air of stupefaction mingled with derision, which gave her a silly look.

It would have been a wonderful meal if Setter had not ruined it in advance. That pie, salad, a stilton cheese, burgundy — just the sort of things I loved, and Jenny would never understand.

We all ate, but mechanically. There was no talk at all, except for the please-pass-the-butter variety. Emily grew pinker and pinker, and was obviously angry. Setter munched. Bernard messed around with his plate and pushed it back. Jenny looked from one to the other with infantile, terrified eyes.

When we had got our coffee, Setter began again. We might have been a board meeting.

'I've told you my plans, or rather, my decision not to have any plans, any more. I don't want any argument, because it's useless. So you two——'

'What do you mean, "we two"?' Emily demanded. 'Anybody would think Bernard and I were——'

'Look here, Bill, this is simply silly,' Bernard broke in smoothly but rather gingerly, as if inserting a knife into a cake to see if it was done. 'Victor and Jenny will think the most peculiar things. We've all known each other for years and years, and——'

'Quite. All I am saying is, that I'm giving up my work. If Emily wants to make any different plans in the circumstances, you and she can talk it over. But not with me.'

'You are being quite preposterous——' Emily began, flushing, making as if to rise, but he shook his head and she stopped speaking.

He turned to Jenny, gave her an affectionate smile. 'This is a nuisance for you. But it means nothing more than my own brand of bad behaviour. Emily will tell you what that is. I can hardly ever bring myself to make a decision at all. When I do manage it, it seems to me so epoch-making that I never choose the right time and place for an announcement. Sorry, Victor.' His smile disappeared. He said to Emily, 'Good meal. Now then, what does everyone want to do this afternoon? Sleep? I know I shall.'

He got up, patting Jenny on the head in a fatherly, compassionate way, and went straight upstairs. We heard his feet along the gallery and then, with a touch of shock, a bolt rammed home.

Emily decided to pretend that *nothing whatsoever had happened* except for Setter's plain statement about his work.

'Isn't he silly?' she beamed at us. 'God knows what's got into him. But he'll have forgotten it by tomorrow, thank Heavens.'

I had often wondered what happens in the lull which follows big scenes. I can tell you what happened in this one. Emily, Jenny and I played Scrabble till teatime (Jenny won hands down). Bernard got out some work from his brief-case and settled down to it in Setter's study, occasionally wandering in on us to ask how the game was going.

At half-past four, Jenny made tea. At twenty to five Setter appeared, looking rested and bland. We talked politics in a very animated and civilised sort of way. It began to rain heavens hard outside. At five o'clock precisely, the telephone started to ring.

Emily answered it, called out to Jenny, 'Darling, your sister wants you.'

Jenny turned white.

We do know when these things are coming. Anyway, Jenny knew. Guilt had sharpened her sixth sense: she had almost been expecting it. There could have been three or four reasons why Fay could be ringing her, but of course she hit on the right one.

She went into the study and I went with her.

Stephanie had died an hour ago.

Jenny said, 'I'll come at once.'

She hung up the receiver, and without a glance at me walked back with a curious wide stance, as if she had wet herself between the legs, into the hall. Her face was quite blank. Catching up with her, holding her tightly, I said what I should never have said: 'You're not to blame yourself. You could never have known.'

For this suggested to her at once the idea that she might blame herself, and that she ought to have known.

'What——' Setter began.

'Jenny's mother has died,' I said.

Emily came in in a barnyard rush. 'Oh my dear, my poor dear——'

'Good God, I'm sorry,' said Bernard, looking curiously oafish, with his mouth open.

Jenny just stood and stared.

Setter took her right away from me into the study and shut the door. There was a long silence. After a while we heard her crying violently on a high, reaping note as if she were cutting corn with her voice, then shudderingly, then in a steady gasp and heave, heave and gasp, till all of a sudden she stopped.

He came out again. 'You look after her,' he said, 'I've given her a pill to take the edge off. I'll get the car. There may be a train from Sudbury.'

Jenny was lying on a sofa, her eyes dark and dilated, her hair streaming down her wet cheeks. She looked bloated and old and beautiful. Even in my distress, I thought it extraordinary that 'beautiful' was the word I should find: she had always been very pretty, but very pretty people are not beautiful at all. She raised her hand and I took it, sitting wretchedly beside her, not knowing what to say.

'If I hadn't made her go,' said Jenny. She gritted her teeth. All her facial muscles twitched. Then she said in a scream, 'Oh no, no, no, no, no!' She gasped, was quiet again.

I said, 'You'll make yourself ill.'

She whispered, 'Myself ill! I made her die.'

'It would have happened anyhow.'

'I can never know.'

I kissed her. She let me do it, after a while responding greedily, her cheeks sticky against mine.

Emily put her head in. 'If I can help——'

'Thank you,' Jenny said stiffly. 'No.'

The door shut again.

'The fire in the bedroom, just as we hoped; all *that*: making love, and she was going to die. Oh God, oh God, oh God, I shall never be able to see a bedroom fire again without seeing her!'

Hysteria was rising once more. In her throat, the apple moved up and down like a bubble on a jet at one of those fairground things. I was helpless.

Setter came in and sat beside her.

'There's a train from Sudbury to Mark's Tey in an hour. Take your time. We'll do it easily. Emily will pack your bag. And now listen to me.'

She turned to him the dark, tragic olive of her eyes.

'You didn't kill Stephanie, my girl. My guess is that she's had a cerebral haemorrhage, which no one can anticipate. You did everything for her, held her up when your father kicked the bucket, you've held her up ever since, far beyond the call of duty. She loved you, she always told me so. Too much. But she'd go mad if she could see you now, breaking yourself to bits for her sake. She was bloody selfish, Stephanie was, she was sucking you both dry, but she wasn't a cruel woman. Only a cruel woman could want you to suffer like this. Stephanie was good fun, when her bones didn't ache. Aches and pains made her bloody, but that was a sort of disguise. Under it, she was always the way you liked her.'

(I can remember all right, pretty well word for word. I don't know how much Jenny took in.)

'If you must kick yourself, just remember this. She kicked you, both of you, and damned hard. Don't start being a masochistic little bitch, because if you do you'll drive Vic off his nut. Remember: at this moment both he and I are talking sense, but you can't *think* sense. Remember that.' He said loudly, 'Don't think of what you did to her, but of what she did to you, of all

89

the things she did to you. Be a bitch, but not a grizzling sort of bitch.'

He hauled her up and to her feet. 'Get your things on.'

I went up with her to the bedroom, where she powdered over the tears, combed her hair, put on her hat and coat. All dry-eyed, till she noticed the ashes in the grate. Then she burst out into another great, uncontrollable flood of tears, and we rolled together on to the bed where we lay, Jenny storming with grief, myself trying to quieten her, till Setter called to us.

She went delicately down those stately stairs, as if they or she were made of glass. With dignity she kissed Emily and thanked her, made her apologies, shook hands with Bernard. We went out into the drumming rain and into the car: Setter drove us in silence to the station.

All I remember of that journey home is Jenny's set and seething face, the rain slashing in silver against the carriage windows. The moment when she said, 'I shall have to look at her, and see her dead.'

# Chapter 14

WE never knew whether Setter was right about the cause of Stephanie's death. Our doctor wanted an inquest, but Jenny wouldn't permit it. Her beastly sisters disapproved, anyway, and did nothing to discourage her from the self-condemnation which for a couple of months made our lives almost intolerable. I had always thought of Jenny as a pretty lightweight character, and shouldn't have married her, I think, if my impressions had been different. I don't like the Siddons touch around the house. But there was nothing light about the awful, howling grief with which I had to contend. Her skin seemed to be sore with it: she kept bumping into things as she went around the house, and giving great shuddering winces as though someone had stripped off a bit of skin with a razor blade. She was entirely sunken in guilt; it beautified her, and made her look like death. She cried for hours in the night.

After the funeral we had to return to our house, which was redolent of Stephanie: her clothes, her multiple pill-boxes, her bundles of old letters, her violetty smell, which lay in the folds of underwear Jenny dragged out and thrust upon the charwoman. We found a packet with two squashed cigarettes in it. A locket neither of us knew she had, containing a photograph of Jenny aged three. A silver caddy-spoon, broken, tarnished, which must for some reason have been prized. A flowery box containing two marshmallows. I found Jenny one night weeping over that box, her hair trailing into the flour from the sweets. I had to pick her up bodily, and as I did so she flopped over like a rag doll.

However, the worst of it passed as these things do, though she had nightmares. She woke me at four one morning: she was shaking all over. She had been sliding into hell, with Stephanie, a grin on her face, tugging her by the feet. Stephanie was wearing her best blue frock, Cambridge-blue, the one with the marcasite buttons.

'How furious she'd be,' I said, 'if she knew you were making a bogey of her. She'd boil with rage. She was far too vain to want to be a bogey. Anyone would be.'

Jenny admitted the truth of this, though she was too afraid to sleep again till it was time for us to get up. It was only the first of such dreams.

Setter, of course, was always in and out, watching Jenny when he thought she wasn't watching him. He gave her some dexedrine tablets, not too often: half a tablet every two days. 'It's not really for her benefit,' he told me, 'it's for yours. She's got to sweat this out her own way, but I see no reason why you should have to sweat too. You had enough of poor old Stephanie during her lifetime.'

Meanwhile, apparently, to the accompaniment of alarums and excursions in circles not known to me, he had done as he said he would: he had given up his work. He had sold his Harley Street lease, his plate was down. He was doing, he told me, nothing at all: just seeing old friends. Malpass told us that the club nights were still going strong and that Sammy Underwood never missed one.

Then we heard, from Setter himself, that Emily had left him, that she meant to marry Bernard. 'So she's upped and gone. I realize now that the only thing keeping her was the thought of my possible glory in the future. There's no glory going now.' He looked at me with small, hot, inflamed eyes. 'It is pretty monstrous,' he said.

I asked him what was monstrous.

He replied: that he should have made such a damned fool of himself. He had believed in her practical, her physical, fidelity. He had wanted to believe it: he had done so. And all the time cold little Emily was in rut, sleeping around with that triping estate agent, a friend of his, or more or less a friend of his.

'You must have known,' I said.

'No. I don't think I knew. Anyway, I didn't want to know. And if you don't want to know things, then you don't. See infant teacher's first discovery in the teaching of arithmetic.'

He asked me to dine that night at his club. 'I'm sick of Jenny,' he said, 'I can't stand her misery. And you must be sicker of it, since you live with it all the time. In any case, I need to talk.'

So we met down by Whitehall Court, had a chop and some claret, retired not to the library but to an alcove in one of the landings of the great draughty staircase, where we drank Guinness.

I think I had better give what he told me as straight as I can remember it, calling it

## SETTER'S STORY (1)

*(Setter speaking)*

When I was about eighteen I used to go down to Eastbourne to take my nephew out; he was nine, he went to a prep school there. His mother could only stand half-holidays in summertime; the grey, bitter, bracing rainstorms, the sweeping-the-Front ones, those she left to me. Anyway, he liked me. One Sunday I found out that the cinemas were open at 3.30, so I thought I'd take him, to fill in time and save money. Otherwise, it meant feeding slot-machines on the pier, hour after hour. It was a beastly day, winter, half a gale blowing, dark, wet, the sea stinking of itself, *you* know. I hadn't got to take him back till 8.30, wild horses wouldn't make him go before, as well I knew. We stumbled across a sort of flea-pit in a back street. Anything, I thought, to get in out of the wet. The big feature seemed all right, cowboys and Indians. Then I saw the second feature was an old one, vampire film, it had scared me stiff when I was a child. I nearly said — 'Let's go somewhere else,' but by now it was pouring heavens hard and he was cavorting joyfully round the box office, waiting for me to pay. So I thought, but I don't remember the progression of my thoughts — He won't mind it, he's totally insensitive anyway; I can't disappoint the kid; it would be interesting to see him react; it would be psychologically *valuable* to compare how he takes it with how I took it; it would hurt him, it would be interesting and rich to hurt him, a positive duty to hurt him.

So in we went, and the cowboys, thank God, were first, because, although I was watching the film intently, as thrilled as he was (I told you, I was only eighteen), a second set of thoughts was churning below the top ones, making a sort of hot pain and excitement. In those thoughts was something ugly about the kid (how flabby he was, what a silly face he had, such faces needed a good healthy shock to give them an *expression*) and something ugly about myself, which made me feel sick and powerful at the same time. Then I began to think *above* the cowboy film, and it was quite clear: You are not going to let him stay for the vampires. All right. But then an internal debate began on that level, and the cowboys faded away. This sort of thing:

A. Obviously you won't let him stay.
B. But it's raining cats and dogs outside.
A. Rain or no rain, you won't do it. Obviously.
B. You can't get dinner till 7. What will you do with him for hours on end?
A. I don't care what I do with him. Of course I have to get him out.

94

B. And you will miss the treat, your own succulent little treat?

A. It's no treat. I *swear* that.

B. No? Then does it occur to you that you may be making the boy soft? (It will be water off a duck's back to him, in any case.)

A. I've no right to take the risk.

B. However much you long to. (He is a filthy brat, isn't he? He picks his nose and puts it in his mouth.)

At that moment, the lights went up. Fondant-coloured ads for furniture shops, dancing classes, cycle stores, chocolate, beauty parlours. He had an ice cream, and the news reel began.

I said, 'We won't wait for the other film.'

Well, of course, that started it. By the time he'd argued and I'd argued, I'd yanked at him and he'd kicked my shins, the B. feature was on: tombstones in a fog, far, far away a white thing, like a blowing newspaper, flickering between trees, then coming nearer and nearer, with a glide, a hop, a skip and a jump.

'Come on, damn you,' I said, and grabbed at him.

With that he gave a yell of rage you could hear all over the cinema. People shush'd us. Growing out of the screen was the face of a beastly woman with long black hair and her mouth filled with blood as if someone had just kicked her teeth out.

He said, 'Think I'm going to miss this?'

We had a sort of running fight to the door. The rain had stopped, but it was as cold as death, the sea mist made one cough. I walked him about, took him to the pier, bought him one of those filthy candy-floss things, dished out to us bare-handed by a girl with acne. He wouldn't talk to me. He sulked himself sick. It was a hellish evening. But I, I felt saved. I felt good. My God, I felt good! Holy! *Good!*

You mustn't think, though, that this was, for me, a moment of revelation. I had known it all for a long time, without raising it to Thought Level One (there being three, you understand), had known that deep in my nature (oh, for what it is, for what it is), like one of those slimy great fat stones in an avocado pear, there was a core of pure rich hate. I could hate anything, or anyone. And when I let that hate rise, then I wanted to revenge myself on anything, or anyone. When I was a small boy, sixish, or so, I remember hating a pebble for its beastly colour. And I carried it along, wanting to revenge myself on it, till I found a cowturd, and ground it in. That served it right. To be buried in a cowturd, just right for that filthy pebble, just what it deserved, for being grey with turd yellow blotches on it. And then I turned back, dug the beast out with a stick and washed it in a puddle till it was clean, and stuck it back with the other pebbles. I could not carry it through. *I have never carried it through.* But someone knows about it, about the pebble, about me. It isn't private to myself, or to you, even, now I am drunk enough (but not all that drunk) to talk about it. It doesn't matter if I tell you, you understand? It wouldn't matter if I told the entire British Isles and the United States put together. Because so long as I never carry it through, I am all right with people. I shall never be all right with myself.

Inside I am extremely dirty. I knew that young. It isn't easy to live with. It is all the filth of hell to live with, like a dirty mouth in the morning, and bugger chlorophyll.

A vampire for a favourite nephew, a pebble stuck in dung. Not much. But there were other things. Such as enjoying books that jerked me up like a red-hot poker. *Pleasures of the Torture Chamber*—— Oh yes, we all go through that stage, you too, you too. But we ought to get out of it. And so we do, so I did. But for show, only for show.

In the Medical Schools, I got a bit of peace, till I understood what I was up to. Pain and disease and death were not only permitted but obligatory; I looked on them with such a calm, shocked, delighted eye. Calm and shocked — one can be both. It's common. *Et puis?* (Excuse my French.) *Et puis*, I was there to help, I was there to overcome pain and disease and (up to a point) death. What a blessing that was! I could have my fate and eat it. Why did I take up medicine? To enjoy, I think, pain and disease and death. But also, to destroy them. I could do, for salvation, what my nature denied me the right to do: heal.

Fine. Then what? It struck me — 'but you don't believe in God.' For whose benefit, then, are you putting on this act? Caught you there. (I mean, I caught myself.) For whose benefit? I tell you, I don't know, I don't know, but there is *something* which knows about me. As I said, not you, it doesn't matter your knowing, or the British Isles, or the United States of America.

I am watched. I am deeply, steadily watched. Something has its pale and lidless eye on that greasy core of avocado. I could go mad sometimes under that watching. Whatever I do, it makes no difference. It is what I am. And nothing can alter that. Not what I am.

I remember reading, about 1933, in the magazine *Time*, about the Nazi persecution of the Jews in Germany. It made me sick and excited, and I sweated cold all over. I loathed it: and I had to go back and back and sneak yet another look at those things, because I could not help myself. In the thirties I was an active politico: not a demonstration that I wasn't on. At one end of every banner was me. I hated Hell because I understood it. When the rest of them didn't, not really. Because it was in me. Let me tell you something.

One day I discovered that what I hated was pain and disease and death.

A triumph? Ah, you think you've come to Chapter the End. Bells ring out. Half a dozen rhubarb-faced cherubim with an army blanket arrive to accomplish the apotheosis of Setter.

97

You are wrong. Because I also discovered in myself the desire to *torture* Pain and Disease and Death. And at the same time, I discovered the distressing position of the Damned. For whatever they do, they can't achieve Election. Calvin was dead right. Grace, that's what you want, my boy. And it's no good trying to work for it. You have it or you haven't, like a club foot or a wall eye. BUT — but — but — you have to go on working for it, just the same. There's the bad joke. I try to heal, to cure myself of the urge to destroy. Then I find I am healing *in order to destroy*. Round we go again. And furthermore, I discover that whatever I do, it profits me nothing. Giving my body to be burned and having not charity, profits me nothing. Oh yes, I was the son of a parson, but alas, alas, I have forgotten the words. My father was a dull man, a droning man, my mother was bored with him and longed to be a smart girl wearing nice clothes to restaurants. Also he had hay-coloured hair growing out of his ears. 'Do cut it,' she used to say, 'it's so easy, just let me take a little snip with my scissors——' But no, it was part of him, that hay was. Like my young cousin's snot, he couldn't bear to lose it. He refused to christen babies if their parents didn't come to church like clockwork, and what a parade he made of it! Imagine Moses steaming down from Sinai, lightning in his beard, arms creaking-full of stone and then saying, 'I am sorry, Mrs. Smith, the sacrament of baptism is a serious matter, Mrs. Smith, it is not just a social occasion.' So I forgot the words pretty early, as I say, and I don't think my mother ever learned them. But a little bit of it sticks even among the barbarians (did you enjoy *Stalky*? I did, naturally) and I think I understand Saint Paul better than the Corinthians did. If they had understood, they'd have fled him like the plague after what he said to them. They didn't, because it was too terrible for them to grasp. It's a fine recitation piece, that, it sounds comfortable. In sober fact, the thing's a Commination. For *me*, a Commination. No charity, so I may

give my body to be burned. I have to, in fact. But it profiteth
me nothing. Poor old William Cowper, if he read Corinthians
Fourteen in any cosy spirit, I should be surprised. It profited him
nothing.

Let me tell you something else.

I was a brilliant boy, flower of my family. What the rest
did with blood and sweat and tears, I did on my head. I was the
most dazzling student of my year, always. And I prospered
in my profession. I became the man to go to. Up went my
plate: go to Setter, go to old doggy-woggy, he *knows*. Also, I had
a lot of money, legacy from my mother's sister.

I started off first of all in partnership, in a county town, very
rich, lots of old women. I had a white Georgian house with
yew-hedges, lilacs and syringa, a cosy waiting-room with all the
magazines up to date. I met Emily at that time, she liked the
house, we got married. At the end of the passage leading to the
garden was a door with a pane of orange glass in it. When the
sun shone and the door was open, the whole hall was orange,
and the greenery dazzled you outside. Emily loved that glass
door, I think she married it.

She never had the normal strain of being a doctor's wife; I
had the money to spare her that. She was beautiful, she was
cool as a cucumber; you remember the orange moon making
Proust thirsty for orangeade? (What a drink!) Emily made me
thirsty for cucumbers.

But I was going to tell you something. A woman came to see
me one evening, a visitor to the town. I never saw a brute I
hated so (Browning). She was pious, she whined, she was a
prude, she was rude. She had a sebaceous cyst in her armpit,
nothing of interest. I said I'd better cut it out for her. That's
no job, a snip, all over. She went white, said she'd prefer it to be
done by her doctor in London. After all, she didn't know me
(she said), she didn't want to offend me, but I seemed very

young, and one did trust the London people better. After all, they had the experience.

'Have it your own way,' I said, and shrugged at her as if the Angel of Death was her pigeon.

She went on hesitating, and I went on shrugging.

Then she said, 'All right.'

She got her jumper off. I asked her what deodorant she used, though I don't think she did use one, not with her reek, but it may have been a fear-reek.

I put some stuff on the thing, which was like a dried pea, and I slit the skin for her. Down she went, wallop. I just caught her before she hit the surgery floor. I called my receptionist, and turned the body over to her for reviving.

When I sat down at my desk I was trembling all over, with pleasure and disgust. Because I had hurt her, and yet it was wonderful. She had deserved to be hurt, and I was the only person with a legitimate chance to give her what she deserved. The pleasure was on Thought Level I; it was perfectly plain, I put it mentally into words. I did so for the first time in adult life.

So after a bad night I told Emily the time had come for a change. No more general practice. No more measles, no more babies, no more benzedrine addicts (one of my patients was a farm labourer who took sixty a day), no more piles, no more colds and coughs. At least, not for me to deal with myself. I was going to put my plate up in Harley Street and become a general consultant. I had, in fact, found a way to stop my personal devil in his tracks: I was going to deprive myself of the chance to give, and therefore to enjoy, pain.

Was Emily pleased by the thought of the metropolis? You would have thought so. But not a bit of it. She was in love with that damned house. Remember, this was a smart town, good shops, dressy local life, pots of money, hunting, shooting. She didn't pine for London. 'You're too young,' she said (I was thirty-two) 'no one will pay out good cash for your say-so.'

She piled on the agony till the very day we got our stuff into the removal van. I used to find her standing in the passage, looking at the orange glow on that wall. She would pass her hand up and down the panelling in the dining-room. When she knew I knew she'd seen me, she used to give a jump, blink her eyes rapidly, and beam at me. 'Oh, hullo, darling, I didn't hear you come in.'

When we got to London, she miscarried. She always told me afterwards that it was the strain of the move. In fact, she had hardly lifted a finger. But it made an excuse, the excuse of finding something to make her forget. The men began then, the flirtations. Intellectual companionship, she used to call it. When I can't sleep I don't count sheep, I count Emily's intellectual companions.

Now what have we got? Where am I? A film, a pebble, a tin-pot sebaceous cyst. I got him out of the film, I washed the pebble, I dealt with the damned cyst in an ordinary, careful, gentle manner. I have done nothing. It is what I am that matters.

Victor, I have never been happy. Elated, yes; hilarious, yes. Never happy.

I was in the army during the invasion of France. I saw them shave the heads of four tarts one day, in a village near Rouen. It was as cold as sin that morning. I couldn't stop it, nobody could. But some good chaps went away, they didn't watch. I did, and I was as sick as a dog afterwards. Being doomed to pleasure plus loathing, never one without the other, that's a nasty fate. And to be dirty inside, as I am. One of those girls went dotty, she ran around screaming. The other three stared at her, top-lofty, scornful. She tore across the square, tried to stick her bald head in a hedge outside a café. Nobody laughed,

not the crowds, not the ones who had done it. They pulled
her out, and her face was all over hedge-dust and blood.
Stern they were, the onlookers, very. Like the Puritans staring
at Hester Prynne, not a pleasure among the lot of them, not
likely. Oh no. Not a bit of it. Loins quiescent. That square, I
tell you, was heaving with subterranean pleasure, it was thick
as treacle, it was humming like a swarm of bees. What a day!
What a day to remember! What a good vomit afterwards, what
lovely bad dreams! And I, I watched too, very stern, very cold.
Disapproving. Detached. I wouldn't have missed it for worlds.

The affair wasn't mentioned in the mess: except the C.O.
said, 'I suppose one can see their bloody point of view.' But
it was talked out in the dark, by twos or threes, talked out with
nice thick furry tongues.

You know Whitman: 'Who degrades another, degrades me.'

I had a religious period, it was a purely selfish one. I used to
pray on my knees, big toes together, eyes closed, that I should
find out what happiness meant. Not much to ask, one wouldn't
think. Emily's happy. She wouldn't even think to question
whether she was or not. But I got no answer. All I got was
success. All I got was the reputation of God's good man.

Look: let me put it like this. Despite my incapacity to
believe in God (people who do don't mind looking silly, or if
they do, they brave it out: their sacrifice: but I do mind), it
strikes me that if there were one, this would happen. I should
be brought up before him after queueing for a few million
years calculated by earth-time (time no object in that crystal
desert where it will all take place).

All around would be the multitudes of the earth, and probably
of all the other man-populated stars in other solar systems.
They'd all be standing, because you never get tired up there, and
there's no sickness, so nobody would feel the worse for wear. In
the background, ranges of mountains, dark, as if you're looking

at them through smoked glass. No music. God would have a face like a diamond, quite pure and simple, dazzling, but not off-putting. A triple tiara, gold. Beard, of course — God about seven feet high, very broad. Sitting at a crystal desk, with two secretaries, He would murmur something to one of them, consult the books, run his finger down, stop. Setter, William Setter: nothing but credit items. No crimes. No peccadilloes, no excesses. Pass, Setter, you are good.

And that would be God's error of judgement. For even he, the very last Court of Appeal, would not get the point at all. I should stand there before him, with the dirt, the ordure stinking inside me, and he would simply refuse to take it into account. Pass, Setter, and don't waste my time; pass into bliss, exactly as you are, incurable, into bliss without happiness. Which would be his mistake. 'I shall know as I am known.' *But I shall not be known as I know myself.* So that is why I have opted for the candle snuffed out, for the idea of nothing at all. Why should that terrify a man?

\*　　\*　　\*　　\*　　\*

Let me take over again.

That isn't all Setter told me; I have bowdlerised as I write. I have a queasy stomach: I couldn't write down the whole of it. Setter told me horrors. He told me, for instance, what the fantasy life of his adolescence had been, with what faiths he accompanied his works, as it were. All cruelties: joy in suffering himself. Joy in inflicting it. Not much difference between the two. 'A dog-face,' he said, 'might know why, or say that he knew. But I was made that way, and *I* don't know why. I disliked my father, but I was a reasonably happy child. Perhaps I don't remember? Perhaps what happened, happened when I was in my cradle? Could be. But I doubt it. And the dog-faces would bore and torment me by trying to make it all up for my benefit.' If he believed in God, he said, that would be easy: his misery would then be something seeded in him from the beginning, from God's will, and to some inscrutable (therefore perfectly satisfying) purpose. But he didn't, and he couldn't.

And then, when he seemed to have finished on a phrase which struck me as artistically right (I shouldn't have been thinking of art at that time, but, however, I did), 'Why should that terrify a man?' — he went on talking. It wasn't interesting, though it sounded mad. He began to tell me his hates, America, France, Germany, impaling these countries like so many butterflies on some awful stickpin of his own. I was sorry that he went on, because he had spoiled something, though not something great: he had merely spoiled the art of the moment. Lying back on the scratched leather of his chair, his small eyes sparkling in the lamplight, waving his huge hands about, he raved on. Everyone seemed to have gone home. His is not an enticing club, people tend to go home early. In the Piranese vastnesses of the hall, nothing moved. 'Well,' Setter said at last, shooting up, as if somebody had clapped him on the shoulder, 'time for beddy-byes. That's all for now.'

# Chapter 15

EMILY had gone off to live with Bernard in his flat overlooking Hyde Park. Setter did God knows what all day in
the home they had shared. Towards the middle of April,
he began to ask Jenny to his club nights and failed to invite me.
'You don't need it.'

'What do I need that you're offering?'

'I don't know, but all the same, you don't. And Jenny's
better on her own.'

Jenny came back puzzled but vaguely excited from the first
of such evenings.

'It's dull enough,' she said. 'But such odd fish. Your Miss
Lawson and Purdue seem to get along all right. Anyway, they
sit together.'

I suggested that with luck they might marry.

'Don't be more of a fool than you can help,' said Jenny, 'it's
not like that at all.'

'What is it like?'

'They just need somewhere to go. The trouble with you, you
always have to elaborate. That is all some people want.'

'Do you need somewhere to go?' I was jealous, but not in the
ordinary sort of way.

'I suppose so.'

'And without me, I suppose.'

'I don't think it's your thing,' said Jenny.

I asked her if Sammy Underwood had been there. She said
not. But in the following week he reappeared. And on the next
day Malpass came to see us.

'It was an odd do, wasn't it?' he said to Jenny.

'I couldn't make head nor tail of it.'

'I say head *or* tail.'

'Well, I say *nor*.'

This interchange concluded, and Jenny seeming pleased because she fancied she had routed him, he turned to me. Seriousness always sat oddly on his small and freakish face, but he was serious. They had talked, he said, about capital punishment. Sammy had been all for it, Setter non-committal.

Soft, Sammy had said, that's what people were. For himself, he wouldn't just hang them: if they'd strangled, he'd have them strangled. If they'd shot, then they'd be shot. Or poisoned, poisoned. He'd read about a negro in the American south who had been burned to death with a blow-torch. 'So give 'em the blow-torch.'

Who was to do it? Setter asked. Could you ask a public servant to get out his blow-torch and carry out appropriate execution in the name of the law?

'Let the nigger's relatives do it,' Sammy had replied, 'they'd be glad enough.'

After this, the usual club debate had followed, polite, sensible, so many miles from the practical that it made the head reel. Suddenly Sammy had raised the matter of Addie Engbeck.

Setter said, 'So they catch the chap. And an English peeler is deputed — excuse me, the hangman is deputed — to kick his eyes out. Oh come, Sammy, come!'

'Eye for an eye,' said Sammy, with an air of originality.

Then Setter said, 'Your eye?'

Sammy paused. 'Mine, yes, sure. If I'd done it.'

'He did, you know,' Malpass said to me, as we were talking it over later on.

Jenny cried out, and derided him.

'Oh no. You laugh at the idea of the murderer returning to the scene of the crime. If you substitute "fascination" for "scene", that's just what he will do. It's what Sammy does. Back and back and back. Damn it, why the old woman? It's forgotten. It's probably a closed case.'

I said the Sammys of this world loved to sup full of horrors. Furthermore, for him, it had been a local excitement.

'No,' said Malpass, 'unless you mean local to his own corpus. This has been the only real excitement in Sammy's young life. He can't let it alone.'

I asked him if he had heard from Sandra: up to now, her visit had slipped my memory.

He smiled. 'Oh yes. She made an appointment to come and see me. When she did, she went at me head on. I was a homosexual, chasing after her little brother. She'd been rehearsing her opening speech all the way from Clapham South to East Ham. I let her run on till her breath gave out, and then talked to her sensibly. Sandra deflated. Of course she thinks he did it.'

'Did she say so?' said Jenny.

'No. But it was why she came. To convince herself my interest in Sammy was less dangerous than she feared. Oh, far less. You see, though I have my faults, I don't look queer, or so I think. And when Sandra took a good look at me, she didn't think so either. So she was disappointed. And she went off as scared as before, only more white.'

'But you know——' Jenny began lightly.

I shook my head at her. It was the old question. Why hadn't Malpass married? Vicars usually did, if only for the sake of unpaid labour. The answer, I fancied, was that he was a natural celibate, interested in nothing but his work. It is a contemporary fallacy that there must always be something sexually awry about the unmarried. The males are credited with inversion: the females — if not with that — with multiple and elaborate frustrations. I have known many men and women exquisitely adjusted to life in their own company.

'I don't need sex, duck,' Malpass said to her promptly, 'I never have. And I am perfectly happy and perfectly sane.'

Jenny blushed. 'I wasn't going to question it,' she said with great dignity.

She was at her best that night, the old Jenny, nervously, delightedly conscious of her prettiness, diffident about her own intelligence, forgetting all her sorrows, preening herself because she was with two men, both of whom admired her. It was almost the last time I saw her so, because in the early hours of that morning she had a dream about Hell again.

She fought herself awake, so that I had to hold her arms down, take the force of her butting head on my shoulders, shout at her to make her understand who I was, where we were, what place, what time, what world.

This time, she had been sitting, she told me later, on the edge of a pit, cone-shaped, the open area huge as a football field, golden light streaming upwards from the bottom. Her legs were dangling into the space, and she was gripping the edge tightly with her hands, but without any fear. When the cone grew smaller, till the area of the opening was no bigger than that of our drawing-room, she was interested but still not afraid: she just wanted to see what would happen next. Miles and miles below, but very clearly, she saw Stephanie, wearing a dress she did not know, baby-pink, with a frill round the neck. Her face, stone-dead but very lively, very excited, was turned up to Jenny's. She began to reach for her legs. This did not frighten Jenny yet, for her mother was still so far away. But then Stephanie began to rise up, as on a ladder, up and up, till she touched toes, gripped ankles and began to drag at them. She said nothing, only smiled: gleeful, full of hate and excitement. Her hands were tiny as a doll's. They scuttled up to Jenny's skirts, gripped her knees. She gave a series of little tugs — knees first, then skirt, knees again, while below her the cone glittered down until the gold was swallowed up in the darkness at the point. Her teeth were little and pretty and multiple: the teeth of a crocodile or of an organ manual, and they made a tiny noise as they clipped together. She tickled toes, calves, the ropes behind the knee-cap, not a woman but two spiders, not two spiders but a pair of feather dusters, not feather dusters but grappling irons, secure now, ready for action. Jenny's hands were torn from the edge and as she began to slip she struggled, not against the irons but against the giggling, the hilarity, the obscene intention, and against something monstrous with no body but only a giant personality, who was called Fall.

That was when she woke.

All I could get out of her at first was, 'It's Fall. Fall. He's called Fall.'

Later, when I had extracted the whole thing (which I should never have done if the slime of the dream had not still been upon her) I tried to pull her together by scolding. What would Stephanie have thought of it? To be made into a nightmare? Wouldn't she have loathed it? Furthermore, wouldn't it have seemed to her idiotic?

'Oh, and she meant to plait my hair,' Jenny screamed, her pupils enormous with tears and terror.

I shook her. 'Come on, wake up properly. Sit up. Get out of bed, go on. I'm here, don't you know that? I am. Me.'

I walked her around the room, but this was a mistake. She was so upset to find herself on her feet (where she didn't normally expect to be at 3 a.m.) that she thought she was still dreaming, and so burst out crying again. I dared not leave her to make a cup of tea. I got her back into bed, made her drink some water, put a cigarette between her lips.

'Ah, but one isn't allowed to smoke in Hell,' she said at last, 'or not like that, anyway, so I can't be there. I'm not, am I? I'm with you? Vic? I'm not going to sleep again. Don't turn the light off. Promise me you won't. I shall sit up, here.'

I didn't, but in half an hour she had dropped to sleep again. She woke at eight o'clock with heavy, reddened eyes, and didn't refer to her nightmare. I shall never know whether she really had forgotten or not. On the whole, I think she had.

Anyhow, later that day she said she would like to see Setter. Couldn't we ask him to supper? I tried, but he was away. 'Then Emily,' said Jenny, 'let's ask Emily.'

Bernard, too, was away, on business, so Emily said she would come alone.

'Good,' Jenny said.

I asked why she wanted her.

'Why not? I like to have people. And Emily's all right.'

I thought, You wanted him. She's the next best thing.

I suggested that Emily and Setter were far too unlike in every possible way for Emily to be a satisfactory substitute, especially now the marriage had snapped.

'Oh, he's still where she is, really,' Jenny told me, with a curious matter-of-fact kind of briskness. 'That doesn't disappear overnight.'

I did not ask why she had wanted to see Setter. I knew. She wanted something he gave to his lame dogs, without understanding what it was that he gave: without their understanding it either. She wanted to be with him.

It was a blustering night. Emily, big, flowery, beautified by rain, stepped in, scattering water from her crimson mackintosh all over the hall. She said, 'Beware, you two, I'm wet.'

She had never looked more radiant nor in higher spirits. I had regarded her always as serene and light of heart: but then,

I had never seen her when she was utterly so. She reminded me, crudely, of those brighter than white advertisements: I had thought the old Emily bright until I saw the new one.

She hugged Jenny and told her she was losing weight. 'Butter, you need, and lots of cream, all the things I mustn't have. Look, I've found you what you wanted.'

It was a Wedgwood plaque, icing-sugar on pale green, very pretty indeed. 'You know the one you liked? This is its double. I picked it up this morning.'

Jenny squealed with pleasure; then said, 'But Emily, it cost pots! We honestly can't let you——'

'I didn't say it was a present, love.' Emily swept us both into the drawing-room, as if it were her own.

'Well, then, *I* can't afford it. I told you I couldn't.'

'I don't suppose you could, at ——'s,' she named an antique dealer's in Kensington. 'But I picked this up at that shop just by your own silly station, and I only paid seven and six for it, which you *can* afford.'

'Emily, you know perfectly well . . . Suppose I go in and ask him what you paid?'

'Then he will tell you lies and treble it, just to put his own stock up. I beat him down. I can always haggle, you can't.'

'I don't believe——'

'Seven and six, please.'

Jenny paid, grinning. The dream seemed to have left her. She was flushed and girlish, they were girlishly excluding me. I didn't mind, I was relieved.

The meal was rather worse than usual, but Emily didn't seem to care. I'd been rather worried about my stomach recently, so I shared the wine between her and Jenny, in proportions of 2 : 1. After that, Emily drank a good deal of our whisky and basked before the small spring fire.

Jenny began to drink too. It was unnatural, it was not like her at all, it was defeat. I saw her glance sideways at me as she went with exquisite precision between sofa and sideboard.

She and Emily talked of happiness. How good to feel settled! In a world without war (so far as one could see, so far as one could hope)! In a gentle, unstressed, domestic world.

'But I had a hell of a dream last night,' said Jenny, remembering.

'Did you? I never dream.'

A big girl, a big smart girl, Emily began to talk as smart girls never should. In our too-small, too-white room, the atmosphere thickened like mustard. Again they were excluding me: but this time I did mind.

'You see, he was a terrible strain. Always on the move. We began so nicely: he was a pet. A pet lamb. Oh yes, a pet,' Emily reiterated. 'But darling, coarse though I may be, I do like to have it when *I* want it, only he . . . Oh, when *he* did. More than according to the books. And then leaving our quite lovely house — you don't know what I'd put into that house. Oh, Jenny, I'm a house-girl!' (Her fine thick legs wriggled, re-crossed themselves.) 'Like you, I love decorating it. The house, I mean. Tarting it up. Everything in its place. But he would move. And then he didn't seem to care what I did, so, loves —' (plural this time, including me) —'occasionally I did it. But when *I* wanted to. On my terms.' She was a big appealing girl now, all open to us, Danaë to the stars. 'Then it got worse, his silly club — darling, I couldn't understand it. You see, it is not that I am callous or cruel, but if I don't understand things I am desperately unhappy. Most people think only sensitive people are unhappy, people who do understand things. But people like me get unhappy because we don't. Worry, worry, puzzle, puzzle, how can you sleep with a puzzle? You're thinking too hard to have fun. Bernard is a pet lamb, I understand him. We'll get married when Bill files a suit. Easy for Bill, I'm not defending. Easy for Bernard, nobody cares about the morals of estate agents.'

She had been sitting on the floor, the light shining pink on to her hair, looking very pretty, very large, very lucid. Now she moved in some serpentine fashion backward, so that she could lay her head on Jenny's knees (Jenny was sitting on the sofa), exposing her throat which was as solid, as greenish white, as a stick of endive.

'But darling, darling, I loved him once. Just as you love Victor. But one must love a man with a name, not a man called X. "My heart is sad and lonely, for you I cry, for you dear, only——" '

' "Body and soul",' Jenny completed it, with a gulp and a faint shine of sweat. She was going to feel worse than Emily. She was not used to drinking. Also, she had endured much during the past twenty-four hours.

'Exactly,' said Emily. She brightened, sat up refreshed, as after a night's sleep. 'But who were we talking about?'

'I thought,' said Jenny, 'that you were talking about Bill.'

'Could be, could be. All completely forgotten. So you dream?'

Jenny shivered.

'I don't. I never dream. That's my piece of luck.' Emily jumped up, with scarcely a stagger. 'Dears, I must go. You are so terribly in the wilds, you know. Can I get a taxi? Or must I go to the silly little station?'

I called a cab, and in a few minutes it came.

The rain had ceased, our privet hedge sparkled in the steady lamplight. Emily walked briskly down the path, her arm round Jenny's neck. She kissed us both.

'Wonderful evening. I have drunk too much. Loves, I have been tremendously happy tonight.'

Jenny and I went back into the house.

She said in a false, light voice, 'Excuse me, darling, I must go upstairs and get a handkerchief. I'm sure I've got a cold coming.'

'We're both going up. It's twenty to one.'

'I said,' Jenny told me in a high, frantic voice, 'that *I* had to go up. Not you.'

She broke from me, ran on balletic tip-toes upstairs.

I heard hideous noises and the sound of the flush.

When she came down she was all right, but very pale.

'So silly, Vic. Let me confess it, let me admit it without shame, I drank too much.'

I kissed her, for she was sad and weak. She had had too much to bear.

# Chapter 16

SO I called on Setter. The house looked like a tidy rubbish heap: full of dusty stacks of books and papers Emily would have thrown out weeks ago.

I told him about Jenny.

'Not much I can do. I'm not a dog-face. It could be the start of menopause: she's older than you, isn't she?' She was: four years: but I seldom thought of it and never mentioned it to people when I did, for she looked a dozen years younger than she was (or so it struck me) and she moved and behaved like a young woman. She did not like to remember her birthdays and never kept them. I used to give her a present, but never on the day.

I asked him how he knew, and he asked me what I took him for, grinning just a little.

'She doesn't look it,' I said, feeling a touch of disappointment, of humiliation, for Jenny's sake: she did so love to be a girl.

'Not to most people. But I can tell. There, don't look so surly. Jenny's a marvel. Forget it.'

'She comes to you for help,' I said.

'No, she doesn't. She comes to my *conversaziones*.' He underlined the word heavily, grinned again. 'Just see she goes on coming. And get your doc to give her an overhaul. Is she getting enough sex?'

I said, with some pride, that she was getting plenty. She liked it, so did I.

'Good. Because if they feel you don't want them so often at that time of life, it often breaks them up. They think you don't love them because they're not so pretty, or that they show it around the neck or the midriff. Ever seen a handsome, well-set-up, still sexy woman in her upper forties starting to put herself with her back to the light, getting a sort of meek look when she sits down? That's heartrending,' said Setter. 'One has to admire Lawson. She's too proud to get out of the light, so she makes a deliberate fool of herself while she's in it. You give Jenny bed, her doc will give her little pills, I'll give her a refuge of pure boredom once a week.'

He pushed at a pile of papers on the floor by his chair as if he wanted to do something about it, but only succeeded in toppling it over.

'She hasn't even a child to build her self-esteem. She must mind that.'

It was a sore point. I said that when we married we had agreed that it wouldn't matter if no children came: after all, she was thirty-nine then, and at that age you needed a bit of luck.

'Before that?' Setter asked me.

I told him she had been widowed in the war. There hadn't been children of that marriage, either.

'Rough luck. Anyway, get her along on Wednesday. You can come if you like.'

'Very nice of you,' I said with irony. 'Are you quite sure I may come?'

'Oh yes,' said Setter, 'in fact, I want you to.' He added, 'What was the husband like?'

'Big chap. Handsome chap. Paragon of most of the virtues.'

'What virtues missing?'

'Too fond of the women.'

'Did she mind?'

I replied that she had minded: so much that she had dropped out of love with him five years before his death.

She had suffered so much, she said, that just when it seemed unendurable this thought had occurred to her: there was no need to suffer any more. She could simply stop loving. She had done so, at a certain hour on a certain morning. It was like stepping out into the sun on a spring day, without an obligation in the world and nothing but pleasure ahead. For the first time in months, she was *not at all tired*. It had given her husband a frightful shock, of course. Her only regret was that she was unable to comfort him with pity. She just couldn't be sorry for him at all.

'Poor old Jenny,' said Setter. He paused. 'Did Stephanie like the first chap?'

'She detested him,' I answered. 'That was my piece of luck.'

'You saw Emily last night.'

I felt obscurely caught out. 'Yes, in fact we did.'

'She told me. She rings me every morning. Extraordinary, isn't it?'

He sat back on the sofa, heavy, calm, faintly smiling. He was seeing her face, as if swollen up on a cinema screen. He smiled at the lips that spoke to him so nicely over the telephone, cool and considerate lips. 'Very kind of her,' said Setter. 'She thinks it makes the break easier. We chit and we chat. About this, that and the other. So many domestic details to arrange, property held in common, which of us has what. It isn't only civilised, it is thoroughly humane. Because, of course, nothing unites two people more than the sharing of loot. There's a lithograph, one of those Frenchmen, I forget which. Horses and carriages. It's hers, but I liked it. Emily won't take it back. "*You* have it," she says. "No, dear, I say, *you* have it." And then there are minor matters, suitcases, which are hers, which are mine. We have long, long talks. What I am thinking about is her in bed with Bernard. I can see every square inch. There's a lithograph for you.'

He went on smiling.

'I know,' I said.

'No, you don't.'

'One has to go on.'

'Oh, has one? Well, perhaps.' He got up, dismissing me. 'See you both day after tomorrow.' He droned under his breath, 'The thoughts of youth are long, long thoughts. The talks of Emily are long, long talks. The ——s of Bernard are long, long, long ——s.'

He stopped. He went downstairs with me into the hall.

'What do you do with yourself all day?' I asked him.

Opening the door, he said briskly that he found plenty to do. 'You'd be surprised how much: this, that and the other. Oh, I hardly know where the time goes to!'

# Chapter 17

WE waited and waited: no Setter.

Lawson and Purdue were there; the girl with the rose-garden; Sammy Underwood and another boy, older than Sammy, with a fair blank face and pear-shaped hips; the woman who was nearly blind; two men I didn't know. Jenny and me. The man who owned the place came in to ask for orders: he implied, with a touch of insult, that they were on Setter's bill.

Lawson and Purdue did, in fact, sit side by side, not talking much. They seemed ill-pleased by the sight of me. The room looked even dingier than before, I think nobody had taken a broom to it, let alone a vacuum cleaner, since I had seen it last.

Sammy recognised me with a wriggle and a nod of pleasure and crossed to my side, motioning his friend to come with him.

'Nice to see you, Mr. Hendrey. This is Cliff Waters.'

Cliff made a noise of acknowledgment. I introduced them both to Jenny.

'Where's the great man tonight?' Sammy enquired.

'I don't know,' I said. 'He'll be along.'

A committee meeting without an agenda. That's what it was like.

Miss Lawson said, 'How do you do, Mr. Hendrey? And Mrs. Hendrey too, I see!' She smiled at Jenny, whom she had met once before.

'Drinking his coke, him not here, that doesn't seem manners,' said Sammy.

The blind woman, the rose girl and the two men went on talking in undertones.

When Jenny spoke up, she seemed to me like a stranger. Obviously, this was a place she now knew, a familiar place, a stamping ground. She knew the *mores*. And I was out of it.

She said, in a high brisk voice, 'Dr. Setter seems to have been delayed. But I don't see why we shouldn't start. Has anyone an idea for a topic?'

No one but myself appeared to think this was mad.

A tall woman with a terrible lead-coloured face replied readily, 'Last time we were discussing whether there was a teenage problem nowadays — terrible term!' she laughed, fingering seed-pearls — 'any different to any problem of young people which has *ever* existed.' She had an overstrong, cultivated voice. 'May I begin on that? I was speaking of the "roaring boys" of the Eighteenth Century, if you remember from last time.'

'Two teenagers here,' said Sammy brightly. 'Seventeen and — no, Cliff has left us behind. Cliff is an adult, aren't you, Cliff?'

Cliff smiled and said nothing.

'Twenty-one last week,' Sammy chanted. 'He was twenty-one last week — that's right, Cliff, isn't it?'

'Well,' said the woman made of lead, 'we have at least one representative, then, of the group under discussion.'

'And not all that representative, Mrs. Brigham,' Sammy said cheerfully, 'because this isn't where most of them go for a night out.'

Mrs. Brigham said, 'I have perfect faith in the young.'

Sammy grinned from ear to ear.

'More than I have,' said Lawson. 'I see a damn sight more of 'em, I dare say.'

'That's right,' said Ulick Purdue.

'But we can't,' said the girl with the rose-garden, projecting her delicate, faded face, 'start talking without Dr. Setter.'

They all began to fidget, except Jenny. She just sat there, her eyes on the door.

Setter walked in, said he was sorry. His taxi had collided with a van, no harm done, but much talk. 'Where had you all got to?'

'Mrs. Brigham showing faith in the young,' said Sammy.

Setter said, 'I don't see why she should.' He got himself a drink.

'Come on, Guv,' said Sammy, 'remember the company you keep.'

'Yes, you just do!' one of them whom I had not identified called out.

They began to tease Setter, Jenny too, even Lawson: and it seemed to me that they were derisive. They might not be able to begin without him, but when he appeared, he lost his *mana*. Large, grey, stolid, even stupid-looking, he sat in his extraordinary club, taking the impudence without seeming to notice it.

I said to him under my breath, 'Only Mrs. Brigham behaves herself seemlily.'

'Oh, she's a newcomer,' he replied, 'she'll learn.'

The talk, as before, drifted on till past ten o'clock. It had drifted from teenagers to *apartheid*, from there to the coming Presidential elections in America. They all seemed to me equally dreary, equally ill-informed. Everyone took part except Cliff Waters, who maintained his blonde smile and uttered only once, when he asked Jenny if she wanted another drink.

'This is the bin,' I whispered to Jenny.

She said, not looking at me, her voice soft and furious, 'Then go home!' She rose suddenly, left me, and went to sit next to Setter. I felt a horrible pang, as if she had gone for ever; my side was cold all the way down. I might have been sitting in a draught. He did not look at her, just went on talking and listening. Yet somehow, to me, they looked like king and queen. I was out of it, right out.

As usual, Setter's rising was the general signal. They said goodnight, they trailed out. Setter stopped Sammy at the door.

'Get along and see Father Malpass. Not tomorrow, tonight. You've got time.'

'What for?'

'Do as I tell you.'

Sammy went white. He said, 'Muck along, Cliff. I'll see you tomorrow.'

Setter was shaking hands like a parson after service. 'Goodnight, Miss Lawson. Ulick. Mrs. Brigham. Miss Dewes.' He stopped me. 'You and Jenny come round to my place. I want to talk to you.'

As we walked off in search of a taxi, Miss Dewes of the rose-garden ran after us. She touched Setter on the arm. She said, as if it were some private joke, 'An outward and visible sign. Don't forget, will you?'

Setter said, 'Not me. Not up my street. How often have I got to tell you?'

She laughed, a theatrical, tinkling, chandelier laugh, and for a moment gripped his arm with both her hands. Then she was gone, too, after the others, who had waited for her.

'Damn fool,' said Setter.

We went to his house. It was a warm night, no need for a fire. The drawing-room looked sadder and even more derelict than I had seen it before, newspapers on every flat surface, books tumbled out of the cases.

'For God's sake,' said Jenny, in her Mother Hubbard voice, 'have you even sacked the char?'

He told her no, but that when he wanted things cleaned he would clean them up himself. He knew exactly where everything was kept. The woman could clean round them, he had no objection to that.

'What was that about Sammy?' Jenny asked him.

'Oh, that'll keep. I wanted to talk to you about something quite different.'

He swept some papers off the sofa so that we could sit down, gave us a drink. Then he began to speak.

I wish I were writing *War and Peace*. It looks such a straightforward book, even though it isn't. Take that white top hat on the battlefield: it's a signpost, something to hang on to. I find it hard to hang on to Setter. Let me try to describe, at least, how he was looking when he told us about Emily. He was looking exactly as I had first seen him, except that his clothes weren't so tidy. Quite different from the dominant, derided man of the Phryne Club. Calm, grey, a bit rock-like, a bit frog-like: not handsome, not not-handsome either. A reliable man, he looked: past his prime, but not so far past it that you wondered what his age was. A distinguished physician in a distinguished way of business, bang on the job, private life his own, what wasn't private at the devoted service of the moaners, groaners, shrug-it-offers, take-it-with-a-smilers; the innocent, the anticipatory, the optimistic, the desperate. But all that was past. He wore the shell of the past still: which made the whole thing more maddening.

Total recall is no gift of mine. But patching together my recollections of what he said (as, pushing himself between us on the sofa, he embraced us in a Father-Christmassy fashion) with the way I think he said, or would have said it, I shall put it down as

# An Error of Judgement
## SETTER'S STORY (2)

(*Setter speaking*)

I told you, Emily and I have been having a sort of game: me as the Man of Property. Sorting out, settling up. Her books, my books. Her pictures, my—— I don't know about pictures, I told you I didn't. She can have them. But there was a little desk I did like, we bought it together in the early days, before we were married, and I wanted to keep that little desk. So did Emily. Morning after morning on the 'phone. So I said to her, 'Look, you come round, we'd better talk it over.' And she said, 'All right, Bernard's away, I'll be with you about nine this evening.' Nine, and no Emily. Half-past nine, nine forty-five, no Emily. Ten o'clock, yes: bell rings: Emily. Bounces upstairs as if she owned the place. Coat on the floor, hat on the back of her head — 'Bill, darling, NO malice!' Naturally not. Gin for both. Discussion about that little desk.

(*In answer to Jenny*) No, not bloody Chippendale. Ugly little beast, a bit florid. But useful.

Useful, however, to Emily, too. There was a small drawer just right for odd photographs. Odd bits. And you always knew, she said, where things were.

Believe me, you would not believe — (badly put) — that that bloody little desk could cause such argument. But half-way through the argument, I would have let her have it (if she'd just stopped talking for a second) because I'd stopped wanting it.

It's stuffy tonight: you know how cold last night was. I had the electric fire on. I'd got it good and hot in here. We drank a lot, we were warm as toast. Emily was a million miles away, in that liberated world of hers. She'd flown away. Oh, she knew I was an old friend, she remembered all the good times: but I wasn't there any more. When you are madly in love with someone else, how nice you can be to the one you've kicked out on his arse! And *vice versa*, no charity about it.

124

Emily wasn't there in a charitable spirit. She was just enjoying the haggle, and liking it there with me, and feeling I was really a very good chap whom, after all, she *knew*.

Do you know how beautiful Emily is? Big-beautiful. You're smallish people. She and I are big ones. Rhinos — like rhinos. But she sat there, so big and beautiful, so much at ease, her legs stuck out as if she were in the stocks and quite comfortable there, thank you, so much at ease because it was only me. . . .

So I began a drunken manoeuvre. Her coat on the floor wouldn't do. I said, 'Damn it, you do make a mess of things, don't you? I'll put this where it belongs.' Up I got, and stalked off to the bedroom and threw it on the bed.

Time passed, desk still unwon. (I was going to pitch it off to her tomorrow in any case, though she didn't know that.) Both of us tight — Bernard drinks too much, anyway, and makes her drink more. Emily tight is like a big, beautiful, wobbly bonfire.

We heard the chimes of midnight, Master Shallow, from that ghastly clock with the exposed intestines, Emily's father gave it to us. (I used to say to her, 'I see insides at the damned hospital, I don't want them in the house.' But no go. We kept the clock.)

Emily said she must go. I had been longing for her to say that. I had been willing her to do it, I think.

'Where's my coat?'

'On the bed,' I said, 'and not in a mucky heap on the floor.'

So she went into the bedroom and I followed. Down she sat in the old way, at the dressing-table, to comb her hair. Got up, went to the loo (all, all are gone, the old familiar noises), came back, picked up the coat. I took it away again.

She giggled, told me not to be silly. So much at home, so EMILY.

So I threw her on the bed, and she started to fight and laugh, only as cool as a cucumber she was: it was only my fun, of course.

You see, dear Vic, dear Jenny, the trend this narrative is taking, its indelicate trend. I told you, I was the Man of Property. I think all that telephone haggle must have put it into my head. Anyway, there was Emily, burning like a bonfire, and I wanted her. So.

But the ridiculous thing is this. In my younger days, many a witness box have I seen. Many an outraged poppet. So I should have known the answers.

(*To Jenny's query:* 'Rape. Never believe in it. Not if the girl's in full possession of her health and faculties.')

It is dark in that room, we've never got it properly lit. And it was warm, because the radiators were on. I wanted Emily so much I could have died, or seen her die, or anything, so long as I could have her, or so long as neither of us could have anything.

Then what happened?

You may well ask.

Emily is a sensible girl, level-headed. In full possession of her health and faculties.

Take your wretched child: she may be too scared to do it. Or your drunk, perhaps.

Emily was neither a child, nor drunk.

She did what the real victims always do. I mean, the ones who really don't want it.

(*To Jenny's query:* 'What? Oh, she used her knee.')

So that was that. Emily rebounding from the springs, outraged but flattered and triumphant, me in some physical pain, but feeling degraded beyond . . . beyond anything your innocent rapist could possibly feel, because I might have known it. Soames *take* (I love 'take') Irene? She'd have used

her knee. It's easy. Either Soames gave out that he was successful to buck himself up, or Irene didn't mind for once. That's
just possible, she was a liar anyway. But I don't imagine for one
moment that Soames brought it off.

Yes. Well. Where was I? (Oh yes, embarrassing you both.)
I was looking a damn fool and feeling like a damned soul.
Emily was combing her hair again, getting into her coat.

I went downstairs with her. She kissed me goodnight,
nicely. It was the measure of my failure, that she dared to kiss
me, knowing I was powerless as a gelded tomcat.

When she had gone, I lay on that bed in my clothes, for hours,
it seemed, until I went to sleep.

It is a bloody horror. We only know what love is when it is
politely denied us.

Mark 'politely'. A violent refusal does something to satisfy
the ego. So does contempt. But politeness — you can only be
polite if you really don't care, right down to the core don't
care — that is murder. 'I appreciate so much the honour you
do me in offering me your hand . . .' which means, '—— your
hand!' Murder, murder.

I wish I had died last night.

# Chapter 18

THEN, of course, the subject had to be changed. So I
said, 'What's all this about Sammy?'

Setter would not come out of his horrible dream.
'Oh, him,' he said glumly, 'leave that to Malpass!'

He began to talk about love again. Jenny and I grew bored,
after the initial shock, since nobody's love affair is of the smallest
interest except one's own.

Love, he said, was so much more rare than one thought. The
general view was that anyone could love: just as the general
view was that anyone had one novel in him simply because
anyone could write, i.e. perform the physical act of writing.

Nobody suggested that anyone had one picture in him, or
one sonata, or one piece of sculpture. But love — to most
people, that was a synonym for getting on all right and being
pleasant in bed. 'To damn few people, love is possible. The
real stuff, aching to your wrists not for a week, not for a year,
aching always. The awful nights and days.'

He had been married to Emily for a good many years. All the
same, her key in the lock had set his pulses going at a rate: and
once, thinking he saw her in Bruton Street, where he hadn't
expected her to be, his heart had seemed to reverse itself and
stand on its valves. 'Love seated in the liver, my foot. Love is
in the heart: it does tricks, it sends up your blood pressure.
Love is something different.'

They had been married for twelve years then, had just made
the move to London. He had wanted a walk — it was a fine,

douce day in spring ('You know what I mean, douce'). He had walked all the way from Harley Street, down Bond Street, meaning to buy her something, and through Bruton Street in the direction of Berkeley Square. There, he thought, she was, walking at an idle, springtime lope, past the pub, her head bare, pinkish in the sunlight.

His pulses had stopped. Then raced: as during the first few months of their love affair.

But it wasn't Emily's coat. She hadn't a blue one at that time — he might have known it. He drew level with the false Emily, and under the pinkish hair saw a pig's face.

'I don't know love, not like that,' said Jenny.

He was on her like a flash. 'Don't you go forgetting!'

'Well, not what you meant.' She looked prim. Her mouth closed, as if by press-studs.

I was stifled by his warm room, and by the terrible thing I had heard. For Jenny had left me. There had been love between us once, and it was like Setter's. His kind of love.

I said, 'I want to know about Sammy.'

'Oh,' said Setter, 'that's like a bad detective story. Malpass drew him out about the old lady. Sammy revelled in it, scared though he was. Danger is heaven to Sammy, if he thinks he won't get caught. Imaginative flights, that's what he went in for. Poor old bitch, he could just see her in that gutter, her little strip of cat . . . but she *had* a little strip of cat. How did he know?'

I said Addie Engbeck had been a local figure.

'Ah, but . . . biting it?'

Jenny sat up, her face like fire. It was the first time this sort of horror had really touched her.

'What do you mean, biting it?'

'It was a little collar. When they were kicking her, she got it between her teeth.'

She asked him how he knew. 'Oh, I don't. But Malpass knows. He's in with the police. He asked them.'

'It's not Sammy,' I said.

'Oh yes. I'm sure enough. Sammy, his pal Cliff, possibly, but I don't think so. And the others.'

Setter rose up, ready for us to go. Years in Harley Street had made him very good at dismissal.

'I tell him to go and see Malpass, and he jumps to it. He knows why.'

'Is this fun for you?' Jenny broke in.

'More or less. Fun in a good cause. And that has not come easy to me.'

Jenny said, with the thoughtful air of an aspiring female detective, that if Sammy had just mentioned cat, it was of no significance. Had Sammy said she was biting it?

'No, no,' said Setter, 'Sammy is a little too clever. But you see, he did mention it. Fur in itself wouldn't impress him. But fur between the teeth — I'm quite sure.'

Of course, if a man is going to be romantic in one way, he will be in all the others. Malpass was not, I discovered, 'in with the police'. He knew about the bitten fur because it had been reported in the newspapers. So Sammy could have seen the report too, probably had.

I talked to him on the telephone, the night after Setter's Soames story and the dismissing of Sammy.

'You know,' said Malpass, 'that there are things I can't tell you.'

I persisted: 'Does Sammy admit to this nonsense?'

'If I now said my lips were sealed, you would immediately assume he had admitted it. The answer is, no admissions at all.'

'Setter is sure.'

'Maybe.'

'What do you think?'

'No validity to my thoughts,' said Malpass.

I told him to come off it.

I was completely in the dark. In any case, it was none of my business: but the things that aren't one's business are infinitely more fascinating than the ones that are. Also, it was a relief to play detective, just to get Jenny's disclaimer of love out of my mind. For I knew that, believing it only at the moment of saying, she had nevertheless used this moment of belief to revenge herself on me. Since Stephanie's death, she had ached to give pain, so as to draw a little of the pain away from herself. Therefore everything rough and delicate and delightful between us, everything coarse, visceral, adorable, deep-rooted, the roots of our life together, she had denied before Setter and before me.

# Chapter 19

BUT you can't worry about someone all the time, not if you are with them in intimate and above all domestic relations. There is so much to do in a house you share, if you are childless. There are so many details. When will the curtains be done? How long are we going to stand that damned broken fence? Grocer's bill this week, £4 11 3½. Precisely 10s. 0½d. up on last week's. Why? Did we have something extra, or have they got their books wrong again?

And so forth.

At that time, the idea that she was rejecting me, in front of Setter, to let Setter know she was free for him, lasted about a couple of hours and then blew away. For we were united, Jenny and I, in the piddling facts of a long-shared domestic life, our fingers in the same pie and fast stuck in it.

In May we went to Italy, taking our holidays early, and lay on the beach at Stresa pretending it was all exactly the same as it had once been, when we were first in love. I was impressed, when I read *Elmer Gantry*, by the passage in which Sister Falconer, out with her lover, once again became little Katie Jonas, girlish, nautical, all pleats and tam-o'-shanter. Jenny became girlish too, as light as if she had shed half a stone, jumping up like a girl, skittering all over the sand into the sea — middle-aged Jenny, but looking like a girl, concerned, because she knew I loved her, that she should go on looking like one. But she talked about Setter rather too much. It was surprising how gifted she was at lugging him into any context, however implausible. It was like some awful parlour game.

132

## An Error of Judgement

I had hoped for much of Stresa since, before this, it had merely been a place seen from the window of a train, a place at which one would have loved to stop. Flowers in tubs on the platform (I think), and beyond it pinky, chalky or khaki villas jolting down to the cobalt sea. Well, here we were, playing like hell at the game of pretending it was all we had hoped for.

I wasn't sorry when we got back to London.

London enclosed me like the womb, liver-coloured, restrictive, gentle in its deplorable suction. We returned to our house; and, hosanna! the curtains were all wrong. The chap had made a mess of the fence, we had an infinite number of things to talk about. Down-to-earth things, which are the tent-pegs of a potentially rebellious life.

Oh, what a marvellous time we had in Stresa! — we told our friends. We made them drool with envy.

But it was such a comfort to be home that on our first night I slept for nearly eleven hours without a single dream.

# Chapter 20

IN the summer two things happened.

Setter abandoned his club. I heard this from Malpass, who told me bleak notices to that effect had gone out to all members. No explanation. Nothing. Only, the evenings were off, and for good.

Purdue and Lawson got married.

Now I suppose this is the only practical happening for which Setter had been accountable, up to that time: if, indeed, he was accountable for it.

I learned this one fine morning at the office. Lawson asked to speak to me. She came briskly into my office, her cardboard tweeds creaking as usual. She was no prettier than usual. No less grotesque. She was businesslike.

'I have to tell you, Mr. Hendrey, that I am going to be married in September.'

I took the shock. 'A handsome timepiece from us all,' I said, 'handed over formally by Mr. Bickerton. Congratulations, Miss Lawson. I'm so pleased. Who's it to?'

'Mr. Purdue.'

I suppose I should not have been surprised. At least they had been in each other's company after office hours. But he was certainly seven years her junior, and they would make a bizarre couple.

'I know,' said Lawson, 'that it must seem odd. I'm not so young. But we're lonely people and we get on together. Even if there wasn't anything else to it.'

She sat down rather suddenly. Her face flushed, a faint silvering of sweat beaded her forehead.

I repeated that I was so glad.

'Being lonely is something, it makes you feel anything's better. And Mr. Purdue hasn't a very happy home life.'

I asked her if she knew why the club had broken up.

'Oh, I think Mr. Setter just lost interest. If it hadn't broken up, I don't know whether Ulick would have thought about — she hesitated — 'other arrangements.'

Then she laid her big palm upward on my desk as if giving me a present. The fingers quivered. I did not know what I was supposed to do. Take it? Hardly. Put ash in it? I looked at it. She said, 'They'll laugh in the office, I suppose.' Her throat moved. She shut her eyes quickly, squeezing the lids together. Then she flicked them open again and stared at me: no tears. 'Bloody lot if they do, but they will.'

I told her most people got laughed at the moment they announced an intention to get married. All the world didn't love a lover: it hated a lover. Jealousy crawled in the world's intestines whenever some besotted maverick laid claim to personal happiness.

'Yes,' said Lawson, immovably, 'but I look an odd fish. Some people even think I'm one of those women — you know. I'm not. I can't stand women. Well, let them laugh!'

We agreed to do so. I had a sentimental fancy that I might have kissed her, just to make a little ring-a-rosy celebration out of it all. However, I didn't. She would have hated it, and it might have made her tearful. She was pretty shot-up already, at the thought of marrying Purdue, but she would go through with it. Because she loved him. Lawson, no less than Cleopatra, no less than Helen (in fact, a damned sight more than either of them, I suspect), was in love.

I had not made contact with Setter since the Soames evening.

Now I wanted to do so, to tell him of his success: but when I dialled, the operator told me the number had been changed. The new one was *Pimlico* 3069. I dialled PIM, but no answer.

I meant to try again later, but I had a busy day and no chance to amuse myself. When I got home I told Jenny the news, and said I must get it to Setter somehow.

'Find out what he's doing in Pimlico and ask him round,' she said casually; which at once made me counter suggestible. I probably shouldn't have discovered his whereabouts for some time if Emily hadn't asked me to lunch with her that week — not, by the way, asking Jenny. It was all a bit hush-hush.

She was bonny as ever, as untouched by any sort of strain. Being with Emily was like sitting back in a chair whose springs have very gently collapsed: it was rock-bottom repose. The divorce proceedings, she told me, were under way: the hearing was fixed for November.

'Poor old Bill,' she said, 'we've virtually ceased communication. Not that I wouldn't go and see him, if I thought he'd like it, only one has to worry about King's Proctors from the word go, as it were.' She brooded for a moment, pushing out her creamy-rose lips. In the muted lights of the restaurant, where everyone else looked etiolated, Emily seemed about to burst into some huge bloom, some inordinate, inappropriate, grotesquely fertile flower.

'You know he's given up the house? Oh yes, he has. He's living in three rooms down by the river, not far from the Dolphin.' (Dolphin Square.) She gave me the address. 'He's crazy, poor old thing, quite crazy. One can't cope. *I* couldn't.'

'And he won't get his K now.'

She looked up sharply. Her eyes sparkled. 'No, he won't, will he?' She paused. 'And what did you mean by that? That it's all I ever really wanted?'

I said nothing.

'Well, I did want it; I think it must help one to jump the gun at the hairdresser's.'

'If I thought you were as horrible as you pretend to be,' I said, 'I'd pay the bill and go home.'

'Nonsense, you're lunching with me.' She beamed. 'Why am I horrible? It was never any good with Bill and me, not for quite five years past.'

'He's in love with you,' I said, 'which is respect-worthy.'

'I did go and see him not so long ago,' Emily said. She added, with her usual air of thoughtful immodesty, 'He was so odd then. He tried to *take me*, as I believe the phrase goes. But he was pretty tight and so was I. I just said no.'

I said she had no need to tell me all this.

'Oh, but I want to. You're so uninvolved, aren't you? You are the only completely uninvolved person I have ever met. That is, outside your own home. You and Jenny — that's different. But you and everyone else — just no contact.'

The idea seemed to make her even happier. She waved a marbled arm in the air, knocking a lampshade askew as she did so, and ordered brandies for us both.

'I don't drink in the middle of the day.'

'Oh yes, you do,' said Emily.

I asked her directly why she had wanted Jenny left out of this particular party.

For the first time the social air, the ebullience as formalised as a trade-mark, deserted her. 'That's the hell of it. I've been worrying myself silly about this. Bernard and I have had it out time and time again, and he's always said, "You leave well alone." But I say, it isn't as if it's *serious*, only Victor ought to know. I mean, it's not unfaithfulness, or anything, it couldn't be, but you do love Jenny and so do I, and I *do* think you ought to know.'

During this speech I had felt my blood seeping away, my stomach turning sour.

'But I'll only tell you *if* you think you ought.'

I told her furiously that I couldn't have an opinion one way or the other, without knowing what she was talking about.

'It's only that she never has been quite well since that maddening mum of hers died, and that I do want to help if I can.'

After some few sickening minutes of this kind of hedging, Emily came out with it, as nakedly, as unashamedly, as I might have known she would.

When Setter left the flat some four or five weeks ago, he had left Emily the business of cleaning up and reletting it. So every few days she had gone along there, to do the odds and ends and collect mail. What she found, almost every day, was a letter from Jenny. Out of pure curiosity, she had at last steamed one open. 'It's very dishonest, Vic, but I just can't help it. I am not jealous of Bill, I don't care what he does; I'd hate Jenny to hurt you, but I wouldn't have done it on that account. I was just mad curious.'

I told her sharply to tell me what the letter had contained. She opened her bag and gave it to me. 'There were a couple of others, too. I read those. Just the same.'

They were not love-letters, though something passionate lay beneath them. They were simply bald pleas for a meeting, any time, anywhere. Jenny wrote, 'I think I shall break down if I don't see you. I don't want to burden you with my sorrows, such as they are, I don't want you even to listen. But when I see you I feel safe. Just let me talk about anything, give me a drink, and tell me whatever you like, about the weather, or what you're doing, or just, well, whatever.'

Emily watched me anxiously. 'Did I do wrong?'

'Yes,' I said.

'But she sounds so on edge. And of course, he *won't* see her.'

'How do you know?'

'I sent on the first four, the ones I didn't open. He phoned me. He told me what was in them — they were the same as this one. He said he wasn't going to answer, he was fed up with doing harm. He hadn't tried this time, he'd just done it by accident. Oh, Vic!'

She was peering into my face, as if it were a newspaper. I suppose it was, of a sort.

'Never mind,' I said.

'It's not as if she was in love with him.'

'No.'

The room felt like a furnace. I wanted to take my coat off, my tie, open my shirt. I believed I was really going to be sick, so I left Emily abruptly and went to the Men's. I wasn't sick, however.

When I got back to the table she was sitting in a huddled position, looking appalled.

'Oh, Vic! Vic, it's nothing but Jenny in a state. I simply thought you ought to know.'

I told her she was probably right.

She walked with me up St. James's Street, very silent, now and then stealing glances at me.

'I'd stop opening other people's letters if I were you,' I said at last.

'Yes, I see I shall have to. It seems a crime to the majority, I know. Vic, I'm so sorry.'

I said it was all right.

'You won't tell Jenny?' she cried absurdly.

I said of course I should bloody well tell her. If she didn't want that, what was the object of the whole exercise? To drive *me* silly?

'But then she'll know——' Emily stopped.

'You're not dead to shame, I see.'

Brightness inflated her again. She squeezed my hand. 'Bless you, I suppose I can't be! Dear Vic, you do know that *I* know there's nothing in it!'

I asked her whether she honestly had had no intention but to help Jenny and me. 'Can you seriously say that?'

She answered quite seriously, 'Well, yes. I suppose I don't think things through much. But I hadn't any *arrière pensée*. What *pensée* could I have? I'm not in love with Bill, so I don't want to queer his pitch, and though I deeply adore you, I'm not in love with you, so I don't want to queer yours.'

I called a taxi and put her in it.

'Oh, forget the whole thing!' she screamed at me out of the window, as she drove off. 'Please! Please!'

Emily was, it struck me, a remarkably obtuse woman in all the important things, even if she were as clever as a monkey in the little ones. I wished her dead. I walked round and about in the hot summer day, in the blue, untroubled air, and everything swam before me and my hearing went bad. A troop of Life Guards bobbled by, shooting off sunshine like pain. Lovers rolling in the grass of the Green Park made me so sick I wanted to kick at them. Everything was filthy, not only the blown newspaper, the dog's turd on the path, the mad workman in the baize apron gobbing furiously as he walked: the flowers were filthy, and the sun, and the faces of all men and women.

I hadn't to go back to work. I went home, where I found nobody. Jenny was out at the hairdresser's. I had a bath and lay in it for half an hour. Afterwards, I slept. I woke up with a headache, but feeling calm. I had to stare at myself in the glass to see what on earth I could look like when I was feeling as calm as all that.

I waited for her at the gate, as I often did if I happened to be before her, and the weather was fine. Across the road, they had been digging up the water pipes, and the work-dust lay grey on our privet hedge. She came along soon, walking with her light straight step, her head thrown back to catch the warmth of the falling sun. Her hair was glossy and neat, somewhat redder than usual. The light picked out the few very fine lines between her eyes and at the corners of her mouth, showed a minute puckering of flesh below the underlip. I noticed the scooping out of her legs over the shin-bones. She saw me and smiled, quickened pace, took the last few yards at a run.

She said how nice it was that I should be early, kissed me and linked her arm in mine as we went back into the house. She had had some tea under the dryer. Had I had mine?

I said I didn't want any.

She touched her hair. 'Too gaudy? I don't think so. I won't go grey, not yet. Not too gaudy?'

I said no.

Jenny looked at me. 'And what's the matter with you?'

So I told her, as calmly and as carefully as I could. I could see no change in her face. But when I had finished, she sat down abruptly, and went white with anger.

'What does all that add up to?' When Jenny was angry she spoke like that.

'You'd better tell me.'

'And you'd better tell dear Emily that of all the vulgar, sneaking, miserable tricks——'

'Tell me what it adds up to,' I said.

'Why should I? Why should I reward sneaks? You should have shut her up at once.'

'I'm human.'

She cried scornfully, 'Do you suggest I'm *in love* with Setter?'

'I hope not.'

'You damned fool!'

She struck the edge of the table such a bang with her fist that the glass bowl in the middle of it gave out a ringing note, a beautiful coloratura sound, straight from La Scala.

'Tell me what it adds up to.'

Then she stormed at me, in tears, that all she wanted was someone who had a faint understanding of all she was going through. Setter wasn't a glamour boy (again, the terminology of Jenny's rage), he was flat-faced, getting fat, even boring, but somehow he helped her — was there anything in that? If I had any perception at all I'd thank him on my damned knees, because there were times when she might have done *anything* if he hadn't been there to help. . . .

'What things?'

The tears disappeared. Her shoulders drooped. She said quietly, 'Kill myself, I think.'

I made no comment and she blushed, as well she might have. Silence ticked in the room like a grandfather clock.

I put my arms round her and she rocked herself about in them, laying her cheek against mine.

'You wouldn't,' I said, 'and you know it.' She did know it. I would not allow her to act at me.

She moaned, 'You can't really know.'

'Yes, I can.'

'Anyway, when I used to feel horrible, he helped. Now I never see him. He means nothing to me, except as a doctor.' She pulled away, smiling at me wanly. 'Well, a dog-face.'

I asked her if she were in love with him.

This time she answered, 'No. But I have to see him. I'm sorry for what I did, it would have been all right if I'd told you. Wouldn't it have been all right?'

'I don't know.'

'Oh Vic, I couldn't be in love with him! He's so absurd, he's such a clown, him and his clubs . . . you see?'

'But you can't do without him.'

'I don't *want* to,' said Jenny, very carefully and tightly, setting her jaw.

'Would you go to a proper dog-face?'

She flashed at me, 'I'm not mad!'

'What you did seems a little dotty to me.'

But then I had to apologise, for I had gone too far: so she had the upper hand of me, for a while. After an exhausting hour of real and fake emotions, tears, smiles, rages, Lake District calms, I had to agree, of course, to forget about the whole thing. Naturally, I had been making a mountain out of a molehill, Jenny explained, adding indulgently, 'What man wouldn't?' She said she would like to see Setter, that was all: she would like him to come to dinner with us. She had never wanted to see him *alone* — that was quite irrelevant. She loved only me — had I forgotten? Silly old Victor. Silly Jenny. She admitted that she had been silly.

She did not, however, propose to forgive Emily.

I had such a raging headache by this time that I had a cup of tea and went straight to bed.

# Chapter 21

WHEN I telephoned Setter at last, he sounded remote. He was still settling in, there was so much to be done. A mess to clear up. No, he didn't go out much. He told me why he had moved: to save money. He was well enough off, yes — but he wasn't likely to earn any more, and there was no point in living in state. 'I live in *a* state,' he explained, 'which is different.'

I asked him to come and see me and Jenny. He temporised. He would, all right, when things were straighter.

So I told him I knew about the letters.

He said heavily, 'Yes. She's been trying to make a transference without benefit of dog-face. I don't do her any good now. But she's not really interested in me, though she thinks she is. Get her out more.'

I got her out more: three times a week. We saw all the kitchen-sink plays, all the jolly films about rape or plague, or drug-addiction. Jenny was grateful and sociable, extremely nice to me. I took her to a couple of musicals, for a change. She was just as sociable and nice. At the end of a fortnight of this, I rang Setter again.

'Oh, all right,' he said, 'if you ask other people too.'

So we asked him, and Malpass, the civil servant next door and his wife (Arnold and Rosemary Borton), and a friend of Jenny's called Nina.

I don't know what I expected him to look like, after the oddities of his recent life, the move from grandeur to Pimlico.

## An Error of Judgement

What I didn't expect was the reappearance of the well-dressed, calm, huge-handed, distinguished consultant, obviously far more distinguished than anyone in the room — possibly excluding Borton, who, though he had a dim and smudgy look, even a trifle Pooterish, was tipped for big things one of these days. Setter moved in upon us with stately tread, smiling and slow.

Glancing at Jenny, I saw her relaxed, as if even her bones had softened. Her smile shone back at him, spontaneous and happy. As she passed by me on her way to get him a drink, she slid her hand for a second into mine.

This was her night of hopefulness. What she hoped for precisely, I did not know, I'm sure she didn't; it was the unmaterial, thunderous, Emily Dickinson hope, the hope of an event: a coronation, even a calvary, perhaps a prodigious birth. It exalted her. Pimpishly, I felt a touch of that exaltation exalting me.

Setter began to talk to Nina, a handsome beanpole of a girl with a small bright cone of yellow hair at the top of her head, and to Rosemary Borton who had one of those very dark, very pretty and very hard little faces, as if she had once suffered very much and had now built her defences against the world. (So far as I know, she had never suffered at all.) He managed to give a 'how happy could I be with either' impression that pleased them both.

Malpass arrived, birdlike, dishevelled, with roses for Jenny. He asked Setter how the world was treating him.

'Oh,' said Setter, awakening histrionically from his social flirtation, 'none too bad, none too bad. I find plenty to interest me.'

'Haven't you given up medicine?' Borton asked, with the directness of the experienced interviewer.

Setter said yes, and nothing else, which left Borton looking puzzled.

'He has retired from life,' said Jenny, all little-girl, taking her place on a stool near his feet, 'and he hardly comes to see us any more. We are very cross with him. Here we wait, in our lonely cot, day after day, hour after hour — "Where's Bill?" we say, but no one answers, no ring at the bell. . . .' Her voice trailed away, she looked at nothing.

'I've been busy,' said Setter.

'Even now you've wound up our little club?' Jenny's voice prodded at him.

'Oh, what club? Do tell.' This was Nina, imagining gaieties from which she had been excluded.

'Just a talk-club. I started it. But we talked ourselves out.' He picked up Nina's hand. 'You've got a wart coming on that finger. I know a man who charms them off for you, remote control, two and six a time.'

She gave a flitter of laughter. 'And you a scientist!'

'He can,' said Setter. 'It maddens me. But he can. He lives in Luton. Two and six a time, just send him a P.O.'

He lured the conversation on to superstitions. Everyone had stories to tell. Rosemary confessed to her horror when confronted with the back of a hay-cart.

'That's why we live in London,' said Borton, 'so few of them.'

I said to Malpass under cover of the talk, 'What's happened to Sammy?'

'He pursues me. But Bill won't see him. Sammy doesn't like it.'

'You still think——?'

'Could be.'

'Father Malpass,' Rosemary said with unbecoming archness, 'surely *you* can't believe in witchcraft?'

He feathered his hair through his fingers so that, like quills, it looked damp as well as stiff. 'I believe in bad men.'

146

'In the devil?'

'The devil is bad men.'

'And you only believe in sick men.' This time she addressed Setter, and she sounded impertinent.

'No. Like Malpass, I believe in bad men, too.'

'And bad women, perhaps?' Jenny said. The too-red hair bounced on the top-knot of her spine. She looked delicate and pretty about the wrists.

'There are fewer of them.' He patted her shoulder, and she relaxed again.

'I'll tell you,' he said, 'what I believe.' Now he had wholly captured the attention of the room. They listened respectfully, as patients to the doctor. He gave a sudden stretched grin, and his blue, sequin eyes sparkled in the heavy surround of flesh. 'I believe in silly men. In posturing men. And there are far more of those than of bad ones. *Ergo*, they're more dangerous. If this world gets blown up, or that portion of it the physicists think plausible——'

'Oh, don't,' said Nina, affectedly.

'— it will be because of silly men and posturing men, all saying "our side is good and the other side is bad, and people would far rather be dead than live in any other way but ours".'

Borton began to speak, but Setter went on.

'For the first time we may be hit, not by something calling itself an ideological war, but by something that is.' His eyes deadened. 'Before any of us start taking lethal moral decisions, we have to ask the children what they think.' He began an inept, embarrassing mimicry. 'George, you are having a fine time, aged seven. Ivan, you seem to be enjoying yourself, aged eight. You'd both much rather be dead than red, wouldn't you? Of course you would. I shall see to it myself, little man. Personally. Leave it to Daddy.'

His voice changed.

'I'm getting on. I now say what I think. There has only been one war in the history of man worth fighting, and that was the Second World War. Because of the camps, and the killing, and what is unspeakable. And because there was no counter-balance.'

Jenny moved restlessly. She seemed to be searching for something to do. She found it in the hearthrug, an employment for her fingers; some ash spilled fine which she proceeded to remove by spitting, by rubbing, by sprucing up the pile with her thumbnail. She had the pouchy, ominous look of a child who damned well proposes to cry, and do it loudly.

Borton asked a question.

'The written-in belief,' said Setter, 'that colour and race don't count, and that men are equal.'

'Does it always work out in practice?' Borton said, his air dry, enquiring.

'No. Often not. But a statement of faith, *written in*, is the final safeguard. Better a decent hypocrisy than a bold, truthful cruelty. The moment a man accepts the appearance of decency, he has to spend a certain proportion of his public time behaving in a decent manner. And a hypocritical good example is better than a sincere bad one.'

There was silence. He seemed to have come to an end.

Jenny said hastily, 'Politics! A new line for you, Bill.' There were tears in her eyes. 'Could it really be that I am the only person in the world bored stiff, bored pallid, by politics?'

The miracle was not going to happen and she knew it now. There was to be no Event, no stop-sensation in Jenny's soul.

'No,' he said, 'we all are, those of us who aren't politicians. That's why we're the prey of the silly men, the posturing men. They don't get bored, not ever. They will never get bored. We are the victims of their professional excitement.'

He was not talking to her, but out into the room. It had begun to rain. I heard the heavy splashing and pitting of water on the gravel beyond the window. Some of them were going to get damned wet going home.

'So when I get bored,' he said, 'and can't face thinking of the big filthy things, I think about the small filthy ones. For instance, I know a youth of eighteen who almost certainly took part in kicking an elderly female alcoholic to death in a gutter. I devote a good deal of my thought to him.'

Malpass was silent, poking through his hair.

Everyone else laughed on the wrong side of his face, pretending not to believe a word of it.

Then Jenny said, 'But Bill, you can't *know*!'

'Oh, I shall. Here, give me another drink. You're slipping as a hostess.' He was not looking at her, but holding his glass sideways, under her nose.

She burst out, 'You are slipping as a guest!' Her face was red and furious. She had forgotten us. She cared nothing for what we might think.

'Sorry,' he said. 'What have I done wrong?'

'Nothing.' She took his glass and refilled it. Setter said, 'I shall show you a card trick.'

Nina giggled. When he took a pack of cards from his pocket she gave a yelp of mirth. Jenny sat down on her heels beside him, pale again.

Setter spread the cards before Borton. 'You pick.'

Borton said, 'Now this is what I must see. I believe it is called "forcing a card" on one. Can you force one on me?'

'Just take one,' said Setter.

'It's pouring!' Jenny exclaimed. 'Listen to it!'

Borton took a card. He smiled.

'Like another?' Setter said.

'Certainly I would.'

'Go ahead.'

Borton returned the first card, took another from the fan slackly held.

Setter asked him if he approved of that one. 'No? Try another then.'

Borton returned the second, took a third.

'Look at it. It's red, I think.'

'Yes.'

'Diamonds.'

'Yes.'

We all stared at Setter with that wholehearted wonder one accords to professional magicians. Now, however, he looked uneasy. 'Could be a — no. Not . . . no, not a ten. A nine? No.'

Breaths were held.

Borton said, 'Now tell me in confidence, are you really puzzled, or is this part of the act?'

'Part of the act,' Setter replied promptly. 'Of course I know what it is. I always do. It is the eight of diamonds.'

Demonstrated, face upwards, the card sparkled the scarlet mystery. We all stared at it.

Nina and Rosemary began to clap.

'But if I'd put the third one back, and taken another?' Borton was analytic.

Setter grinned at him. 'It would have made no difference. Shall I tell you how it's done?'

We crowded in on him, enthusiasts upon the Eleusinian threshold.

'I don't think I will,' he said. 'I never give away my answers.'

Soon after that, perhaps because the throbbing rain had ceased, the party broke up. Everyone seemed happy. Jenny smiled her way blissfully to bed. Within half an hour I was aware that she was crying her eyes out, but of course there was nothing I could do, so I pretended to be asleep. She half-wanted me to discover her misery, half-wanted me not to. I respected the second of these wants. I was tired, so tired that when I closed my eyes gentle bursts of fireworks sprang and sprayed, delightful, but ephemeral. Blue, white and red. Sprayed into oceans, into oceanic sleep itself.

# Chapter 22

MALPASS wrote to me: 'Sammy Underwood has acquired a taste for club life. He has become a clubman. He comes to my club twice a week after work, all the way to Plaistow. I think you'd better come down and take a look.'

So I went to the church hall, nicely done up with a lick of paint and arty travel posters, and watched Sammy playing pingpong.

He was good at it, jumping around like a half-grown cat, taking astonishing balls from just below the table-edge and flicking them back with grinning skill. In jeans and a black sweater he looked uncommonly catlike, as if he had just taken off a furry head after an appearance in pantomime. The hall was three-quarters empty; the whole thing seemed something of a failure. Some depressed, sinless-looking lads were playing chess. Some girls were heaving about round a gramophone, surging, dancing a bit.

Sammy, showing off, waved a hand at me even as he returned a smash. Waiting for service, he crouched down low, teeth bared, his eyes glinting. He won game and set.

His opponent slouched into a raincoat and went off. Sammy came over to me.

'Well, well, if it isn't Mr. H.,' he said familiarly. 'I'm sweating.' He flopped down beside Malpass and me, on a hard chair by the wall.

'He's getting so good,' Malpass said, 'that if he liked to take up the game seriously he could probably get into the area championships.'

Sammy derided this. A game was a game. He did it for the exercise. Sitting at a bench all day you got gummed up, see?

'How's your girl?' Malpass asked him.

'All off. She was a snob, and I don't like snobs. Either she plays things my way or we don't play. I told her so straight.'

'How's the family?' I asked.

'Oh, them! It's a fine old muck at present. Sandra got a concert-party job, meant leaving the kid with Mum, and he's had all the things he could have — measles, chicken-pox, and —' he enunciated carefully — 'gastro-enteritis. Sick! You never saw anything like it. He's all right now, though.'

He fished out a packet of cigarettes, offered them to us.

'You ever see the doc?' he asked me suddenly.

Malpass watched him.

I said I did.

'Now he's a snob, that's what.' Sammy's face darkened. 'I didn't think he was, but he is. What I say is, why start something you can't go on with?'

I suggested this was not snobbery.

'Ah,' said Malpass, 'but he won't see Sammy.'

'Oh no, it's me he's dropped like a hot potato. He sees you and Mrs. H., doesn't he? And I bet he sees some of the others. But not me, oh no. I'm common.' He brooded. 'Like a hot potato. Let's go round to the pub.'

'No pub,' Malpass said, 'not on club nights.'

Sammy said fretfully, 'This lot aren't doing anything. Why don't they clear out?'

'I'm here until they want to.'

I asked the boy why he minded being dropped by Setter. What had he got out of the Phryne? What had Setter done for him?

'And a silly damned idea that was. Bored — it was all I could do not to drop off.'

'Why did you go?'

'Oh, I don't know. Because it was round the bend, I suppose, the whole thing was. That crummy piece with her rose-garden . . . the rest of them. I sort of found myself waiting for something to happen next. But it never did.'

I pressed him about Setter himself.

He glowered at me. 'That's nothing to do with it, see? Only he's a snob. Thinks he can pick you up and drop you.' He sneered. 'I wrote him a letter in my very best handwriting, fine Italian hand, as they say. Does he answer? Not a smell of it. If you ask me, he's round the bend, too.'

Getting up, he took a ball, stood at the table and began to spin it expertly so that it came repeatedly back to him.

Malpass said idly, 'You ever hear any more talk about the old woman?'

The ball dropped to the floor. Sammy didn't pick it up. Instead, he lounged back to us. He looked at me, his eyes sparkling.

'Do you know, Mr. H., the Father really seems to think I done that — did it. Don't you, Father?'

Malpass smiled.

'I have him on a bit. But it's not much to think of a man, is it?'

'I only thought you might have picked something out of the air, Sammy. You've got pals.'

The boy looked virtuous. 'Now is that a nice thing to say, suggesting I'd have mates like that?'

'She had a conviction once. I bet you didn't know.'

Sammy, alert: 'What for?'

'Shoplifting. Only the once.'

'Well, there you are! They talk about her, such an old dear, only a bit of a boozer, always pennies for the kids. But she was a crook, wasn't she?' He looked excited.

'A hard penalty to pay for a bit of shoplifting. Not much like the justice of God, Sammy.'

The boy looked at him affectionately, with a glance drew me, too, into a condescending kind of love. 'There he goes. The Father's got a direct line to God, he knows how he works. You have, haven't you, Father?'

'Well, I do know He isn't ridiculous. He wouldn't arrange for thugs to kick an old woman's eyes out because she once pinched a hair-net and a packet of Jello from Woolworth's. The punishment doesn't fit the crime, don't you agree, Sammy?'

'You've got it on the brain. That's morbid, see?'

The record had finished: the pop-singer was silent. The girls were drifting off. Only the chess-game continued.

'Mr. Setter has it on his.'

'Well, if I do get a line, I might tell him something. But he's — ' Sammy, like Henry James, sought conscientiously for a word — 'incognito.'

'*Incommunicado*,' I said.

'Same thing.'

I persisted, pedantic as always, 'Not the same thing.'

'What the bloody hell do I care?'

At this sign of temper, Malpass stirred. 'No bad language within these walls. You know what I've said.'

Sammy looked round. 'And what walls! I tell you, padre, you give me a few cans of paint and I'll tart them up a bit better for you than that.' His eyes rested dreamily on the posters. 'Venice. *O Sole Mio!* — that's a square number, that is. Bruges,' (he called it Broog) 'Venice of the north. Got Venice on the brain. Gay Paree.' He added practically, 'You should have had them cracks filled in before you did any painting.'

'No money,' said Malpass.

Now the chess players were packing up.

'Ten minutes in the pub,' I said.

Sammy chose to sulk. 'No, thanks. I can't swill it down like that. I like to take my time.' To Malpass — 'Why is the doc *incommunicado*?' He was smart. Put him right once, and he would never forget it.

'I don't know,' Malpass said, 'I'm not in his confidence.'

'Well, tell him God's got good manners — right? — and that he ought to . . . Tell him to answer his bloody letters.'

He got up. 'Goodnight, all.' Stripping off the black sweater, he put on a jacket. 'I'm off.'

And he was gone, almost without visible disappearance.

'You'd better come round to my house,' Malpass said, 'and tell me what you think.'

The rectory was dingy outside, comfortable within. He had spent on it the only legacy he had ever received since his father died (his patrimony had gone somewhere or other years ago), two hundred pounds from an aunt. He gave me whiskey, and repeated his question.

'I don't believe a word of it,' I said.

'Why does he want to see Setter?'

'Setter,' I said rather bitterly, 'is gifted as a wrecker of lives.'

'Jenny?'

'Yes.'

'That will pass.'

He didn't pretend not to understand me. Poor Jenny's secret, which she believed quite undetected, was in fact as open as a football stadium.

I asked him what right Setter had to garner and then to reject. Malpass replied that he rejected when he thought he was doing harm.

'To Sammy?'

'I don't know why he won't see Sammy. Sammy's eaten up with resentment. I think he ought to see him. But he won't till he's ready.'

# Chapter 23

I ONLY once saw Setter in a rage. It was in his scruffy flat where he had asked me to spend the evening, Jenny being out with a friend. When I got there he was listening to a record, Leonard Bernstein playing the Ravel Piano Concerto in G Major. 'This I like,' Setter said. 'Some music I do. Fix yourself a drink. You don't mind waiting.'

We sat in the limey, grainy dust of his room, in the sadness of all that is beyond repair, books whose covers are torn, ceilings that stain at the corners, and I heard the thinly romantic limp of the second movement, talking, I thought, about the sadness of rooms such as Setter's but with only half the mind given to it, the other half being given to dead infantas.

I had forgotten his claim to be musical. Perhaps he wasn't, in a lofty sense: but to this music he drooped his large head, and his hands hung down, and his little blue eyes were Russian and vague. The cigarette poking from the corner of his mouth was like something stuck on to a surrealist picture, stuck on to give a jolt from one dimension into another. The jellied-madrilène notes rippled up and down, so sad, so touching, all about love, taking love gravely but (thank God) not too seriously. At that time I hated taking anything too seriously.

I like Ravel. He gives us sweetness without straining us too much. But he does strain us just a pleasurable bit.

Then we got to the violence, the sneer, the Spanish stuff, very exciting and all, pianist playing at the top of his joy. Setter's eyes sparkled. I had a grotesque fancy of Setter with castanets,

whirling in skirts. More and more excited I got, and that is why
I made my mistake later.

Setter waved a huge hand — 'Grumbling away, now that I
like —' and he raised his head; exciting music stirred him to
something or other, to *hope*, I think; as it stirs me. I get taken
by the delusion that some preposterous sexual triumph is
within my grasp, a piece of cake. Ripple, ripple, slash, crash!
That's the end. A fountain overflowed.

A slide, a sigh and the record stopped.

'At your service,' said Setter.

'Miss Dewes says you're a saint.'

'Miss who?'

I told him, the girl who grew roses. I had met her at my bus
stop. She had told me of her disappointment. She had met
Setter and known him for a saint. When she had been with him,
she had felt an absolute peace, an absolute knowledge of right
and wrong. Wrong, mind you, she had felt unable to resist
upon occasion: but Right — oh yes — *Right*, Setter had taught
her. And he had gone away. Betraying her, he had gone away.
'He ditched us all,' she had said, bitterly, colloquially, 'he went
away.'

His face burst into flame. Bardolph-colour overflowed it,
throwing into colour of terrible intensity the little rounded blue
of his eyes.

'Damn her,' said Setter, 'that's one load I won't carry!'

Feeling caught up in a wave of self-confidence (as one does
sometimes, quite meaninglessly) I told him in a loud voice what
other claims Miss Dewes had made for him. For instance,
Purdue and Lawson.

'That?' Setter said, blazing. 'I got them to sit on the same
sofa. God help them both! Purdue is almost certainly impotent.
Lawson wants it like hell. If they are lucky, they will get a sort
of happiness out of shoring each other up, like two broken

buildings which happen to have collapsed at the same time in opposite directions. But if you think a damned saint would have arranged that—— ! Victor, I don't arrange. That's one bloodiness I've tried to avoid. Arrangements, by one human being, of two or more others, are pure devilment. All I did was to offer nothing at all except a sit-down out of the cold, no money passing. I was offering the cleanest of all things: Nothing. If you start on that saint tack, you can get out of here!'

While he was talking he had without thinking reversed the record. Shostakovitch was spouting out at us, circus horses, high-stepping, gay, clean, but — again — exciting. I couldn't stand it. I got up and turned the thing off.

'For God's sake,' said Setter, 'don't you want a drink? It's over there. Go and get it.'

So I did. I said, 'Suppose you do get through, as you hoped, without doing any harm? Isn't that a triumph?'

He said he didn't understand.

' "An outward and visible sign",' I said. 'That's what Miss Dewes thought you'd got for her. And she thought you had confiscated it, like taking a gobstopper from a schoolboy.'

'You drink that up,' said Setter, 'and get out. There's no triumph for me. Almighty God, what words you use! "Triumph", egad, begorrah! I tell you, my aim is to do *nothing*. Ergo, nothing wrong. Nothing right, either. But I tell you, Victor — something I have got. Something I shall find. Bring me Sammy. I know Sammy. I know all about it.'

I saw for the first time (and I daresay more acute persons would have seen it before) the disintegration of Setter. He was farther gone than I had thought. Look for the physical signs first: we become psychologically peculiar later, much later. Setter was going to flab. His collar wasn't clean. Certainly his rooms weren't.

He burst out, 'And I know all about Jenny! I've done that girl nothing but harm. As for you, you'll be fed up with her soon. She grieves. She mourns. You go home and tell her, you'll be fed up with her soon unless she snaps out of it.'

I retorted that I should never get fed up with Jenny and didn't mean to pretend otherwise. Faking an emotion was too hard to keep up, even though it might be good therapy.

His eyes were inflamed. 'You're a man. Don't you know what men want? "Bring on my dancing girls." That's the basis of their desire. Jenny's aching and weeping and yearning will get your sympathy for a while, and then she'll lose you entirely. A woman grieving,' said Setter, more steadily, sententiously, with a literary, aphoristic touch, 'is to a man a pain in the neck.'

I suggested that all men were not alike.

'Well,' he said reasonably, rage subsiding, 'there are the sadists. But you'd be surprised how easily *they* get fed up — that is, with the same weeper. But — "Bring on my dancing girls" — that's it for most of us. Do you know why I'm so crazy about Emily? Because she never grieves. She hasn't the capacity. She rides high, Emily does, with a cloud between her legs. She isn't scared of heights, she's no imagination. She doesn't even need a saddle and reins. She's up there, up in the sky, all the time. My God, I wish I could have been the one to drag her down! But I'm too difficult, too twisted, me. She likes Bernard because he is a simple oaf. He makes no demands, he wouldn't know how to make them. He's too stupid. The oafs get the sky-riders, every time, every time.' He ruminated and looked ugly. 'Saint Setter. That's a joke.'

He added suddenly, 'Let's walk. I didn't ask you round here for nothing, not even for the pleasure of your company. I've got something to tell you, strong drama. Come on.'

The night was mild and overcast. Swansdown of rust-coloured smoke fluffed out from the chimneys of the power-station. There was a star or two, nothing much. The barges trailed their fairy-lights along the satiny, smelly water. The plane trees were stagey green under the lamps.

Setter's walk was light and silent. I noticed, in the light from a passing bus, that there was a button missing from his overcoat. He needed a woman's care, Setter did. And wouldn't my wife have loved to give it him! (Let me catch her.)

'What about the strong drama?' I asked him. He told me about it. As I dislike trying to remember monologues in detail (in fact, one can't) and have decided that it only means faking if you try, I shall make some sort of narrative out of it and call it

## SETTER'S STORY (3)

For weeks, Sammy had been trying to see him. He had dropped hints *via* Malpass, and finally demands. Setter had not answered. Sammy had tried the resources of the mails. Letters (polite), letters (impolite), postcards (carneying or insulting), even anonymous postcards, if that is what Sammy really imagined they were. Still Setter was unresponsive. He was waiting for Sammy to get to such a pitch of frustrated vanity that he would do anything, *anything*, to gain attention. He had learned from Malpass that the boy was in a surly and unsettled state, that he was idling at his work, that the shine was slipping from him, little by little. His father and mother were at their wits' end.

Setter waited patiently till Malpass assured him that Sammy was just getting ripe for some act of public mischief, something which would draw him back into the limelight. Then he acted. He dropped Sammy a card and told him to call.

(The following happened on the night before I saw Setter myself.)

Punctual to the minute, nine o'clock, Sammy turned up at the Pimlico flat. He was shiny again, clean, his hair bright with tiny prismatic sparkles of oil. He wore light trousers of the Ivy League variety and a huge, bulky black sweater, which gave him the misleading impression of having a chest. He wore orange suede shoes without laces. He stopped dead, dramatically, on Setter's threshold.

'God, what a muckheap! You know what, Doc, if I had your money I wouldn't put my dog in here.'

'Glad to see me?' Setter enquired.

Sammy was taken aback. He opened his mouth, and the cigarette, by some conjuring trick, remained stuck by a mere fleck of paper to his lower lip. He pulled it off, looked at it, and squashed it in a tray. He shrugged. 'Could be.'

'Been going to some trouble about it, haven't you? Sit down, and look through your assorted correspondence. I like this Brighton postcard. I like the inscription on the back. Why didn't you sign it, Sammy? I know your elegant scrawl.'

Sammy denied sending it.

'Oh, shut up. Don't be a fool. Here, you can have a coke.'

'Fancy the great doc drinking that nasty, habit-forming, common, kid's stuff.'

'Oh, but I got it in for you.'

Sammy said he'd rather have a glass of water. He sat down on the littered sofa, hands between his knees, rocking thoughtfully back and forth. Setter, who was used to waiting for Sammy, continued to wait.

The boy spoke at last, gritting his teeth like a gangster in a film. 'I don't know why you have to start things if you don't mean to carry on. That club. It wasn't exactly the "full glam"——'

'You mix with theatrical persons, I see.'

'— but it was something for them all to do, poor sods. They liked it. And you clear off and leave them standing. I don't know what you wanted to do it for.'

'So you don't like my room, Sammy?'

'I wouldn't be seen dead in a place like this.'

'I think you were accusing me of snobbery to Mr. Malpass. Do my surroundings chime with that idea?'

'You talk so fancy, I don't know if I'm on my arse or my elbow.'

'Snobbish surroundings, I suggested.'

'Snobs can live anywhere. They do it to show off.'

'Come, come. You must have a better reason.'

'Dropped me, didn't you?'

'Yes.'

'Why?'

Setter said slowly, 'Because I thought you might be interesting, Sammy. In fact, you turned out to be a bore.'

Sammy's face flushed into violent, baffled life. He swore nastily.

'You aren't interesting at all,' said Setter. 'Your mind's not interesting. You haven't done anything interesting.'

Sammy looked as if he were about to burst. He resembled one of the cherubs in Botticelli's *Birth of Venus*, getting up wind. For the moment he was speechless.

'Not social snobbery,' Setter pursued, 'interest-snobbery. When people cease to interest me I drop them. I dropped a very long-established duke once, if that soothes your infantile mind.'

'There are people as would do you.' Sammy's voice seemed not to come from his mouth, but some congested cavity in his lungs.

'I dare say. But not you. You couldn't "do" a pussy-cat.'

Sammy was filthy on the subject of Setter's pussy-cats.

163

'So as you don't interest me, I don't want to go on seeing you. Is that clear?'

'I did it to her face. I didn't do her, though.' Sammy was pernicketty.

Setter lay back, closed his eyes, pushed disbelieving breath out from a buttonhole of lips.

'Go away.'

'I tell you, I did! Didn't you think so at one time? Weren't you chasing after me to find out?'

'You're a bore.'

The boy got up. He was trembling, the scanty hair bristling on his scalp. He started to swear. Setter rose too. 'Oh, get up and go home. I've heard all those words before, you fool. And I don't want to listen to your fantasies.'

'Fantasies, was it? If that's it, how do I *know* what happened?'

'You don't. . . . But I expect you can make up a horror-comic when you put your mind to it.' He went towards the door. He was conscious only for a fraction of a second that Sammy, if he had a weapon, could be dangerous. Without one, he couldn't. He was too small, Setter too big. Unsure of himself, feeling like a hero, which was the only way he could compensate for that flash of fear, he turned his back on the boy, and walked over to the door. Nothing happened. Sammy had no weapon.

'You listen,' said Sammy.

'I don't want to. You tell it to the marines.'

The boy sat down again with a thump. 'I said, you listen!'

'Red Riding Hood's a good story. I'd rather have that.'

Sammy said, 'I know what wasn't in the papers.'

Setter walked back.

'What?'

'Her teeth fell out. Someone stamped on 'em in the gutter.'

'Perce?'

'Perce my arse! You think that fat——? Oh no. And don't think you're going to get me to give my mates away. Say there was A, B and me.'

Setter said, 'Toosey-pegs is a good guess.' He sat down.

Sammy's eyes brightened and grew moist. His adam's apple rose and fell like the indicator of a lift.

He murmured, 'You'd better listen, see? And don't think you can do nothing about it. What you want is to know the way it was. It was because she scared me, see? That old bag. If she hadn't scared me, I wouldn't have done it.'

Setter did not interrupt again. He sat very still, like some Brobdingnagian mouse, and breathed only delicately, not wanting to awaken the boy from his memorial dream.

# Chapter 24

## SAMMY'S STORY

(*Oratio obliqua*, as I can't reproduce his sort of speech.
I'm too old to have learnt it.)

A, B and he were wandering along about an hour after
closing time, fed up to the marrow. They were bored, there
was nowhere to go. They mooched down the side-streets, not
thinking where and not caring. They had run out of cash. They
hadn't much to begin with, Sammy and B hadn't: A had drunk
a bit, because it was pay-day. The other two had had only a pint
and a half apiece.

Out from a side turning came Addie Engbeck, weaving and
tottering, stinking to high heaven. She had a great big handbag
dangling from her arm; it looked like the sort of thing you went
round collecting scraps in. It was very shiny, and the meagre
light of a street lamp bounced off it. Just for fun, A grabbed at
it. Addie hung on. She addressed him in round terms. 'Filthy,
it was,' said Sammy, with genuine if grotesque distaste. Just
for fun, B tripped her. Over she went, smack on her face,
sicked up a mouthful, then got hold of the nearest thing, which
was one of Sammy's ankles.

(All this took some time to tell, but the actual event was a
matter of a couple of minutes. Someone might have come
along, so it had to be quick. Sammy tried to convey that the
guilt lay with the person who might have come along: if there

166

had been no such person, and they had been sure of that, it wouldn't have happened.)

Sammy freed himself, stamping on her hand as he did so. This sent A wild, it was A who really started it. He kicked out, just to quieten her really, and then B joined in. The old girl's teeth were out, B jumped on them. There wasn't much noise. She hardly groaned. She'd got her bit of fur between her gums and somehow clenched on to that.

She seemed to be flat out. They were going just to run for it, when she did something that gave Sammy the horrors. She reared up suddenly, like a bundle of old umbrella-covers, only reeking, stinking, pawed about till she'd got Sammy's foot again (he had been the last to leave her, thinking perhaps he ought to see she wasn't in too bad a way), and climbed up from it to his calf. She hung on, all blood and muck (reeking, stinking, he reiterated), with her sagging white face turned up to his, and the bit of fur running out from each side of her mouth like a sort of moustache. He kneed her with his free leg, had her over backwards. And because she seemed to glare at him ('It was like it was insulting!' Sammy insisted) he couldn't stand it; he was crazy mad with fright, with the horrors, he couldn't go on being scared, so he shut her eyes for her. Then he ran on after the others, even yelling out, 'Wait for me!' — though it was in-sane to make a noise.

They went without much said to their separate homes. No one heard Sammy come in, they probably didn't even know he'd been out, glued to the telly, as they always were. He washed himself, inspected his clothes, couldn't find anything on them. But he did wash his shoes in the lavatory flush. They were nasty.

The boys had never been in trouble before, not he, or A or B. That seemed to him important. He slept without dreaming. He had never dreamed about it. It had never got on his nerves, that was the funny thing. No, he hadn't felt sorry about her. She had scared him out of his wits till he didn't know what he was doing, so it wasn't his fault.

'One of those big hairy moths, it flies in your face. You slap out without thinking, see? You can't be blamed for that.' No, he hadn't lost a moment's sleep about Addie.

Why had he come out with it now?

'You jeering,' he said to Setter.

## SETTER'S STORY (3) *contd.*

He might have been terrified by Addie Engbeck, rearing up like old umbrella covers in the vomit and the blood, but not half so terrified as he was by Setter, once the story was out. He tried at once to cover up. He tried to laugh.

'Believe it or not, as you like,' Sammy said, hare-eyes protruding, 'it's up to you. But remember, I got imagination. I used to get good marks for essay-writing, when I was at school.'

Setter pondered for a little, then replied that the whole thing seemed plausible.

'Those are nice details, Sammy. Especially the teeth. Did they ever make you read Edgar Allen Poe?'

'Just my guess. Anyone could make that sort of guess.'

'The police would be interested.'

'You won't go running to the police. They'd get nothing on me.'

Setter said at once, 'No, I shan't tell the police. So get out of here, Sammy. Just clear.'

Certain situations seem insoluble, in terms of drama. Full stops come when you least expect them, and then, and *then*, you are gummed up. To Setter's speech there should have been some good answer, some viable answer, so that the scene could proceed. But there wasn't. Anyway, Sammy didn't find one, and Setter couldn't think of any answer he would have made, had he been Sammy.

The boy got up and went to the door. He said one thing only. 'You let everyone down, that's what you do. And don't you think we don't know it.'

# Chapter 25

'WHAT will you do?' I asked Setter.
We were leaning on the parapet above the tide. It had begun to rain, so thinly that there was no sensation of damp, only of glitter.

'Oh, I don't know yet. And you'll tell nobody, of course. Not even Jenny. Nor Malpass.'

I would have to go to the police, I told him, feeling a curious surge of responsible, sadistic citizenship quite new in my experience. I felt like a householder. Like a judge. Not entirely unlike God.

'Hangings aren't my line,' Setter said.

I asked him curiously what he would actually like to do.

He turned towards me his white moon face, sparkled over with the silver dust of the rain. 'You can guess what I would like.' His mouth stretched in a smile. He looked down, stuck out his foot and pounded his heel into a mishmash of leaves. 'For Master Sammy. But naturally not. We can make ourselves act as better men than in fact we are — that's our hope: and I shall do so.'

He frightened me. I told him rapidly that he had had his triumph: by battening down his desire for cruelty, by chaining it up, he had won. He ought to be at peace with himself. (So fatuous can one get, when one doesn't try.)

He shook his head. 'Oh no. I behave. But inside, it's the same. You take Jenny away, will you? Take her on a trip. You can make the firm pay.'

He walked off so suddenly that for a moment I thought he had caught sight of someone he knew. But it wasn't that. Alone, he went away from me, vaguely purposeful as a policeman pounding a beat, left me standing as though we had quarrelled. I saw his figure diminishing under the lamps, saw his big black back all scurfed over with the diamond dust of the rain.

It may seem odd to you that the occasion for taking Jenny away arose almost immediately, in fact that autumn. I had one of my regular trips to make, and when, muscling my courage, I broached the subject of my wife, my boss agreed, with an air of one permitted by divine providence to demonstrate how good a man he had been all along, that of course I must take her, it was good that I should take her, in fact I was something of a cad because I hadn't taken her before.

I must say the thought of it rallied her. We were to go by sea, which meant that she needed clothes; three evening dresses at least, and something which she called 'separates'. It was an expensive time for me.

When we got aboard the liner, Jenny seemed to go slightly mad. Youth overcame her, and archness; she tripped around the decks, into the stuffy palm-court lounges, the floral cocktail bars, metaphorically clapping her little hands. Her colour was high, her hair even redder than usual. Seeing the attention she attracted, I was at first afraid that she was simply making a little-girl fool of herself. I soon realised that, just as she was attractive to me, so she was attractive to other men. She proved to be an excellent sailor, a damned sight better than I was. On the first night out I preferred to read a good book in the stateroom. Jenny went up and played Bingo, won fifty dollars, and danced with a breathing host of enthusiastic elderly and middle-aged gentlemen.

I must say my hopes, and therefore my spirits, were rising. Jenny seemed entranced by the novelty of life on a ship. She laughed more than I had heard her laugh for months, and didn't drag Setter's name persistently into our conversation. (She had recently developed a very cunning casual line about him, which would not have deceived anyone with a mental age of over four.) To see her coming down to dinner was a fine sight. She would never use the lift — the sea was pretty choppy, so I did — but liked to trail in her new finery all down those plunging stairs to be received by the photographers at the bottom. Jenny, imperial in violet chiffon! Jenny severe, duchessy, in black! Jenny bridal in white! She drew glances not only of admiration but of amused indulgence from experienced travellers. A child at a birthday party she was, and while I sat toying with Vichyssoise and an omelette, Jenny gobbled up *foie gras* and duck as though we were sailing on a lake. 'Feeling sick,' she said to me scornfully, 'is purely psychological. You only feel sick because you think it's the thing to do.'

She had me up on the boat deck, in a tearing wind, with gulfs of grey and pounding horror below us, the damned ship pitching like someone having sex. 'One of my great uncles was a sailor,' she told me dreamily, leaning her head on my shoulder and almost knocking me over, 'it may be hereditary.'

I said there was no such heredity in my family and went to bed. She went off to dance. She liked it to be rough. She enjoyed climbing up the dance floor one way and making a *glissando* down it the other. She had the gift of balance, and her partners appreciated her skill in keeping theirs. Flushed, bright-eyed, she went from one admirer to another, treating the young and handsome ones (though there weren't many) with the same flirtatious, armoured comradeship she gave to the old and uncomely. Or so she told me. I never watched her for long.

She woke me at 3 a.m. by banging on the stateroom door. I blinked at her through the dazzle of sleep.

She had been up in the Verandah Grill with a retired spaghetti tycoon, he was at least seventy, she said, and I was not to be jealous. I was not. There had been Spanish dancers and a calypso singer. The singer had made up a song about her — she hadn't known where to look, or rather, to be honest, she had. Something like 'Lovely lady with the red hair. Best on land or sea anywhere, Lovely lady with the eyes so bright, I'll carry you off in my dream tonight.' Jenny was capable of making this incident up, of course, but I didn't think she had.

'Where did you look?' I asked her out of pure curiosity.

She replied, 'Down my neck.'

She was stripping her clothes off, tumbling them anywhere, though ordinarily she was a neat girl. She said, 'Move over,' and pushed in beside me, still as slender as a stick ('peeled white wand,' I think William Morris said) and reeking of *Vol de Nuit*. She turned out the light. Pushing the pyjama jacket back from my shoulder she laid her cheek there, so I should know that cheek was wet with tears.

I cuddled her. 'Want it?'

'I don't know. Oh Vic, oh Vic, I do love you! But it's so lonely, this world is so bloody lonely.'

She was drunk, or partially so. Nevertheless, Jenny, when she had had a drink, was always perfectly capable of listening to reason.

'Fine old lonely time you've been having,' I said boisterously, bluff King Hal.

Around us the ship creaked in all its senile joints. The wash of the sea was a tremendous, sick sighing. Underneath us was so much sea that it frightened me to think of it, miles of it going downwards. Waves dashed against the portholes, first a glassy thrust, then a collapse into huge salty weeping, the grief of the hysteric sea, the overgrown, the too fat, female sea.

'Vic, Vic, do help me, I'm so lonely.'

173

'Nothing like love for that,' I said. 'Better than poppy or mandragora, much nicer.'

I kissed her in the preliminary way we both understood, but she reared away from me, sat up on the rolling bed and burst into a sweat of tears. I couldn't see her clearly, but my hand touched her face.

I said, 'Lie down and shut up. I know who you're lonely for, and you can get over it. Setter's a pretty crazy man by now, and anyway he only wants Emily. He won't get her, you won't get him. Lie down, be quiet, listen to the creaks and the sea, and go to sleep.'

She did lie down for a moment or two, snuffling into the pillow. Then I felt her leave me, heard her stumbling over the floor to her own bed, knocking things over on the way. I heard nothing more of her that night. I didn't sleep much myself, because I was wondering how we were going to carry on. Not that I had lost hope: I pinned hope to every distraction in store for us. A change of scene, of atmosphere, of friends, a change in the colour of the day, a peculiarity in the night sky, anything might do it. I had never hoped so hard. And there is nothing like hope for promoting insomnia.

In the morning she was breezy. 'You know, Vic? I was tiddly last night, yes, *me*! My mind is a complete blank from the moment I left the Grill to when I woke up just now. I don't even remember undressing.'

Of course she did. She had forgotten nothing.

The sea had moderated, and the sun had tipped the grey Atlantic with a *douceur* of dubious gold. We sat in our deck chairs and read books from the library. The elderly gentlemen all greeted Jenny as they rolled by on their constitutionals. She was gentle and polite with me, shut up tight within herself. She didn't make much of a meal at lunchtime.

When we got to New York, she declared it a disappointment.

'It's flashy,' she said, 'but not interesting.' She pouted as we drove up the chilly canyon of Fifth Avenue.

The trouble was, on this sort of trip, that I had to leave her alone a good deal. I thought she would have enjoyed the shops, but after one essay she developed a reluctance to go out alone. She was stupid, she said, about the money. She sat all day looking at TV in the hotel room, and getting sandwiches from Room Service when she was hungry. Wives of my opposite numbers asked her out sometimes, of course, and though she never wanted to go with them, she always seemed to have enjoyed herself when she got back. Still, I can't say either of us was having a good time. When I got a free night, I took her to Times Square to see the lights.

I suppose it was quite the wrong thing to do, though it would have been a brilliant dog-face who could have predicted it. For some reason the glare, the colour, the whizzing brilliance, seemed to infuriate her. She stood on the pavement near to tears, denouncing the United States of America. It appeared, somehow or other, that all Jenny's sorrows could be laid at the door of the United States, a country designed from its inception, from the first landing of the Pilgrim Fathers, via the Declaration of Independence, via the Monroe Doctrine to the MacCarran Act, to lay her life in ruins. No one in Times Square could ever in the whole of its history have been so lonely as Jenny. I was at my wits' end.

If Setter had appeared at that moment I would have been the most *complaisant* of *maris*. Simply for her sake, I would have implored him to take her away, make love to her, satisfy all her delusions about his strength, his mastery, and the rest of it. But then, he wouldn't have taken her. He didn't want her, never had, never would.

That night, however, she let me make love to her and for an hour or so we were surprisingly happy. Hope, that sickener, rose in me again. I never do learn. I never learn any thing.

Next morning, though, Jenny got a surprise, for someone telephoned, and it was Emily.

She was with Bernard on a trip — no, not business, just fun, just a holiday. Bill had told her where we would be staying. She wanted the four of us to go on the town.

Jenny was so transfigured that she might have heard from Setter himself. Her little white face shone at me. She tripped over her words, as if she were suffering from aphasia.

I, as it happened, couldn't go on any town, because I had to attend some horrible business dinner. But Jenny accepted.

We had only four more days in New York, and I had to spend a couple of them in Detroit. During that period Jenny passed from me to Emily; as far as I could make out they went everywhere together, snug as kittens in a basket. There was nothing wrong with America now. 'I've got the *rhythm* of it,' Jenny said, 'I've got the feel!'

On our last evening Bernard was otherwise engaged, so Emily took Jenny and me to dine in the Village. It was a semi-basement restaurant under one of those old liver-coloured houses where laurels still grow in the front yard, and the air is close and brown. It was almost inconceivably airless, noisy and hot. The food was rotten, but the atmosphere fine.

'I can't bear to leave here now,' Jenny told Emily, 'not now I've just got the rhythm!'

Emily said, 'Then don't. Stay with Bernard and me for another week, and fly back with us. Victor won't mind. It would do you good.'

But I had some vestigial sense left, and I said no. After dinner we went to a pitch-dark place where one could dance. Off went Jenny with some unsnubbable stranger, and Emily began on me at once.

'Why not?'

'She's too disturbed,' I said. 'Haven't you noticed it?'

Emily's blue, prefectorial eyes widened. 'She's as gay as a trivet! — Why are trivets gay?'

'Why are owls drunk?' I asked in return. 'But let's not be semantic.'

'I didn't say anything about the Jews!' Emily was indignant.

'Nor did I. Look, I'm taking her home.'

'She's having fun here.'

'She's in love with Bill.'

'Well, for God's sake!' Emily took some time to digest this. She then said, with an air of reasonableness, that out of sight was out of mind. I said no, out of sight, in such a city, meant the growth of fantasy. In New York, Jenny never left Setter's side, day and night, night and day. That was the tune they happened to be playing at the moment, and I ached to it as I hadn't done since the 1930's. I had become wary of tunes attached to moments in the past, as middle-aged persons should: for they have a habit of turning rotten. They are like peaches, which are fine if you get them the right side up, but with a wasp burrowed into the festering flesh if you turn them the other way.

'Poor old thing, I didn't tell you, or I don't think so. He tried to make love to me, you know, after we'd parted. So silly. He didn't get to first base.' She grinned. 'Oh, I'm becoming very American again. Bernard and I are always wondering whether we wouldn't like to live here.'

I told her as earnestly as I could, that I was real, our house was real, the fiddle-faddles of our common life were real: all this wasn't. Jenny had got to come home.

Emily swung her big, beautiful leg. 'It's too complicated for me. But if you say so, all right. I have enormous faith in your judgement, Vic. Yes, I have. And so has Bill. He won't let me come to that awful flat of his, you know. He won't even see me now. So silly. After all, things were over long before they *were* over, if you know what I mean.'

I thought this was the common face-saver, conscience-saver, of adulterous persons. They hadn't hurt anyone, had they: because it had all been over anyway? If Jenny ever could get Setter (which she couldn't) she would go to considerable lengths to persuade herself that it had been all over for herself, and for me too, long, long since.

At one in the morning we walked through the brown and blazing night, past the laurels, the crumbling steps, the odorous dustbins, back towards Fifth Avenue, where we would get a taxi.

'If you do change your mind—— ' Emily said to Jenny.

She answered at once. She looked peaky under the lights of a restaurant. 'I won't,' she said, 'I'd better go home. Vic would only make a muck-up without me.' She walked with us as though she were arthritic, as though her feet hurt.

# Chapter 26

'MRS. PURDUE has a touch of gastric flu,' Ulick explained. He always spoke of his wife in this mid-Victorian fashion, according her not only the benefit of her new status but, I fancied, the status of her job also. It never mattered to him now that he sat at the bottom of the room, she at the top, still supervisor, still the boss. Despite Setter's reflections upon the probable complications of their sex-life, I was sure the two of them were hitting it off very nicely. The automatic smiles on drawing-office faces had already begun to dim, like the smiles of so many cheshire cats melting away in branches. It was all right. She was Mrs. Purdue. Grotesque as she still was, as hairy in her tweeds, she had a local habitation and a name.

It was a nuisance about her gastric flu, however, because her second-in-command wasn't much use and the place tended to go to pot without her. This, of course, only concerned me in so much as complaints got made, headaches were developed, people wanted time off when it was least convenient for them to have it. There were even moments when I had considered suggesting the promotion of Purdue. He wasn't bright, but since his marriage he had become remarkably steady. However, I imagined the stupefied glances I should get if I did anything of the sort, and as I have never been much of a moral hero, I left him where he was.

My office wasn't particularly peaceful during Lawson's absence (Lawson she was to me) but my home was. I praised myself for insisting that Jenny should return there. She pottered about on her ordinary avocations, she didn't cry any more, she didn't mention her mother, she had rationed her mentions of Setter to the very minimum.

What he was up to, God only knew. Not Sammy. Not even Malpass. Sammy haunted my sleep a bit, or rather the minutes immediately before and after sleep, but that was all. I felt as if someone had taken away the book I was reading just when I'd got to the exciting part. Jenny and I went to the theatre a great deal, but usually to extroverted shows, such as musicals and the less talented reviews.

At the core of my life (I don't know about Jenny's) was a deep, horrible ache, a sag and a rottenness. We were extremely nice to each other, which helped, and there was always a moment in bed when we both felt (I think) that a miracle had happened, a special flash of pleasure, which had put everything right again. But in the morning all was politeness — the domestic minuet, the strain which is so great because there is no reason why the material submitted to it should ever reach breaking-point. People can go on for much longer than we think, some people until they die. That is where some novelists go so wrong. *Pauvres petits*, they believe there is always an answer, always a resolution. The majority of novels, it seems to me, end on a protracted *coda*, bang, bang, bang, Umpah, umpah, umpah, umpah:

Bang——

BANG!!

In fact, in a marriage, a murder, a suicide, a triumph, a disaster. The majority of lives, however, fade gently away without a noticeable peroration or a final curtain. With the excitement wrung out of them, they just go on and on and on.

You should have seen Jenny and me washing up. There was a minuet, if you like! A perfect formality, advance and retreat, one, two, three — thank you — curtsey, polish, polish, polish, and into the cupboard. We never left dishes in the draining-rack overnight, not us. The kitchen had to be ship-shape before we retired. In my masochistic dreams, I saw myself in a frilly apron.

For some reason I never liked to let Jenny out of my sight, and I think she didn't like me out of hers. The house was pretty claustrophobic. Though I loved her, I used to long to get away by myself, if only for twenty-four hours.

I got an opportunity when Malpass asked me to go up to Cambridge with him and dine in our old college. We usually did this once a year, and, though I had faint misgivings, I thought I might accept the chance of a break.

It was November, and a thin fog hung over the city, making great dizzy aureoles round the lamps. Malpass hadn't travelled with me, so I met him in the rooms of Bob Speeder, a youngish historian and amateur theologian, with whom Malpass had once collaborated in a book. He was already installed when I went in, buttery with crumpets before the electric fire, a break-fast cup of very strong tea at his feet. 'I was telling Bob something about our Sammy,' he said.

'It's my belief 'e done the old girl in,' Bob misquoted with a grin. 'That's Mal's belief anyhow. I must say I doubt it myself. It's a show-off. He seems to go around dropping so many little hints that the police would have been on to him months ago if there had been anything in it.'

In consternation at what I happened to know and couldn't tell I made a show of being very hungry. One thing: the boy had never said anything to Malpass. I'd wondered about that. In a way, I felt relieved; even though Malpass was a priest and could no more tell me some things than an official of M.I.5, I had nevertheless felt shut out. Most of us resent the fortunate tenants of the confessional box, the doctor and the priest. It makes them so smug. Special knowledge puffs them up, like gas in toy balloons, and they float with it, bobbing over the heads of us all.

He smoothed his crest of hair, leaving butter on it. 'I wish I were sure one way or another. I suppose I'll know one day.'

'Why do you suppose that?' Bob asked him, his country-man's face cunning and bright. 'You're like a child, Mal. You always think there must be answers. Don't you realise you'll die bristling all over with question marks, as we all shall?'

Malpass said that was probably true, though he hated to think it.

'Afterwards, it is said, and I'm sure I have no need to remind you, we shall *know*.'

'I want to know now,' said Malpass, disconsolately.

It turned out to be a perfectly beastly night, rain pouring down through the fog, making puddles in the court. It was cold, too. I didn't want to catch a chill because I was a bit worried about gastric flu. I could have caught it via the office, where it was going the rounds. The hall wasn't warm, either; great gusts of wet, cold, mouldy air rushed through the swing doors every time a servant came in or went out. I began to wish they would stop trying to feed us, just let us stay warm and in good health. The dinner was good, however. Bob Speeder was poetic about the wine (I never had much of a palate, so wouldn't know); in fact, I heard some of the most preposterous wine-nonsense in my life that evening. The alcohol part did me good, I forgot to shiver, and after the first hour my anxieties began to drop away from me in gauzy layers, rather like the dance of the Seven Veils. I forgot about Sammy, Setter, Jenny even.

There were many faces, of course, that I didn't know. I was attracted by a lean, humorous one with very bright eyes in it and I asked a question.

'Rotblatt,' said Speeder, 'physicist.'

'He's making jokes,' I said. 'I never think physicists ought. Their responsibilities are too serious. And much too dirty.'

Speeder told me that was why this man had thrown them off. He had worked on atomic energy at Liverpool, then at Los Alamos; and had suddenly given all this up for health physics.

I said, good for him.

'Not easy to chuck your career away like that, not if it's been as dazzling as his was.'

I looked at the face again; it was by no means an abstracted one; it was vivid with enjoyment, yet a little sardonic. I thought of Setter, who had also tried to castrate his own power to do harm, and was finding it difficult. But Setter was not a sure man, not as this man was. And his enemy was not the tools of harm, but the harm he fancied within himself, built into his own being, as much part of the total structure as rib-cage or spinal column.

We went into the Combination Room for a bit and then back to Bob's. Bob was in the middle of one of his love-affairs. He was an incurable and incautious womaniser, and I had never seen him free of some kind of trouble. It went all right with the history, but not with the theology. People talked about him, deplored him, but always, in the end, left him alone— perhaps because they were sorry for him; his exploits never ended in anything but disaster. He had just been called away to talk on the telephone to some girl or other, so Malpass and I were alone for the best part of half an hour.

'Why doesn't he marry one of them?' I asked.

Malpass laughed. 'I've tried to urge it. But he can never make up his mind. So he tires them out to the point when they have to throw him over, and then he's absolutely stupefied, and

quite appallingly miserable. Then, after about three months'
pause, he begins again on exactly the same process with somebody else. How are things with you and Jenny?'

I said fine, fine.

'Good.' He didn't seem to believe it. He was silent for a
while. He said, 'You didn't talk much at tea.'

'I was hungry.'

'You didn't talk at all *au sujet de* Sammy.'

I looked up to see his beady eyes intent upon my face.

'Nothing to say.'

'You've always got something to say,' said Malpass. 'Have
you seen Setter?'

'Not recently.'

'But you have. Does *he* know?'

'You keep your secrets,' I said. 'I suppose Setter keeps his.'

'But I don't believe he did keep them.' Malpass began to
talk rapidly in a way quite unfamiliar to me, hurrying along as
though there were some terrible urgency, time was running out.
Sammy was on his mind, he never got him off it.

He had tried to make him talk, but the boy had just danced
rings around him, rings of malice, of conceit, of quiet triumph.
'If he did it,' said Malpass, 'then he'll do it again. I want to
catch him before he can. I must know.'

'There was a time when I believed you did.'

'You haven't heard me on the subject of damnation, it's not
quite right for sociable evenings. I don't suppose it has ever
occurred to you and Jenny that I might even believe in it. With
part of me I don't, but something sticks. I get fits of fright in
the night — not often, just now and then.' He went on: 'Let
me tell you, that boy is damned, because he is sane. If he were
a crazy boy, I wouldn't say it. But if I don't catch him, if God
can't catch him — Manley Hopkins, Herbert too, they think of
God as the Catcher — then he's damned.'

'The catcher in the sky,' I said, not because it was the right
time to be funny or even because I thought it *was* funny, but
because I was embarrassed and a bit scared. It's not an uncommon experience for an agnostic suddenly to spot the idea
of damnation and shy a mile off. Which doesn't mean that there
is anything to it. But supporting this idea, which can look for a
moment as solid as the world we live in, are the Atlas shoulders
of Dante, Calvin, Luther, John Knox, thousands of other
shoulders of the same calibre; and say what you like about
those people, they weren't fools.

Malpass gave himself another drink.

'No, thanks,' I said.

'I have got to get him somehow. And if you do know——'
He stopped, and looked at me.

'Why the devil you should think——'

'Oh, you're hedging! So you do.'

I said, 'I tell you, I don't.'

Speeder came back, flushed, out of conceit with himself. 'To
hell with her,' he said.

We asked him, who?

She was the Master's niece, which made it difficult, fifteen
years younger than Speeder, virgin, pie-faced. He had toyed
with the idea of marrying her, but she had tended to rush her
fences. 'After all, it would be a considerable change in my way
of life.'

He glanced round for an euphoric moment at his curtains of
sage-green plush, his boring but reputable mezzotints.

I suggested it might mean a change in hers.

'But the usual change,' said Speeder, 'only what young
women expect. Still, I may have to do it.' He fancied himself,
momentarily, as a married man. A soft, connubial shine spread
across his face. 'I always wanted a daughter. Or a son. I don't
suppose I'd mind when the time came.'

He saw himself pushing a perambulator across Parker's Piece on Sunday mornings, while the little woman cooked beef and Yorkshire pudding. He would succeed, as so few men do, in *strolling* with the pram, as if it were an aid to dignity, like a malacca cane or a furled umbrella. In pink or blue bonnet his infant would beam at him windily, and old, unmarried friends would come and envy him.

Malpass went to bed on the stroke of midnight. 'Back to my rags,' he said, 'no more glass slippers.' He had to catch an early train.

Speeder and I sat up for an hour or so longer, talking about girls. Listening to him, I felt like a bachelor again, joyfully caddish, out for all I could get with the least to pay; a man banded with males against all women, willing to play Nuts-in-May, to snatch one out of the ring for a bit, but nothing more; prideful in sexual fraudulence, cunning in the preservation of freedom. Ah, freedom!

It is probably only fair to say that I was never, at any time, in the least like this. Even in adolescence, I had gone in for what is now called the 'heavy date': one heavy girl after another had stood on the toes of my spirit for very considerable periods, and I had treated them with solemn, earnest, and later on with expensive, consideration. Jenny had been the last of this respectable series, this testimony to a youth of comparative rectitude. Like most uncaddish people, I often regretted what I was, and passionately envied people like Bob Speeder; as, so Jenny once told me, women who are temperamentally constant admire, envy, and therefore hate, the girls who go sleeping around with every Tom, Dick and Harry. 'I'd have loved it!' she had cried out, to punish me for something or the other. 'Only I wasn't made that way, I'm a different sort of animal, damn it.' 'A swan,' I suggested. 'They're monogamous.' 'A pen,' she replied bitterly, 'a damned, boring pen.'

Speeder and I were both a little drunk by this time. At one point he stumbled up, hurled up the window and shouted out into the sleeping court — 'Stop that, do you hear? You can bloody well stop it!'

I asked him who he was talking to.

He said, 'The rain.'

# Chapter 27

I MENTIONED before that Setter had a son. One Sunday afternoon, early in December, I met him. It was a mild, dampish day with an oysterlike sun in the sky, and Jenny and I had decided to go to the Zoo. As we were coming out from the boom and ammonia of the lion house, we saw Emily walking with a large, shuttered-looking youth, so like Setter that no one could have doubted who he was. He was growing out of a Daniel Neal suit, and his hands and feet looked very big; but he had something of his father's weighty, unsought dignity, and when he walked placed his feet firmly on the ground as if in a constant boring process downhill towards the centre of the earth.

We went up to them. Emily introduced Roger, who gave us a dull, correct greeting.

'My big boy,' she said archly, using a different tone in his presence from any we had heard from her. 'He is going to be a zoologist, so I thought he might do a bit of field work.'

Roger toothed a smile on and off.

I was reminded of a little man I had known in my youth, a poet of *fin de siècle* charm, with a big, beautiful, dominant wife. He was above the mechanics of daily living. When he needed clothes, she bought them for him. He stood silent, on Parnassus, while she made the choice. Yet he was not utterly unnoticing. 'Gracia bought me some shoes this morning. We went into the shop, and I sat down, and she had me fitted. The chap selling them didn't think I could talk. He pressed my toes and said to Gracia, "Do you think they pinch him, Madam?" '

Rather like Roger.

## An Error of Judgement

We went the rounds together, all four of us, Emily and Jenny in front, myself and the boy behind. He must have been sixteen, but he looked much older than that. He dressed himself messily.

The Zoo in winter is a melancholy place, though most of the beasts seem to enjoy it. Emily and her son, it appeared, came there often: they knew some of the animals like intimate friends. They could make (or Emily could make) a rhinoceros called Lorna sit down, by shouting objurgations in a military, upper-class voice. Lorna, a snob, collapsed obediently three or four times into her own impenetrable concrete. Roger fed the gerenuk with apples, seeming to enjoy the creature's fragile friendliness, the lovely crunch of the white teeth, the luscious drip of pale green foamy juices. His face was suddenly tender, open with fondness and responsibility.

In the monkey-house we stood in silence before that huge black sad gorilla called Guy, in whom seven devils are pent, who looks out at us all in his enormous hate. 'Poor sod,' said Roger rather surprisingly: he did not look like a profane boy. He walked quickly past a cage in which monkeys were joyful in masturbation, though Emily stopped and admired their vivacity. I don't think she realised what they were up to. We went into the coloured pandemonium of the parrots.

'I believe you know my father,' Roger said, motionless before a white cockatoo with a syllabub crest of lemons and whipped cream.

I assented.

'I ought to be at school. I've had bronchitis. I go back next week.'

I asked him fatuously whether he would be glad to go.

'Oh: yes and no.'

We passed on to a cage of tanagers. Emily caught up with us, and Roger instantly looked the other way. 'Now, that's a drawing I'd do for *The New Yorker*, if only I could draw!'

189

Jenny asked her what drawing.

'Oh, of a bank, staffed by birds, all the customers are birds. One comes up to the cashier and says, "I want to see the Tanager".'

We laughed: not the boy. He simply stretched his mouth in a polite but insulting acknowledgment.

'Bernard laughed *more*,' said Emily, in a little-girl voice. At this, he flinched and walked away to study the hyacinthine macaw. 'I can't get him adjusted to Bernard,' she said to us plaintively. 'He is being such a trial, you can't imagine.'

As if deliberately giving her the chance to talk about him, he mooched along far ahead of us, his shoulders hunched and bulky. He would be a stout man in middle-age.

'Does he like it better with Bill?' Jenny asked, pleased to speak the name.

'He doesn't seem to. Anyway, he can't live in Bill's pigsty, can he? They sometimes go out together.' She added plaintively, 'I've made him such a nice room, Bernard took so much trouble with it. It's by far and away the nicest room in the flat.'

'They don't care for what we give them,' Jenny said with a stuffy experienced air, 'not the material things. They don't give a rap.'

'Then what *do* they want?' Emily demanded, pausing before the violet bird which had engaged her son's attention. It circled on its perch, bore down with its huge yellow beak, contemplated a step on to her shoulder. She backed away. 'What *do* they want? Love? I'd give Roger pots of that, if I got half the chance. But I'm not even allowed to kiss him!'

The parrot house burst out into one of its more grandiose rackets, which make the normal racket seem like dead silence. Croaks, whistles, great rattles, rasps and hawkings, split the air; the little birds fluttered wildly about in their cages, sparkling like fireflies.

'Oh God,' said Emily, 'let's get out of here! I'm getting a headache. I need my tea.'

She took us to the Fellows' restaurant. We were on the late side, and it was crowded, so we had to split up two and two, Jenny and Emily at one table, Roger and I at another. He was morose at first, mumbling at me, calling me 'Sir', but food brightened him up. His appetite was hearty. Brown and white bread and butter, sandwiches, plain cake and fruit cake, jam sponge. 'I believe you know my father,' he said. He had forgotten saying it before.

I said yes.

'He talks about you a lot.'

'I've lost touch with him lately,' I said, hoping for news. I got it.

'He's in Paris.' He shifted uncomfortably. 'Anyway, he said that's where he was going.'

I asked, what was he doing there?

'He said something about taking a patient,' Roger gave me a swift, anxious, lowering look. 'As a matter of fact, I thought he'd given all that up.'

The conclusion I jumped to gave me such a turn that I felt, beyond all reason, it must be the right one.

'I thought you might know, sir,' the boy said.

I could not help him. He gave me another dark look, then began his tea all over again, brown and white, sandwiches, etc. Two tables beyond us, Emily and Jenny were plunged in gossip, Jenny grave, solicitous, Emily smiling and flirting the rings on her large satiny hand.

This is not, I thought, possible. Even for Setter, obsessed as he is, half-dotty as he is, it isn't possible. And I must obviously be wrong, as it's a chance in a thousand for a hunch to be right. One learns that as life goes on, and it is a great relief, since nearly all hunches are of a disagreeable nature. Fortunately for us, evil never happens on the day of its premonition, or joy on the day we wake up certain of it.

I asked Roger something about school, about his work.

'I'm no great shakes,' he said, 'just average. It's a bore for Mother on Speech Days. I never go up to collect.'

I expressed the usual meaningless and unfounded incredulity, asked him what he meant to be.

'Oh, I may read law, if I can scramble into a university. I shouldn't mind that, I did think of zoology some time back, but I don't want to any more. Mother always forgets.' His face was brightened by a fitful gleam of humour. 'She's always a year behind so far as I'm concerned. She always thinks I'm going to be what I thought I was going to be last Christmas, and she feeds me all the things I grew out of ages ago.'

Not medicine? I asked him.

He withdrew his head between his shoulder blades. His light faded.

'Too messy. I don't like touching things.'

And here our intimacy, such as it was, came to an end. He concluded his second enormous tea in silence, refused politely but with obvious reluctance when I tried to press a third on him. Already the waitress was regarding him with a sort of motherly fascination.

An eating boy: stuffing himself for comfort. The food to supply what? What need? From what Setter had told me, he had never seemed particularly happy even when his father and mother were together. As Emily suggested, half-ironically but meaning it, since for all her airiness she was an affectionate woman, love? No dice. If he wanted it, he refused to accept it. What could one do with him, what could anyone do? Like so many boys in adolescence, unhappiness was in his marrow, a comfortable sort of juice, bitter-sweet, narcotic, habit-forming. Somewhere along the line, someone had disappointed him, but he would never reveal whom, or how. If he did that, matters might be put right, and then he would lose the source of his silence. He would go on making his parents unhappy, and be himself just a little less unhappy, all the time, than they.

Leaving the restaurant, we went out into the falling dusk. The gates were closing, so we had to hurry. Jenny walked with Roger. Emily seized on to me, and drew me on ahead. Just before the other two caught up with us, she whispered passionately to me, 'Vic, I love that boy! I adore that boy! Why doesn't he love me? What's wrong? What have I done?'

# Chapter 28

IT was five days before Christmas, a festival I dislike for its awful monotony. Nor do I care about Christmas food. Jenny and I, being childless, had marked the day rather perfunctorily in previous years (though she, being a believer, had sometimes gone to church); a few bits of holly in a vase, to show the flag, as it were, for the benefit of droppers-in, a bottle of wine, and a small tin of *pâté de foie gras* which we really did enjoy. Mutual gifts, naturally. A shirt for me, a jewel for Jenny.

This year, however, she seemed to go mad about the whole thing. She came home with her shopping basket full of baubles — tinsel, tree ornaments and the rest of it. We were to have a tree this time, she said, even if rather a chichi one: a white one. It could go in the window. She bought a set of fairy lamps with an electric plug attached, blew a fuse when trying it out and dissolved into tears of rage. We were to have a small turkey like other people, and she had made an unsuccessful pudding with sixpences in it. The place seemed to be knee-deep in gift-wrappings. It was all embarrassing to a degree, and I wasn't the only person to feel it. Jenny was embarrassed too, so in defiance went on putting up more and more decorations and whistling at the top of her voice. Whistling beastly carols.

That night, just as she had finished spoiling a batch of mince-pies, which we both detested, and we were sitting together over a drink in that state of sad exhaustion which can seem for seconds together like the purest happiness, the door bell rang, and when I answered it, Setter walked in.

I saw the colour fire Jenny's face; she looked as if she were still bending over the hot stove. She had sprung to her feet, upsetting her glass.

'Oh, Bill!'

'Hullo,' said Setter. He took one of the two hands she had held out to him, and shook it casually. 'I hope I haven't come at an awkward time.' He pulled out a bottle of port and gave it to me. 'Christmas present.'

I thanked him, said he shouldn't have done it, etc. He said I needn't worry; it had been a present to him, but he didn't like the stuff himself.

Jenny was so excited she could hardly speak. His careless greeting had shocked her pale: but now she was rosy once more. 'But it's lovely of you, Bill! Come and sit down. We thought we'd lost you for ever!'

Throwing his coat on to the sofa, he held his hands out to the fire. 'Oh, I don't get lost. I've been in France.'

'What doing?' said Jenny vivaciously, whisky slopping as she poured it. 'Or is it secret?'

'I've been in Paris.'

She insisted that Paris still had a naughty sound for her so that she knew it must be secret, whatever he'd been doing. 'Oo la la,' she said, idiotically.

'Not very,' said Setter. 'I took Sammy.'

Raising his head, he looked straight at me, quartz-like eyes brilliant and steady.

'Sammy?' Jenny said, on something like a screech.

'Sammy Underwood, yes. He hasn't been up to much. He had a week off from work, I took him over there for a change. He'd never been out of England before.'

'Bill!' Jenny really screeched at him this time, heaving her shoulders as if she were shaken with mirth. 'It must have looked just like Oscar Wilde and the boy from Brighton pier with the hat-band——'

'Possibly,' said Setter. 'I shouldn't have noticed.'

She expostulated with him, as if it were all part of a great joke he and she had together. He did not take his eyes from mine. 'He was in a very groggy state,' said Setter, 'a bundle of assorted neuroses were starting to get hold of Sammy. I gave him some good long walks, a little culture, a little phenobarb. I think he feels better.'

'But *Bill*——' Jenny began.

I shut her up. I said, 'What did the Underwoods think about it?'

'The sister thought the worst. She has a fashionable mind. The father and mother thought I was mad, but were worried enough about Sammy to grasp at straws. I was a pretty substantial straw. They were bewildered, but not evil-thinking. They are sensible people. And I don't think I give the wrong impression to sensible people.'

Jenny was lying back in the armchair, her hands locked behind her head, her face brilliant with faked amusement. 'No, but honestly, Bill——'

'I took him to the Louvre, the Luxembourg Gardens, Napoleon's tomb, Notre Dame and the Sainte-Chapelle. He's a quick learner. Pity he never got a decent education. He is quite a pleasure to instruct, Sammy is. You must meet him again.'

Why, I wondered, had Setter come to us like this? He could not talk before Jenny, yet he could not reasonably have hoped to find her out. And if he had wanted to make sure of getting me alone, he could have telephoned.

I was so staggered to see him at all that I had not noticed, till this moment, the marked deterioration in his appearance.

He was so shabby, so ill-cared for, so scruffy now about shirt and shoes, that he might have been a down-and-out. His suit was grimy, his tie frayed at the knot. He needed a hair-cut. Yet under all this was the quiet, steady man who had looked at me in the subterranean light of his consulting room not all that long ago. William Waterfield Setter, M.A., D.M. (Oxon), M.R.C.P., M.R.C.S., in not-so-deep-disguise, ready for the moment when he would fling off his rags and reveal the golden mail.

'Tell me about yourselves,' he said.

'Oh us! What can you expect to be told?' Jenny cried. 'We humdrum old people, stuck here among the Christmas jingle, sickening jingle bells, nothing ever happens to us!'

'Well,' I said, 'we've been to America.' I gave him an account of that.

'Did you enjoy yourself?' he asked Jenny.

'I *loathed* New York! People say it's so stimulating — it didn't stimulate me.'

'Why?'

'It's so show-off! And the noise! And just try to get a letter posted or a zip-fastener repaired——' She was trembling with superiority to the cloud-capped towers, the gorgeous palaces, the Empire State Building.

'Come off it,' I said in a hearty voice, 'you had some good times. And you were the shipboard queen, you know that.'

'I liked it when we met Emily,' she said.

Setter said, 'Was she there? I didn't know.'

We all fell into silence. Then Jenny sat up, clasped her hands around her knees and said quietly, 'We've missed you so much, Bill. You don't want to hide yourself so often.'

'Oh, but I do want to. That's why I do it.'

'It's not kind to other people, though.'

197

The solemnity, the simplicity, of her tone was beautifully managed, but of course it did not deceive him. He merely glanced at her. 'I'm sorry, Jenny.'

'You know we love you?' she cried out at him.

He said nothing.

'We do. And we worry about you. You're not being properly looked after, anyone can see that. Do you expect us to pretend we're blind?'

'It's not important. I'm comfortable enough. I've got things to do.'

'Such as prancing around Paris with that ghastly Sammy?' She had lost control.

'That kind of thing.' His tone was dry; she had him just on the edge of anger. Yet she could not see it, so she rushed on.

'Why do you do it? You owe it to us, to tell us!'

'I don't think I do, Jenny.' He seemed to be speaking from miles away, from some strong cavern, grey as his own flesh. 'But I have, in fact, told you. Sammy needed help and I tried to give it.'

'But why to him? Don't you see what it looks like, you in your position, going off with that squalid——?'

'Sh-sh-sh.' He pursed his lips at her gently. 'Now you're being silly.' She flushed. He looked down at his drink, which he had not tasted. 'Could I beg a cup of coffee, instead?'

'Of course you can! Vic, there's lots in the jug. Do go and heat a cup for Bill.'

It was so obvious, this dismissal, that I glanced at Setter to see if I should accept it. He gave me a faint smile. I went out into the kitchen. I was away for about seven or eight minutes. When I came back, she was sitting quietly at his side and he was holding her hand.

He thanked me for the coffee.

'I told him,' Jenny muttered. She looked very pale, but a long way from tears. Her face was somehow stiff, like wet linen frozen.

'She had to do it,' he said, 'and I thought it was better if she did so now. It is not true, of course, though she thinks it is, and I suppose she'll go on thinking so for a bit longer. But then it will be over and done with.'

I had expected to feel humiliation, and anger. At the sound of his voice, gentle, clinical, sad, I could feel only relief.

'If it were true,' he went on, rubbing her hands between his own as if to restore circulation, 'I should still have to tell Jenny that I have nothing for her, and never could have. Nor for anyone else, either, not again. Not ever again. Poor old Jenny, you will soon know that I am a waste of time. I'm sorry if I hurt you.'

She tried to speak, but could not. I put my arms around her, and she rested her cheek on my shoulder.

'I'm not a dog-face,' said Setter, on a different, rather brisk note, 'I should have been a rotten one. I never tried to be one at all. But I may have done some harm when people didn't understand.' He drank his coffee, though it was still steaming hot. He got up. 'I must go. I'll be out of things for a bit. But I'll ring you in the New Year.'

When he had gone, Jenny washed his cup and the glasses, moving like a sleep-walker, avoiding my eyes. It was hard to imagine, once all was tidied up, the ashtrays emptied, that he had ever been there.

'You're very good to me, Vic,' she said, still not looking at me. 'I know what I've done. It was awful. But I couldn't help it. Only, I do know what I've done. Don't think I don't know.'

I said, 'All right.'

'You do know I'm ashamed.'

'Don't be.'

'I can't help it. I shall never be not ashamed again.'

I told her that would make life extremely boring for us both, and that the sooner she got rid of the emotion, the better I should like it. I also told her that I loved her very much, for what that was worth.

We were both very tired. Something was at an end, over and done with, but whether it was Jenny's life and mine, or whether the spoiling element had been blessedly eradicated — too much to hope? Yet I couldn't help hoping — I don't think either of us knew. We were too tired, in fact, to go to bed. We had another drink, put on the late news, smoked for a bit. Then it all seemed easier, and we turned out the lights and went upstairs. Jenny slept peacefully, not stirring all the night through.

Since there was nothing to be done about us both until I knew what the effect of the confession, and Setter's dismissal, had been, I lay in the dark and wondered furiously (and that is the word, no *cliché*) what he was up to. He believed Sammy was a murderer, and, as murderers go, a sane one. In Sammy was all the cruelty he loathed and feared in himself, the cruelty to which he had never given utterance. And he had taken him away, had walked Paris with this boy quite obviously inferior to him socially, this boy no older than his own son. Had returned him, quietened, with a smutch of culture. What for? What was Setter up to? I had a vision of Sammy, treacle-eyed, smirking, in sweater and jeans, under the bare trees of the Luxembourg Gardens, Sammy by the lake, monstrosity locked within himself. Setter hulking on a green bench, watching him. Little doses of history from Setter. 'Here . . .' and 'here, you see. . . .' The parade through the Louvre, Sammy intelligent before the Winged Victory: 'I see, Doc. Yes, Doc.' Had people stared at them? Or had Setter's shabbiness made it all right? Father and son, perhaps. The egg on Setter's tie, Sammy's lack of tie. I dare say, all right.

Christmas was much like the other Christmasses, as it happened, since after that night, Jenny lost interest in the trimmings, and the fairy-lights never got mended. We ate the turkey and a bit of the pudding. Damp December hung above the hedge, gorged neighbours went for little constitutionals in the deadened light, and after a while, so did we. I held Jenny's arm and she leaned against me, like someone after an illness. She was affectionate and very quiet. She had taken to scooping up her hair into a knot high at the back of her head. It aged her, but she looked the better for it. She was demonstrating to me that her youth was over and that she meant to accept the fact decently. Small, still pretty, still narrow hipped, she stepped softly at my side through the faint drizzle, as the boys kicked their footballs about and lights sprang up first in one window and then another, putting their pink and yellow patchwork all round about us.

'I liked my present,' she said. This year it had been a pendant of olivines in a Victorian setting.

'Good. I liked my shirts.'

# Chapter 29

ON a cold day in the second week of January, Setter telephoned me. He wanted me to have dinner with him in Soho, but I wasn't to bring Jenny. He wouldn't be seeing her again, he told me, in the brisk and conclusive tone of a dentist who has completed a patient's fillings. He named a restaurant in Dean Street, eight o'clock. 'I might be a few minutes late. If you get there before me, ask for my table.'

Snow was beginning to fall, blackening as it touched the pavements. I had been walking so fast to keep myself warm that I was ten minutes early. The little restaurant sparkled, its red sign winked and swung.

'Sharpish, sir,' said the commissionaire, pushing me quickly indoors so that I shouldn't let too much of the cold in with me.

'Sharper for you,' I said.

'I'm used to it.'

I gave Setter's name. 'Yessair,' said a waiter, 'in the back room, sair, very nice table.'

I walked behind him through the diners, through a short passage with serving hatches, past a half-curtain of plush, a screen of potted palms, into the L of the room. It smelled good. The smell of French cigarettes was nice, too, though I never smoke them. Little pink lamps were reflected endlessly in mirrors with gold shells painted on them. Most of the couples looked in love and a bit furtive, which gives a cosy atmosphere to a place whether one feels furtive oneself or not. A good restaurant, not too much garlic. I could never, for

instance, trust Jenny with garlic. To think of her gave me a
pang, not only because she wasn't with me, but because she
simply didn't know where I was. I might have been meeting a
girl. I felt as deceitful as if I were.

Setter's table was right away in the far corner, but Setter
wasn't sitting at it. Sammy was.

He wasn't in his sweater and jeans but in a dark suit with
chalk stripes too widely spaced. He had on a pinkish shirt and
a narrow black knitted tie. He rose like a little gentleman,
greeting me as 'Vic', which maddened me out of all proportion.

'Doc won't be long. He said to get ourselves a drink.' He
motioned in a lordly fashion to a waiter who, having a mind as
fashionable as Sandra's, gave me a faint leer. 'Pink gin for
me,' said Sammy. 'You?'

I had whisky.

'Well, well, well, long time no see.'

'Long time heard disgusting phrase,' I said.

He grinned. He was at ease, or seemed so, but he wasn't
looking well. Something was jumping behind his eyes. His
colour was poor. I thought he seemed very young, younger
than I had remembered. He fascinated me. I saw him kicking
away with his winklepickers at that reeking old body in the
gutter: a moment later, I couldn't see him doing anything of the
sort, and felt a fool because of the hallucination.

'I've been on my travels,' said Sammy. 'Know that?'

I said I had heard about it.

'Not that I'm not grateful, but I don't think Doc's all there.'
He touched his forehead. 'We didn't go V.I.P. exactly, still
it must have cost him a packet. And what for? Damned if I
know.'

He gave me a quick, cunning look. I thought I saw that
gutter again, and wondered how I was going to get through a

meal in his company. He smelled obtrusively of after-shave lotion. I wished Setter would hurry up.

Sammy told me about Paris. What he had liked best, he said, surprising me, was the music.

'He took me to a Lammerer concert. First time I'd ever heard that sort of music live, not canned, can you believe that? Makes a difference to hear it with people around. Doc wanted me to like the Louvre, but I can't get much out of pictures. Well, here's to us.'

He tossed his gin straight down. His gaze was on the palms around the entrance to the room. Looking into middle distance, he took out a bottle and gave himself a little white pill. 'Three a day, he says they keep me steady. Clucks on and on about it. "Taken your phenobarb, Sammy?" he says. "You've got a memory like a sieve."'

Setter was coming towards us now, better groomed than usual, in a clean shirt. 'Sorry, I got held up. Have you looked after yourselves?'

As he sat down he gave Sammy a curious sort of glance, almost affectionate, but not quite that: sympathetic, rather, as if he had bad news to break. He broke none, however, but settled down to ordering the meal. 'I'm hungry. I hope you two are.'

'So-so,' the boy said.

'I am,' I said, and it was true. My hunger had come back again.

After we had ordered, Setter began a run of conversation, dry, anecdotal, amusing. He told stories of bizarre incidents in his country practice, characterizing the various people concerned with a virtuosity of tongue I had never suspected in him. People who had been glancing our way, wondering what on earth we were doing out with Sammy, returned to their own absorptions. To Sammy, I realised, this sort of place was no particular novelty. It wasn't one of the smarter Soho places, certainly, but equally it wasn't one of the places where boys like Sammy usually ate. I supposed Setter had got him used to them in Paris.

Time trickled agreeably but, to me, quite meaninglessly away. When we got to the coffee stage, Setter ordered another bottle of wine. 'Comfortable in here,' he said, 'perishing outside.'

He had been doing most of the talking: Sammy and I hadn't said much. Sammy, indeed, was beginning to look a little sleepy, stretching his eyes from time to time as if to stimulate his eyelid muscles.

'Wake up,' Setter said with sudden roughness, 'you need another drink.'

He plied him, and went on doing it.

Sammy did wake up. A sparkle came over him, a sort of damp sheen. He, in his turn, grew garrulous and grandiose, rehashing his adventures in Paris, announcing to us that he was going to take Hilde there one of these days, give her a bit of fun. He'd got her interested again, he was going to keep her that way this time.

'That's right,' said Setter, 'you do that. No place like Paris for fun.'

'I'd learn to talk French if I was there much. I could pick it up easy.'

'Of course you could.'

'I've got a good ear.'

'Damn good ear, Sammy.'

'Well, haven't I?'

'I said you had.'

'Give me six months and I'd show you.'

'Of course you would.'

'You see?' The boy swung round to me. 'That's what he's like. Humouring me. Can't you tell him I don't have to be humoured?' The wine was stirring him to some obscure anger, and Setter knew it. He gave him some more. Sammy had another silent spell, sipping at his glass, glowering over it at a woman with plump marble shoulders whose appearance displeased him. 'Gorgonzola,' he said, 'that's what she is.'

A couple at the table next to us, a youngish girl out with a dried-up man in early middle age, began a muted but furious quarrel. We could just manage to hear what it was about. She was being taken for granted: who did he think he was, Frank Sinatra, to take her for granted? He needn't think she couldn't spend her evenings better somewhere else. Now, now, said the man, whose voice was B.B.C., she couldn't take that line. She wasn't in a position to take any line at all, and she knew why.

Setter murmured to me, 'No, she isn't in a good position. She's pregnant. But I like her guts.'

Sammy said suddenly, in a quiet, insistent voice, 'Why did you take me there, Doc?'

Setter replied without hesitation. 'To give you a good time.'

'*No*. Why, why? That's what I want to know.'

'I have told you.'

'What did you get out of it?'

'Nothing at all.'

The boy's eyes filled with boozy tears.

'Did you take your phenobarb, Sammy?'' Setter asked him. A gulp and a nod.

'What's the matter, Sammy? Anything on your mind?'

The boy muttered that it was crazy, everyone was crazy, it was just about driving him round the bend.

'Sammy doesn't dream,' said Setter. 'That's very odd. You never do, do you, Sammy?'

'I said not.'

'He ought.' Setter looked at me. 'I wish he did.'

Sammy got up, staggering a bit. He pushed the table out so he could get round it, came behind my chair and peered at Setter. 'That's enough, see? I've had enough. I say I've had enough.'

Setter told him to sit down. This sort of place had plenty of scenes on its hands without him adding to them. I tried to pull the boy into the vacant chair on my left, but he resisted me. We hadn't been talking loudly, but already people had begun to stare.

'Just tell me why you took me, that's all! Vic, you make him tell me!'

Setter answered, 'To give you a good time. Or hope to. That's all it was. And that's all there will be.'

Sammy swayed. His face was opalescent. He put out a hand; whether in appeal or aggression, I don't know. Setter caught it. 'Come on. Gents ahoy. With will-power, you'll make it.'

They went off through the plush curtain, Sammy looking as if he were under arrest, clutched hard to Setter's side. They formed a pyramidal shape, the boy leaning so heavily on the man that he pulled him out of the true. Just as they reached the door, Sammy glanced over his shoulder at me; it was a wild, blinking look, repulsive and at the same time pitiable. His eyes expanded, the pupils enlarged, the whites spread like a negro's. I pretended I hadn't seen. People thought: Drunk: and stopped bothering.

They were a long time gone. I just sat there, feeling like an ass. I hoped they hadn't gone off together, because I hadn't enough in my pockets to pay the bill. I have always worried about that sort of thing happening: me, with no money to pay for something. My mind far from Setter assisting a murderous yob to be sick (but had Sammy ever told the truth, or had it been just his idea of swank?) I wondered whether the *patron* would take my watch, even (I had heard of such things) whether he would let me go quietly into the kitchen and do the washing-up. But if I did the washing-up it would take me all night, and Jenny would worry herself sick. Could I telephone her *before* I offered to wash up, and if I did, what should I say to her? Could she, perhaps, get to me with the money, or had the last tube gone? (Yes.) It seemed to me that our waiter was beginning to spiral about me; the circles narrowing and narrowing.

Setter came back alone, very bright and cheerful. 'I sent him home in a taxi. He's all right now. Let's have another drink, in peace and quiet.'

But I was beginning to feel what I had had already, so I took no risks.

I asked him a question, which had been Sammy's question.

There was only one table other than our own occupied now. The restaurant had that politely yawning air, a yawn of stale breath, sour wine, longing for a good night's sleep, which always makes me pay my bill, over-tip, and run. It did not affect Setter, who asked for brandy.

After a while he answered me. 'Neither of you believe it, but I told you the truth. I wanted to give him pleasure. I wanted to extend his horizons for him. Because I don't think they are likely to be extended much further.'

'Because of——?'

He shrugged. 'I just don't think so.' Now, for the first time, he looked a bit evasive.

'You think he did it?'

'Oh yes. Beyond the slightest doubt.'

'And you think they'll catch him?'

'We've had enough of Sammy,' said Setter, 'for tonight.' He sat back comfortably, as if the best part of the evening lay ahead.

'Why did you want me to see him?'

'I wondered what you'd think.'

I said rather angrily that I thought Sammy was a nasty bit of work with a new line in boasting. It would please him to have a top doctor on a piece of string.

'Could be.' He sighed. 'It's bad for him that he never dreams, though.'

I suggested that Sammy slept the sleep of the just.

'He likes music. He never knew he did, either, not till I put his nose to it. He sat there bright as a daisy, all excited, with his mouth open. Sammy's breath smells, by the way. First he'd watch the conductor, then he'd watch me, to see how I was taking it all. I'm glad I gave him that.'

He repeated then that we had had enough of Sammy, and he turned to something else. He was going abroad pretty soon, he said, by himself: no, he didn't know where, but he was thinking about it. There wasn't much in England to keep him, he might stay away for some time. The boy (Roger) didn't want him, he didn't seem to want Emily, either, but that was hardly the question: he could be of no use to Roger at all, for some reason he never had been.

'Drop me a card,' I said facetiously. I was feeling tired, and, as the drink began to fall away, had started to worry about Jenny again.

'I might.'

'We don't want any "What's become of Waring",' I said.

Setter called for the bill. At last we got up and left.

In the icy street, still gaudy with the light of the dead shops, I realised that he, too, was somewhat the worse for wear. He was walking carefully, with the precision of a sidesman carrying a bounteous plate to the altar rails. A little more dignified than usual, Setter was: a little more grave. I have often thought, in my own cunning, drunken moments, when I have hoped to evade comment, that it is by the 'little more' that we betray ourselves. We have to relax, even to slouch; but never to be slightly more of our natural selves than we naturally are.

A snaggle of prostitutes on a corner had greetings for us.

'No go, dears, no go,' Setter said forlornly, making an over-elaborate *détour* in order to pass them; 'no go, no go, no go,' he went on muttering, as we walked together. He stopped abruptly under a lamp and peered at me. 'Do you know,' he said, 'we haven't, we have never had, one bloody thing in common? But I can talk to you, Vic, because you understand nothing, not one single thing, dear Vic, not one single bloody thing.' His monumental hand came down on my arm. 'I shan't forget, not you, not Vic, not my good old patient, not my Vic. You don't feel ill so often, do you? I told you so. I still remember your face when I showed you the burn I'd got on the oven.'

A taxi came by. He hailed it, put me in and slammed the door. 'We go different ways.'

# Chapter 30

THIS sounds like a valediction, it sounds like last words. It is not. I did see Setter again, but not for some time. In February, to Jenny's stupefaction and mine, we read in the papers that Malpass had been made a canon. He wasn't stupefied in the least: he had, so we discovered, been expecting it. His superiors had always thought well of him, and had disregarded his eccentricities. He wouldn't go any further, of course — he wasn't the stuff from which bishops are made — but this was going quite a long way. He had a little party to celebrate, old friends only. Jenny and me, Bob Speeder, a sonsy-looking cleric named Partridge, who had been the first curate Malpass could call his own, now bossing a handsome parish on the South Coast, and a nice woman who designed stained glass windows, Sally Crocker, I think her name was, or it may have been Crockett.

The party was held in Malpass's big, ugly, comfortable sitting-room, overlooking one of the newer, more cheerful kind of grave-yard, but the bobbled curtains of green chenille, God knows how ancient, were pulled to shut out the view. There were plenty of drinks and some very fancy bits and pieces to eat. 'I had us properly catered for tonight,' said Malpass, in high old form, 'by a catering firm. If I can't quite give the impression of a carousing cardinal in one of those damn awful pictures, I'm going to get the nearest I can to it.'

'Aren't you thrilled, Mal?' Jenny asked him. She was wearing a stately sort of black dress, and her hair was done up on top.

Having grappled with the years and found them too much for her, she was now accepting them defiantly: indeed, her get-up was now a little too old for her. She retained a bit of her deliberate and pretty silliness. 'Or perhaps one oughtn't to be thrilled? Perhaps *awed* would be better?'

'Thrilled will do all right.' He gave her a kiss. Bob Speeder was eyeing her thoughtfully, but without much hope.

The party took off like a jet, in the way some parties do. In the way some parties, unfairly, since all the ingredients seem to be right, don't. It went so well, in fact, that the occasion for it was soon forgotten. Malpass is the only cleric I have never been scared of, for whom I have never felt I must put my best foot forward and watch my language. Speeder was soon talking in low suggestive tones to Sally Crocker, Partridge flirting in (I admit) a somewhat churchy manner with Jenny. When Partridge's wife came in, a pretty, mousy girl with speculative eyes, I flirted with her. It was all fine. I began to think Malpass was in his Heaven, all was right with the world. I felt even better when I saw Jenny looking in a hostile manner at Mrs. Partridge. Could she be jealous of me once more, conceivably? Because if she could——

My spirits soared.

'You women,' I said to Mrs. Partridge, 'parsons' wives or not, you're all the same.'

'The same as what?' she asked me demurely. She had very dark eyes under light lashes, which gave her an odd but alluring appearance, something which was feral, not quite human.

I said, not brilliantly, Same as other women: and regretted audibly what it must be like for her to hold herself down.

'Down?'

'Well,' I evaded, 'you couldn't wear some sorts of hat. The parish would talk.'

'I don't wear a hat.'

'Well, some sorts of make-up.'

'One persuades oneself after a time,' said Mrs. Partridge, 'that one looks infinitely better as one's natural self.' Her lips twitched. 'So superior, too.'

'But does one?'

'One wouldn't dare admit to the contrary.'

I began to wonder how Mrs. Partridge endured what must necessarily, being a public life, be a life of virtue. I would have bet my last sixpence that her husband had snatched her up in the middle of an adventurous career. Now she sat on a pedestal and teased the passers-by. What I could say, if I chose! What I could be! Chase me, Charlie, I'm not to be caught.

Jenny moved firmly in and joined the conversation. I felt better and better and better.

Speeder came over to talk to me, mostly about his love life. The Master's niece had ditched him, and he must say, bloody as he felt, that it was probably a good thing. He didn't want too many ties to the college, he was already tied enough. One day he might want to move, accept a Chair abroad. One never knew. And talking about what one never knew, it almost looked as though Mal had been right about that boy after all, in the light of what had happened.

What boy?

'"Done the old girl in", I forget the name.'

I asked him what had happened and he stared at me. Didn't I know? Hadn't Malpass said anything? It was in the evening papers anyway, just a line or so. No, not tonight, two nights ago; the report of the inquest. Accidental death, by overdose, only it didn't sound much like it.

I supplied the name.

Yes, that was it.

On Newsam Ernest Underwood, aged 18, fitter's apprentice, of something or other Coldfield Lane, S.W.4.

I felt that room, with me in it, wallow like a ship in the trough of a wave. It was not that Sammy had ever been any business of mine, had ever touched my life directly: but in that second I became *shut into* him, that last wild, repulsive look of his flashing back into my mind's eye as if lightning had struck. I could see him in the reeking gutter now, as clearly as if I'd been there myself, lurking in the doorway of a shop, could hear the flap and gasp of the old woman like a whale, wallowing like a whale, a ship, like Malpass's cosy room.

It took me back to what I always thought of as Sarah's dawn.

Before I met Jenny, ten years before, I had been in love with a girl called Sarah White. I was in my middle twenties, she was twenty-one or two. She had silky fair hair, almost apricot-coloured, a fine body, and a plain face. Because her face wasn't pretty, I somehow imagined I had no need to worry about her: by a happy chance she was beautiful in *my* eyes, and I had no reason to worry about any other chaps being as percipient as I. We slept together; it was fine, all very easy and undemanding. I hadn't slept with any of my steady girls before that, only with one or two fly-by-nights. I hadn't actually asked her to marry me, though I assumed she was going to. One summer she went off on holiday abroad, with her mother. I was on my own for three weeks, and bored stiff.

Towards the end of it, one stuffy summer afternoon in the year war broke out, an old schoolfriend of mine came out of the blue, like myself, at a loose end. He suggested we might go on the river at Richmond and then to a dance given by some people he knew, who had a lot of money. We had never been particularly interested in each other: yet today, united by the unexpectedness of the treat, we got on like Roland and Oliver. The hour was dangerous: we knew the intoxication of borrowed time.

His friends were well-heeled all right. They had a house with a lawn running down to the river, and a marquee set up on it. The night was full of moon and afterglow when we arrived there, the willows still holding a reminiscence of pink, the shadows blue on the frocks of the smart girls. We weren't really dressed for that sort of entertainment, but no one seemed to mind. I kissed a girl in the boathouse, and was gloriously happy because Sarah would be back soon and I could kiss her instead. Everything was so beautiful, life so short, yet life so promising, war or no war! I don't think I have ever been so happy, before or since.

Somebody ran us home, about half-past five in a steamy, mercurial dawn. I let myself in, still cocooned in moon-struck bliss. My parents had gone to bed, they had left a Thermos and cup on a tray for me. (I was much spoiled as a young man.) By the tray was a letter from Sarah. I opened it joyfully, and then the room swung, and my world swung, just as Malpass's cosy room, his plushy room, his canon-elect room, was to swing around me, about twenty years later.

It was a very nice letter in its way, jollying me tactfully along in a good-humoured attempt to make me realise that neither of us had been serious about the other, that we had had a marvellous time, that I would wish her luck in her future with a full and overflowing heart. (No, it was not someone she'd met on holiday. It was the young man she'd gone around with some time before she met me, and who had chased her to France in order to grab her again.) It was the kindest, most bloody, most conclusive letter I have ever read in my life.

So, superimposed upon Malpass's chenille curtains with ice and fog and gravestones beyond them, was the fragile haze of earliest morning. The glint of the Thermos flask, the sheet of blue paper, closely written in her rather pernicketty handwriting, typical handwriting of a small-nosed blonde. I remembered the pattern of our coffee-cups, ripply pink roses on a biscuit-coloured ground with meaningless curlicues of brown and gold, very hideous, very cheap, I dare say.

'What's up?' Malpass asked.

'You never told me.'

'Oh, yes. Well, I thought it could wait. Or that you might have spotted it.'

He edged me out of the room, into the untidy kitchen. When Malpass was a canon he would have a better one. He might have a stainless steel sink.

The weather must have changed, because rain, not sleet, was flopping across the window panes.

I asked Malpass what he thought it proved.

He opened his eyes wide, his crest feathered. 'What could it, except bad conscience?'

Oh my baby, I wanted to say, oh my poor baby priest, my infant canon, has your world taught you nothing? Don't you know that for people like Sammy (if I am right about Sammy) there is no such thing as conscience?

Sammy never dreamed. He never had any dreams.

What I did say, of course, was: 'What happened?'

Well, it was no nine days' wonder, not for the world at large, seriously and madly contemplating burning itself to ashes: you couldn't make even a day's wonder out of an item in the local press. A yob taking an overdose on top of too much drink. Who cared who he was, or why he did it?

(Pause for thought: 'seriously and madly' — could that be possible? Were people so crazy? Statesmen so crazy? But then, it was a question of *Losing Face*. Damn funny, when the alternative was no face to lose—— Had somebody said that before? Conceivably. One had to think of individual faces to keep sane. Let us suppose Jenny and I had had a son. He might have been seven, eight, nine. Think of his face. A nice jolly innocent face, trustful as a kitten's.  Now try to burn the skin off that.)

Hurry, hurry, hurry, it's getting dark.

Then what's the point, I asked myself, of hurrying?

No point, unless you mean to get the lights going again. Why doesn't someone do it? What are we sane ones waiting for?

I was in a state, as you will observe.

There had been no complications, Malpass went on. An empty pill bottle, which should have held about half a dozen sodium amytal. A lot of brandy in the stomach: the combination would have finished anyone. Pills prescribed by local physician on the N.H.S. Sammy had visited local physician regularly. But they were all gone, bang off, in one night, and so was Sammy. Verdict as stated, no evidence to support any other.

Inquest?

Oh yes, relations. Nothing of interest from father, mother, sister. Sammy had been under the weather, that was all. Nothing else that they had been able to see.  A very ordinary Sammy, in the best of spirits.

Call Dr. William Waterfield Setter.

Had they?

No.  Dr. William Waterfield Setter hadn't been brought into it. Not by father, mother, or sister Sandra. Why should he have been?

So I told Malpass about the last time I had seen Sammy.

'Perhaps they should have called Dr. William Waterfield Setter,' said Malpass thoughtfully.

'Is Sammy damned, do you suppose?'

I have said that I believe in nothing, certainly not in the fiery pit. Yet I shuddered with a sense of scorching, far, far down, stamped down for ever, deeper even than did plummet sound, etc. etc. Under Malpass's floorboards, under the tacky old carpet, the parquet lino, scorching, scorching, deep down, deep down. Out of earshot, out of forefinger's probe, for ever and ever. Not the least warmth would have reflected itself upon the forefinger, for the heat was a million miles below, a subterranean sun, roaring, sucking, irresistible. Under Malpass's lino it would be comfortable, temperate and nice, for at least a thousand miles down. But then the tickling of the flesh, not unlike sunburn, then the slightest suggestion of scorch, the fast peeling, the second and third sunburn, the stripping away of the flesh, layer by layer, till the burnable soul, the destructible soul, lay bare.

Malpass stretched his mouth, blew out his nostrils. 'No. That I can't believe.'

'Sometimes you do.'

'Not in the best times.'

'For I, thy God, am a Merciful God——' Church with Jenny once or twice, Jenny in a churchy hat, worn at no other time, brow serene, child's eyes open and blue. It struck me then that Jenny took what she wanted from her religion. Christians of her sort do, or it would drive them mad. How many have the guts to take the lot?

*But the whole lot must have been meant*. I clung to my own agnosticism as to a blessed spar in mid-Atlantic.

'Suppose he did it,' I said.

'Suppose,' said Malpass, 'he had gone on? He would have done it again.'

Because Sammy, I thought, didn't dream.

'Not answering my question,' I said.

He replied, 'I can't. No one can.'

He looked terrified. I was terrified.

At that moment Partridge came boisterously in to replenish a jug with Malpass's one modern luxury, ice from the refrigerator. He asked if he had broken in upon a *séance*; if so, he was sorry.

'Not a bit,' said Malpass, 'let's get back to the others.'

I suppose they (Malpass excepted) enjoyed the rest of the party. They must have done, since they knew nothing. They went on celebrating a canonry. Speeder flirted with Jenny, who looked spitefully at me, who looked lasciviously at Mrs. Partridge. . . . Ring-a-ring-o'-roses. We broke up early, because the last tube from that part of the world doesn't keep partified hours.

# Chapter 31

ONE morning I found Jenny sitting at her dressing-table, crying.

'What's the matter?'

For a while she was too choked with tears to answer me. Her red hair was damp with tears, sticking to her cheeks. Her eyelids were swollen already. She kept peering at herself in the glass, then looking down again. Jumbo drops dripped on to her brushes and combs.

She said at last, 'It's too cruel, to have been pretty once, and always to have looked young and then to see yourself growing old.'

'No age for you,' I said heartily, but did not like to touch her.

'You know it for a long time, of course,' she went on, in a controlled and reasonable tone, 'you see your neck going ropey, but you think, "that's just today, tomorrow it will have tightened up again". And your waist — that will be all right too, it's just that you ought to cut down on the starches a bit. But it isn't all right, because it's nothing to do with starch, it's *age*. Age. Age.'

She raised her head, confronting me and herself in the mirror, a drowned girl, sickly as a beached mermaid. 'Oh, Vic, when one knows there will never be another time!'

I didn't ask her what for. I knew.

She swung round on me, raddled with tears and as desirable as I had ever seen her. 'It's so cruel! Men don't know it——'

'Don't you be so sure.'

'— They never do. Vic, I am old.'

Well, yes; she was getting old. She was middle-aged, and a bit more. Setter had taught her this misery, this revelation, Setter who had only meant to do good.

Still, I cuddled her. What else could one do? Also, I loved her, was in love with her still—— Well, was I? That's a rare condition, after a longish marriage. But yes, I think I was, I think I am, in love with her still.

Then she shrank away from me with a hard and terrible look, self-accusing. 'What a fool I am! If I hadn't said it you would never have noticed, would you? You haven't looked at me for years.'

'If you love, you don't look.'

She told me that if you were *in love*, you did: you noticed a new dress, a new hair-style, you noticed! But if you just 'loved', which was dull, which was the last thing, the thing that took all the last light, the afterglow, out of life, then you didn't notice.

Old and comfortable crones in corners, beastly Darbies and Joans ('enough to make one sick!') — she hurled them at me. That was what we were, that was what we had become.

I told her, as quietly as I could, that it was just what we were not. She had taken even a comfortable love from me: had she realised that?

She sprang at me, smacking at my forearms.

'I've taken nothing from you! Only I——'

'You wanted something more,' I said, 'but you couldn't have it.'

Horrible mornings of strife, of weeping, of rapid patchings-up because there was a train to catch. No, I saw nothing wrong with Jenny's neck, Jenny's midriff. (It struck me how boring women could be with their worries about beauty vanishing. As if a husband cares! Boring, boring. . . . Men are terribly bored by women, more often than women like to think, and it is always because women set such store by physical brightness, physical tautness, physical skills. I think they are encouraged in this by all the younger American novelists and a good many of the old ones. This mania for flesh *comme il faut*, for the adolescent image! It is hardly ever a reality in women after the age of twenty.) I loved Jenny. To me, an ounce extra on the waistline was a precious ounce more of Jenny. Could she really not see it?

A horrible morning, this one. I crept off to work, feeling more dead than alive.

You know what it is when your mind is totally dissociated from the duties you have to get through. Somehow, of course, you get through them, by some curious dispensation of providence making fewer errors than you normally do: the pay-off comes next day, when you have completely forgotten what you did, what you omitted, to whom you spoke, and to whom you didn't. A warning to those involved in *Scenes*: you won't feel them that day, but the day after, when all the chickens come home to roost in a flurry of little red and brown feathers, chicken-smelling (i.e. corrupt) and warm.

I worked all right. There was some trouble with Lawson, I mean Mrs. Purdue, who was wholeheartedly determined that I should sack one of the younger draughtsmen, whom she considered inefficient. I dealt with her and with him, leaving both in the *status quo* they had occupied before war broke out, and apparently to the satisfaction of each. Otherwise, the office was sweet to see: I loved the glossy blue paper, the rulers, protractors, compasses, T-squares. Order: that is what I loved. I loved Ulick Purdue, industriously doing his little best. I loved Lawson, industriously doing her considerable best, the light glittering palely upon the ursine pelt of her gents' suiting.

Outside the windows, the mild sun of a sweet March shone on tidy flower-beds, the flowers yet unbudded, but promising such wealth of nasty lobelia, begonia, geranium, what have you! The sky was like milk left a bit too long in the fridge, not curdled exactly, but not fresh either. Right at the top of the sky, a colour like milk just turned, a colour faintly buttery: below, little creamy peaks of cloud, lovelily fragmented: below that, above the privet hedges, a line of skimmed blue. Hundreds of miles away was Jenny, lids still swollen, heart curdling within her, waiting — just waiting! — for me to get in.

Work, work! Work was pure, creamy, dairy-pure, uncomplicated, joyful. I saw several hard cases that afternoon, a draughtsman who wanted a rise and had no right to it, a chap from the Accounts Department to whom some wild injustice (or so he thought) had been done, a girl who was pregnant and wanted time off right away, a typist who wanted a transfer because she hated her immediate boss. A well-balanced, a benign, a tepid Rhadamanthus, even, I dealt justly with them all.

It was half-past five: my knocking-off time. I should have mentioned that my office was on the front of the building, first floor, with the formal gardens, God help them, beyond. I was just packing up to go, reluctantly, I admit, because I was by no means sure what I should find at home, when I saw, on one of the crossing paths, something rigid which seemed human, like a scarecrow.

I do not approve of pinching other men's writing. Obviously it is the fashion to condone it, since pinching is such a rash these days: but I don't pinch, or if I do, I acknowledge it. I acknowledge this to Chesterton. There was, I think, in one of his stories, a scarecrow with a nose made of wax which appeared in a formal garden. My scarecrow had nothing odd about the nose and in fact, being moderately well-dressed, didn't really resemble a scarecrow. But it was a man, standing quite still in the dusk of March, under a lamp (Council of Industrial Design) and beside a rectangle of potential blooms, whom I saw waiting for me, and I knew he was waiting. And I knew who it was.

Refreshed, feeling the end of it all pretty near, I packed up for the day, called my secretary, signed the letters, gave her some stuff for the files, washed my hands and face, put on my hat and coat and walked out to meet Setter.

By the time I left the works, he had deserted the flowers and was waiting for me at the gate.

'Tracked you down,' he said. An unnecessary observation, for the feat could scarcely have been difficult.

He explained that he had not cared to telephone me at home, because of Jenny, nor had he wished to do so at the office.

'Why not?'

'You might have been busy,' he said, 'or said No. Have you got time for a pub?'

In the outer suburb where we have our main works and administrative block, pubs are few and displeasing. However, there was one, outskirts-Tudor, to which I went sometimes. This, like the works, was surrounded by flower-beds, which would be lively and horrible when summer came. It was called 'The Green Man', which was uninspired.

Neon-light on potential dwarf begonias is displeasing, and is worse on faces. Setter and I, mauve, got out of it quickly and found a quiet corner in the private bar which, though exactly like all the other bars, which differ only in a penny on the pint, tends to be shunned.

'I mustn't be too late,' I said. I was feeling an apprehension not unlike thirst: it needed, for relief, to be filled brim-up, until it brimmed over. It would not be true to say that I was afraid of Setter, who was my friend, but that night I would rather have been with somebody else.

Around us, though we could not see through the walls, the homing lights swept piercing and yellow over the freeways, the roundabouts, the flyovers of a modern civilisation. Heavy traffic at this time in the evening, something hot in every oven, the *poule au pot*: pretty little wives in plastic aprons, un-hitching the rollers from their hair: little darlings tucked up for the night, waiting for daddy's benediction. And we weren't yet on our way home, Setter and I, we were in the bar of 'The Green Man', far out, far out on the Northern Line, while my dinner dried in the oven and, I suppose, no dinner waited for him.

'I'm going off tomorrow,' said Setter.

I asked him where.

'France, first. After that, I don't know. I'll keep in touch.'

I said, 'Tell me about Sammy.'

He did.

This is:

### SETTER'S STORY (4)

My own version, with my own comments, some bits filled in, but I think more or less accurate.

From the beginning, he had had not the slightest doubt of Sammy's guilt: and it seemed to him both odious and wonderful. Never in his life had he come up against anything so purely and simply criminal, so untroubled by any back-kick of the soul, by any narcotic side-effects of conscience. He had looked at the boy, into his smooth face, his jeering dark eyes, and marvelled. This was human flesh, each flake precious and delicate, encasing a human mind: but a mind which could not conceive in emotional terms of another mind, of another shrinking and tremulous flesh. Sammy was one thing: all human beings were, to him, something of another order. You squashed a fly, not considering whether or not it could feel pain — if asked, you would say you supposed it couldn't — but it was not a thing you thought about. Now, *fear* was something different: *fear* you understood. If you were Sammy and something frightened you,

you kicked it to death, trampled on it, stamped it into sludge, swilled it down the gutter. For it was intolerable to Sammy to be frightened: no one had a right to frighten him: anyone, or anything, who did so was bad and must be obliterated.

Setter had tried with Sammy; he had worked on him. He had done his best to discover whether, in fact, the boy had the faintest idea of the nature of remorse. He knew that as a rule murderers don't. The remorse of the murderer is a literary invention, with Dostoievski as the worst misleader. It is an error Dickens never made — see Fagin, see Jonas Chuzzlewit. Terror for themselves, yes: but of conscience, no trace. Study Jonas carefully. Did he care for the tender, flaky, crayfish flesh of Tigg, stamped into the leaf-mould of the forest? Jonas cared only for himself and his own danger, was afraid of nothing but to be found out.

Not that Setter had cared whether Sammy, as such, felt remorse. He was not engaged in a clinical study. Sammy would never appear as 'S' in a case history. But Setter believed that if such an emotion were an utter stranger to this boy, then this boy would kill again.

There was something infinitely rare, infinitely marvellous, to Setter about the discovery of a murderer. It was as though he held between his hands a plant hitherto unknown to botanists, or a scrap of paper, brittle as ash, with Shakespeare's signature upon it. An unimaginable object: a murderer. In the form of a bright, blank, merciless, untroubled boy. The important thing was to find out just how untroubled that boy was, and to this he set himself.

He was not, as he had said, a 'dog-face': he distrusted psychologists except those working on the most formal levels, in clinics and hospitals, because he thought they knew too little. One shouldn't play hit-or-miss with human minds. Yet he was himself accomplished enough to extort a confession from

Sammy who, as he had calculated, would probably far rather be hanged than ignored. There had been nothing difficult about it: he had simply picked the boy up and then, conspicuously, dropped him.

I, as I have said, at first doubted that confession. Not so Setter. He had heard the voice behind it, seen the advance guard of the eyes, holding up their shields of glass. But he was not letting on. He wanted to know far, far more than he had been told. He wanted, for instance, to know whether Sammy ever dreamed.

Now it seems to me inconceivable that there are people who don't. I always have: and in colour. It infuriates me to be told that people dream in monochrome — colour is often the most important part of my dreams, the whole story turns on whether some object is red, or yellow, or green. I like dreaming, too, even dreaming bad dreams. When I was a child and had nightmares, I used to think afterwards what a lot of extraordinary things I'd seen that I wouldn't have seen at all, but for them; even if they were bad things, they were wonderful and strange, and I knew I should never find anything like them on earth. It seemed to me that I lived in two worlds, one by day and one by night: and if the second world had some nasty surprises, it had its beauties also. I would not give twopence to be the kind of person with only one world to live in. What poverty! What a thin sort of existence to look forward to, without the forests of the night and the multiplicity of their fauna!

Setter felt as I did. The more he looked at Sammy, who was dreamless, the more he marvelled and the more fearful he became. He longed to awaken Sammy to nightmares: by a single nightmare, just one, Sammy might have been saved.

However: no nightmares. No dreams. Meanwhile, Sammy was getting worn down, but not by conscience, not by the ayenbite of inwit, or anything fancy of that sort. He was being worn down through confrontation with what he thought to be sheer, rocklike disbelief. And this he could not bear. He had so little to offer anyone: no special talents, no exceptional looks. He had had to imagine the love of a girl, Hilde, that dream-girl earning eleven quid a week. He wanted desperately to attract Setter, not, of course, sexually, but intellectually. The great god Setter: what could one do to interest him? Why, be different! And what was the supreme way of being different? Sammy had exposed his supreme way.

And Setter had not seemed to listen.

# Chapter 32

*SETTER'S STORY* (4) *Contd.*

SETTER did listen, however, and he knew there was no hope. He believed Sammy was rotten from birth, like a baby with a built-in cancer. What he had done he would do again, given a shadow of a motive and a ninety-per-cent chance of getting away with it.

'It wasn't accident, it wasn't suicide,' he said to me, looking down into the eyes he had drawn in parchment-coloured beer fluff on the glass top of the table. 'I got rid of Sammy. There was nothing difficult about it.' His own eyes, at that moment, were opaque, the eyes of a clever child who has settled a problem in trigonometry. If you look into the eyes of the very clever, I think you will find that they are pretty pebbly: certainly breeds opacity, as well it might. At the end of all things is the stone, the certainly. But if you look into the eyes of the medium-clever, the hopefully-clever, the aspiring, then you will see clear waters in which all sorts of organisms may breed, all sorts of tiddlers become apparent, ripe for the jam-jar.

Setter had made up his mind round about the end of the year; yet had delayed putting the intention into practice because of his own inner doubt. Built into himself, as killing was built into Sammy, was the desire to give pain. All his adult life he had tried to put himself out of reach of the *opportunity* for doing so. He could not trust himself with scalpels, so he had let the instruments fall from his hands. Then he could not trust himself even to advise, lest he should be advising for cruelty's sake:

so he had thrown up the kind of career that would shortly have brought him to the top. He had given up wife, home, friends, future, order, cleanliness, tidiness, life itself. And here, by a dirty trick of fate, he felt himself (and he did feel it) required to kill.

'I told you, but you wouldn't believe me, that I took him away simply to give him a good time. Because I knew what had to happen to him. And because he couldn't help what he was, I wanted him to be happy first. That is all it was. There was nothing more to it than that.'

Sammy, he told me, had been in a pretty nervy state. If you wanted to drive somebody to drink, Setter said, all you had to do was to refuse to believe something he desperately wanted you to believe. Ever met a doctor, for example, who had a perfectly new line on rheumatism? Or a writer who had perfected a new style, out on its own, like nothing the world had ever seen? Try to disbelieve either of them, put in the one, small, single, qualifying remark, and see how popular you are. Yes, Sammy was jumpy. He might not dream, but neither did he sleep, or not much. So Setter had sent him off to his own doctor, on the N.H.S., with just that information. And the doctor had put Sammy on sodium amytal, one a night.

They had made their rounds of Paris, Sammy soothed by his green pills. The Louvre, the Cluny, Lamoureux Concerts, respectable *boîtes*, *bâteaux mouches*, the works. Nôtre Dame floodlit by night, a sculpture in cream cheese: Sammy's mouth open like an O. Then the return to London and the let-down, Setter too busy for meetings, never available on the telephone.

But he knew where Sammy went, what he did. He went out with his friends three nights in the week: to the local cinema, in solitude, on the fourth, usually on Thursday. One night last week, when Sammy came out from the pictures and had just begun to walk home, whom should he see but Setter.

'You looking for me, by any chance?' said Sammy, lofty, very much on his dignity.

No, said Setter, he wasn't, and it was like Sammy's damned cheek to think so. He, Setter, had a friend living in Clapham Old Town, he had just been to see him. He enquired after Sammy's nerves.

They were all right.

But Sammy still looked jumpy. Did he sleep O.K?

So-so. He snuffled. He thought he had a cold coming.

Wake in the night?

'I put on the light and read.'

'How often?'

'Most nights.'

'What do you read?'

'All sorts of things.'

What was he reading at the moment?

Sammy's face gleamed. They were standing under a lamp, in the press of homegoing crowds. 'I got a good one, about German concentration camps. Makes you sick,' he added unctuously. He offered Setter a lickerish atrocity, his eyelids down. Lips like Sammy's could hardly bear to speak of such things. The words, at the ramparts of those lips, balked, halted, could scarcely be induced to scale them.

'Perhaps they had it coming to them,' said Setter.

'Well, they could have fought back! There were thousands of them. Makes you sick to think of them going to those ovens like a lot of sheep.'

'So it served them right?'

Sammy was silent. They turned into a side street.

'You ought to be sleeping better,' Setter said.

'I won't get much sleep tonight, anyhow.' Sammy was fretful. 'My nose is sore as hell all up at the back. Bet you I'll be streaming tomorrow.'

231

'I think we might fix that.'

'Marvels of modern science?' Sammy said, with a sneer.

'You wait here a moment, and don't go away.'

Setter went down an alley, to the Off Licence of a pub; there was still a quarter of an hour to closing time. Here he bought a quarter bottle of brandy. He could see his way now; he had been feeling for it; but Sammy's prospective cold had put the method into his hands.

He came back again. 'Put that in your pocket. How many of your green pills have you got left?'

'Five, six. He won't let me have many at a time. Don't trust me.'

'Quite right too,' Setter said, distraitly. He prescribed. Sammy was to go straight on up to bed, drink no more than four-fifths of the bottle — 'and not more, if you don't want to be in trouble' — take the remainder of his pills. 'A bit drastic, but it should work. If you're all right again by tomorrow night, sevenish, I'll take you out for a bit of supper. O.K.?'

Sammy looked radiant. So he was not, after all, forgotten! 'If I can make it,' he said, prideful to the last.

'And don't swill the whole lot, mind! Four-fifths.'

Sammy said he wouldn't. He did precisely as Setter had told him, and in the morning he was dead.

Earth dipped under me. I looked at Setter, now six times the size of a man, alienated from me, his face calm behind a shell of glass.

He stared at me, lightless, unblinking. His huge hands moved one over the other, peaceful as the parchment hands of a donor in a painting.

All I could think of, occluding for the moment everything else, was the monstrous risk he had taken.

'What risk? There wasn't much.'

Suppose, I suggested, Sammy had said something to his parents, about the meeting, the advice.

'They're always in bed before he gets in. They're early people.'

'He might not have taken the stuff. He might have got suspicious.'

'You give a lump of sugar to a horse. If it trusts you, it takes it.'

He stuck his hands suddenly into his pockets, driving them hard down. He repeated, almost soundlessly, 'If it trusts you.' He shut his eyes for a second and his mouth hardened, as if he were braced to bear shock. 'It takes the lump of sugar.'

'Someone might have seen the two of you together.'

He opened his eyes, resumed, refreshed, his stare. 'Might have. But no one did.'

There was only one question to ask, but I dared not ask it.

He said, 'I'm seeing Emily tonight. She's coming to say goodbye.'

My thoughts, released from the instant, anaesthetic contemplation of risks taken, of the pure mechanics of what he had done, began to grasp what it was that he had really told me. For a moment I didn't believe one word of it. I believed him no more than I had believed Sammy's tale. It was embarrassing — it was more than embarrassing, shameful — to sit at this beer-slopped table in this featureless pub being fed with a pack of romantic lies by a man who was playing on me some repellent practical joke.

"The only thing that did surprise me,' said Setter, 'was that they brought in accidental death. I suppose they wanted to spare the parents.'

'I must be getting back,' I said, and I never heard anything sound feebler, less apposite. Yet I knew also the strength of the man who has the courage of sane convictions. For some reason I now felt much taller than Setter, taller by a head, far above him, looking down upon absurdity.

Framing the mirror behind the bar ran a string of coloured lights, sapphire, orange and crimson, the sort of colours my aunt used to have in an *art nouveau* pattern in the panels of her front door. I counted them, or tried to, but they ran away from the finger of my thoughts and I found myself chasing them, round and round and round.

Setter answered the question I hadn't asked.

'There was no pleasure in it.'

The lamps stopped racing. I felt a thunderous peace descend. My head was quiet. It was all right, then, all right for him. For he might have been trapped into the cruelty he had fought away from all his life, he might have had upon his conscience the last monstrous, dirty, damning joy. He had no joy in him, not even the joy of the judge, the executioner. He had no more joy in him than the vet. when he puts a dog to sleep.

But what about the error of judgement? Would one be made? This would be on the records, a material fact, a willed action. Setter's factually-minded God, in whom he did not believe, would at least find a significant entry in the books. Would it be better for Setter to be damned for this, an action committed without joy, or to be shoved in among the Elect with the horrors of his heart undetected, because his fingers had never played them out or his lips expressed them?

He got up. 'Let's go home.'

The time of the heavy traffic was past. There was room in the tube to sit down. Since there was nothing more to say, we shared the *Evening Standard*. He had the front pages and the sports columns, I had the human interest and the gossip in the middle. It was curiously absorbing. I followed the fortunes of a deb from her elopement to her extradition by a forceful and level-headed papa. Setter got off the train at Piccadilly Circus and I never saw him again.

# Chapter 33

WHEN I told the story to Jenny she hardly listened. She burst out at me, 'Why did he go *sneaking to you*? Why couldn't he have come here?'

She burst into a tirade about the freemasonry of men, how irritated they were by women, the lengths they would go to to keep them out of all the interesting things. (I wouldn't say there was absolutely nothing in all this, but it makes men dislike women on a very sharp conscious level when women raise the point, which is why things will always be much as they are now.) I was jealous of Setter, probably I'd met him somewhere else at my own suggestion, I was mean, callous, paltry, deceitful——

'Don't make me suffer because of your Ma all my life,' I said.

It checked her. She looked at me with wild, calm eyes, if eyes can be both wild and calm: I know animals' eyes can.

'I don't know what you mean.'

I didn't enlighten her. I think she knew, all right, what was the flash-point of her guilt, and where it had led us. Instead, I reiterated, rather slowly, the facts: that Sammy had killed Aggie Engbeck, and that Setter had killed Sammy.

'Oh, I don't believe it!' She was on her feet now before the glass, pinning her hair and tying a ribbon round the little bun. 'If Bill told you that, he's mad. In fact, *I* think that's just what he is. Do you remember that dotty club? How he had them all around him and then let them down, the Rose Garden, the poor old woman who could hardly see? I'll get the truth out of him!'

'You won't,' I said, 'he's gone.'

'Gone?'

She turned round slowly, self-consciously graceful in her movements, hands still to her shapely little head.

'On holiday. He'll be away a long time.'

She began to laugh at me. What a silly ass I was, being taken in by cock and bull stories! She blushed for me. Honestly she did. She blushed brightly.

Why, I asked her, did she think Sammy should commit suicide? Or even make mistakes? He had loved life, at least, his own.

Oh, she didn't know, it was no use asking her. Adolescents were a different kind of animal. They killed themselves before examinations, sometimes they tied themselves up and hanged themselves by accident. How could she tell what was at the back of Sammy's messy little mind? It was far out of the range of her experience.

She had an inspiration. That girl! The one he had talked so much about. Perhaps she had thrown him over. They ought to have called her at the inquest, that would have been more like it.

She was refusing to face the great indecency: that we had both touched the most profound *romantic* horror of life. People didn't touch such things. (Only judges, doctors, warders, chaplains, hangmen.) She refused to face it because she could not envisage, even by an emotional leap, the sudden locking of the key of thought into the lock of the deed. 'Of course he's off his head,' said Jenny, scornfully at first, then with an air of tender, astonished satisfaction. She knew at last why he had rejected her: it was the one reason it was possible for her to accept and endure. Setter was insane. The idea excited her, made her euphoric. Not for Jenny, as for Malpass, the fear of dying before all the answers had been given to all the problems. A great conclusive answer had just dropped into her lap, miraculous as a bird fallen from the sky. She stroked its easeful softness with her thought, her pulse-rate lessened, the colour moderated in her throat. She came behind me and put her arms round my neck, crossing her hands limply over my chest.

'So don't, please don't, dear, kind, patient Vic, whom I treat so very badly, whom I really love all the time — he knows, he knows, doesn't he? — don't bring that absurd story up again, because I cannot, I will not, bear it.' Then she knelt at my side, hugged me, rested her head on my knees. She looked wonderfully young. She smelled of honey.

That night Malpass telephoned. 'Setter told me. He said I was to tell you he had.'

I asked him if there was anything to be done.

'No. Nothing at all. And the less we talk about it the better.'

I said nothing of this to Jenny.

A week later the hedge began to bud, throwing out into the sunshine the gold and silver paper of its earliest leaves. How long since Sandra and the baby had walked through it?

I had heard something of Sandra. She had been chosen by a film director for a part in a film he meant to make in Rome. I wondered how on earth he meant to teach her the King's English.

Gold and silver first. Then yellowly greening over. That was our beautiful, our sentimental hedge. The almond blossom in the garden across the way was almost done, the pink singed with brown, the flowers like pralines. Some of those evenings of early spring were so mild that we were actually able to take deckchairs on to our little square of front lawn. We heard from nobody: the world seemed to have forgotten us, and a bloody good thing too. We hadn't wanted strong drama, Jenny and I, we had never asked for it. Peaceful, we cultivated our garden metaphorically and literally. Jenny settled down to read *War and Peace*.

My only trouble was a sharp and inexplicable pain which I felt occasionally on the wrong side of my navel, not, I mean, on the appendix side. Jenny refused to pay any attention to this, saying it was only indigestion. She may have been right. I cut down on fats and highly-spiced food.

Soon, however, Emily looked us up again. She and Bernard had been in Spain, near Torre Molinos, they would love to see us.

So we visited them for the first time in their new flat, which was in Mount Street. It was very tasteful and ordinary, just a touch of ostentation about the flowers. Emily looked as much at home there as she had been when she lived with Setter. Bernard was pleasant, amusing, empty. I wondered why he didn't bore her stiff.

She hadn't, she told us, heard from Setter, not a word. 'I do hope the old thing's all right.'

'I hope so too,' said Bernard, his brow wrinkling with solicitude, 'it would comfort Emily to have a line, even on a postcard. One doesn't even know how he manages to live.'

'Oh come,' she said, putting her arm through his in appreciation of his magnanimity, 'Bill had quite a lot put away. And Roger still gets his allowance.'

'I do wish,' said Bernard anxiously, 'that he wouldn't strain himself over that. We can look after Roger perfectly well, and Bill is going to need the money some day. It worries me, I can tell you.' Bill might have been his brother, not his wife's cuckolded husband.

'The poor old thing!' she exclaimed. She bounced round to Jenny and me, beating her fists on her knees. 'Can you beat it? He had everything ahead of him, everything. To give it all up——'

Jenny smiled as if she knew the secret.

238

'Oh well,' said Emily, subsiding, 'if people must be odd, one can only say they have a perfect right to be. It's part of democracy.' Her glance caught Jenny's and held it, eyes upon one double string; it was a mysterious moment. I felt it was and so did Bernard, who cleared his throat and suggested playing some flamenco records which they had brought back with them. These boring records and some boring colour films of Bernard and Emily like seals on rocks and like tourists in flower-markets, holding hands with the infant population, concluded a boring evening. I had time to worry about my stomach, and wonder why Jenny refused to take any notice.

Next week, however, the two women went out together, and Jenny didn't get back till late. When she came in, she had an air of subdued excitement, of an inner disturbance not totally unpleasant. I asked her what had happened.

'Oh, nothing.' She set her lips.

I didn't press her.

We had been in bed about an hour after making love. I wasn't asleep, and I knew she wasn't.

She spoke to me. 'Do you want to hear something about your friend Setter?'

'Yes.'

'I don't know if I ought to tell you. Emily only meant it for me.'

'Only you can know if you ought,' I said. This had always been the best way to get things out of her.

There was a long silence and a pretence of sleep. Then the bed groaned and dipped as she turned over my way. I put my arms round her. There was never much light in our room. Jenny hated to be wakened by the morning sun, so the curtains were double-lined, which made the place airless. They weren't quite drawn, however, so I could see a strip of moonlight printed on a wall, picking out the bevel of the wardrobe glass. A stuffy night in spring, Jenny moist with the night sweats. I could smell the ozone of love, still fresh.

'What, then?'

She told me about Emily's last meeting with Setter. I am calling it:

## EMILY'S STORY

She went to see Setter, bearing him the present of herself, of her lovingkindness, like a cornucopia brimming over with the most select greengrocery. She had never felt more tender to him, not in the whole of their life together: but naturally, with no sex in it. She rejoiced that they could meet so, say goodbye so, as brother and sister, perhaps as kissing-cousins (I believe this is an American phrase, though I never heard an American use it).

It was a warmish, drizzly night, the sort of night which gives Pimlico a curious enticement. The rays from the street lamps speckled the dusk with gold, the pub on the corner glowed like a rajah's ruby. In this early glow, the tattered and scabrous paintwork on the porticos looked like a covering of dead leaves, ivy, or virginia creeper, brittle at the end of autumn. There was a hush about, since few people were in the streets. (Emily gave Jenny a somewhat lyrical description, upon which I have improved.)

There were six names listed beside respective bell pulls on the door of Setter's house. His was the third from the bottom, i.e., first floor up. There were lights in the basement flat, the thud and yowl of a rowdy party. Emily looked up at Setter's window: the curtains were drawn, but a chink of yellow showed along the tops of them. He was there, all right.

He was a long time letting her in.

When he did come he said, 'Sorry, I was in the loo.'

She went upstairs into his dinginess, his pigmuddle, made worse now by a shin-barking clutter of half-finished packing. He had two rooms, kitchenette and bath. The paintwork was dark brown, but the walls had been painted in a manner the owner considered 'Contemporary', i.e., one wall puce, three walls pale green. On the puce wall, over the fireplace, was a notably un-Contemporary print, that one of Lady Butler's with soldiers walking round and round in the slush. There was a small electric fire burning in front of the grate. The grate itself was full of empty cigarette packets, match boxes, spent matches, scrumpled newspaper, the whole heap smothered in cigarette-ash. Not that Setter hadn't tried to make things nice for the occasion. There was a clean cloth on top of the one occasional table, and on it gin, lime juice, two glasses.

'Well, well,' said Emily. She gave him an airy hug and a kiss, which he accepted. 'So this is where you lurk.' She tried not to look shocked, even tried not to feel pity for him, since she believed he would have hated it.

He told her to make herself a drink. He cleared a space for them both on the littered divan.

'It's done me well enough,' he said.

He asked her politely about Bernard, about Roger.

'Look here, where are you *going*?' she said, in that spontaneous, forcing voice one uses in the hope of eliciting a snap response.

'I don't know yet.'

'How long for?'

'That either.'

'I won't question you,' said Emily generously. She put her arm through his. 'We did have some good times, didn't we?'

'They are the ones I can't remember.' This seemed to her so churlish that she felt an upsurge of anger. But she controlled it.

She owed it to him, to herself, to get him out of this mood. Of course he could remember, she said. And nothing which had happened——

'Can spoil those beautiful memories,' said Setter unpleasantly.

She told him sharply that she had come to be nice: if he wasn't going to be nice to her, she would say goodbye to him and go. After all, in view of what had happened at their last meeting, it was sporting of her to risk coming at all.

'Oh, you were all right,' he said, 'you could look after yourself!'

'But I was sorry about that, truly I was.'

'*Opéra bouffe*,' said Setter. He went red.

'You are never going to tell me why you've spoiled so much for yourself.'

'You said you weren't going to question me.'

'That was a statement, not a question.'

'No. You just put in a full stop, but you were questioning me.'

Setter's landlady liked to do things on the cheap. There was a ceiling bowl and a reading lamp, but the bulbs in both were of low voltage and the room swam in a fishy green light. Emily felt suddenly so depressed that for a moment she nearly lost all her good intentions, nearly got up, said goodbye and went. She felt their failure, his and hers also, though hers seemed the lesser of the two: what she had done might have been bad, but at least it had the merit of being sane. People committed adultery all the time, quite nice people, especially when they were lonely, as she had been. For (she insisted to Jenny) she had been lonely with him, lonely enough to die. She had felt he had long lost any need for her. If he had needed her, he would have done things to please her, wouldn't he? Such as not selling the house she loved so much, the lovely house in Suffolk, with the orange pane in the garden door that flared up in the

sun every fine morning, and made the morning seem fine even
when it was wet and dark. And she had been quite open about
seeing Bernard, after all: if Setter had cared about her, would
he have let it go on? She had always thought he knew and
hadn't cared. Perhaps if he had cared, if he had done her the
*honour* of caring, things might have been very different. But
after all, even she had her pride——

He put out his hand and gripped hers very hard.

'Anything *I've* done wrong,' she said, unable to keep stiff-
ness from her voice, 'I am truly sorry for.'

'Thanks,' said Setter, and withdrew the hand.

She felt offended, since he said nothing more. She lit a
cigarette and smoked some of it. 'What about you? Is there
nothing you're sorry for?'

'I've done nothing against you,' he said. 'You might
help me finish packing.'

She was a mild woman: she rarely felt the giddiness of pure
rage. But this time she did. She jumped up: she nearly hit him.
He never budged. She found herself launched upon the tale
of his misdeeds, feeling the words flowing in the exhilarating
rush that sustains the mob orator: she could have swayed
masses, she could have brought down empires.

'Oh, shut up,' said Setter. 'There's only one thing of the
slightest importance.'

She was brought to a halt. The glory of righteousness
drained out of her, the gift of tongues departed. 'What's
that?'

'What we've done to our son.'

'Don't blame me! He was the same long before we split
up——'

'It happened well before that. Years.'

'Well? What do you think it was? Solve the mystery,' said
Emily. 'I'll be grateful.'

'When he was young I loved you too much for his good,' he said. 'Time spent with him was time spent away from you. I know that now. He always knew it.'

'Didn't he have *my* time?'

'What you could spare.'

'Spare from what? Go on, tell me, from what?'

'Your own devices,' said Setter. 'I never knew what they were. Your own friends. Who were they? You never told me. I never asked.'

She was desolate. She didn't know either. She found it hard to imagine what those early years of their marriage had been like, or, at least, to remember her husband and son being part of them.

('Was I selfish, Jenny?' Emily had said. 'I don't think so. I always thought we were quite all right, all three of us. I thought they enjoyed life as I did. *You* know, not huge emotions, not big scenes, just being comfortable.')

Rising, she began to fold a pile of crumpled shirts, to untangle a snarl of socks and ties. None of his clothes looked clean. She was afraid she was going to cry. He watched her, looking grateful. It took quite a long time. When the last case was packed and a new address written over the old labels (an hotel in the rue Dupuytren) she gave herself another drink.

'Thanks, darling,' Setter said.

Her legs were trembling, as if she had walked too far, or come through a crisis. 'Is there anything else I can do for you?'

'Oh yes. You can come to bed with me. It will be the last time, I promise you.'

He lifted her to her feet. His small, brilliant eyes stared into hers. She smelled his familiar flesh. She could not speak.

'It's a bit scruffy,' he said, 'but clean. It's not so bad.'

They went into his bedroom. The double bed hadn't been

made up since he got out of it that morning. There was nothing in the room but a cheap wardrobe, dressing-chest, chair. Dingy walls with a faded flower pattern. Print of the *Mona Lisa*. It was, as he had said, clean.

She undressed and he lay beside her, at first not moving, lying on his face, one arm flung out across her body.

How had she felt then? Without feeling of any sort except to comfort, except to please. For the last time; to please. A touch of vainglory, perhaps, that she should do so much: Saint Emily. She had forgotten how much bodily pleasure he had always given her; she did not look forward even to that. And when he took her she felt none at all, only a deep joy in his joy, a joy in her own cleverness that she could pretend, well enough to deceive him, that he had never given her so much pleasure before.

Afterwards, he slept for a little: perhaps no longer than half an hour. She lay peacefully at his side, surprised to find herself without thoughts, except for thoughts of a fragmented nature, about tomorrow's dinner, a green dress in a shop, a girl in a book she was reading, the last holiday with her father on the coast of Maine. She had just started to worry a little because she thought it must be getting late, when he woke. He looked at his watch. 'Only ten past ten.'

'But I've got to go.'

'Yes, of course. Thanks, Emmy.'

She got up and dressed. He left her alone while she did so.

When she came into the sitting-room he was in shirt and trousers, smoking, on his haunches by the fire. 'I'll get you a taxi,' he said.

'No, don't. There will be one on the rank.' She hesitated, not knowing what to say. 'Come back soon.'

'Not soon. Goodbye, Emmy.'

He did not get up. She kissed the top of his head.

'Thanks,' he said again.

She hesitated for a second or two. Then, as he would not look at her, there seemed to be nothing more for her to do. She went out into the streets, dry now, but still smelling of rain. The pub glowed steadily on. She did not have to walk as far as the rank, because she caught a cruising cab. She was home long before Bernard, in bed, and asleep.

# Chapter 34

AT the beginning of May I was really ill, startling Jenny
out of her wits, making her laugh (I felt, even in the
middle of my own discomfort, my own anxiety) on the
other side of her face. As it turned out, it was nothing to do
with the pain in my stomach. I went to the Oval to watch
cricket and caught cold. (It was a beastly day.) The cold
turned to pneumonia and then I got pleurisy. At first I had
quite a struggle with Jenny before she would call the doctor —
or, come to that, before she would even let me have the thermometer to take my own temperature: she just thought I was
'up to my old tricks' again. I was in bed for three weeks, and
lumbering miserably about the house for another three after
that. I never once pointed out to her how wrong she had been;
she looked remorseful enough without my rubbing it in. There
had, of course, never been the least question of my dying; still
she wasn't to know that, and I certainly wasn't. We were both
pretty badly shaken.

Yet, as soon as I was well enough to go back to the office,
Jenny observed that it was a dreadful nuisance, when you came
to think of it; now I should never feel any confidence in her
again, which meant that I should grow all the more attached to
my aches and pains, and be much more unhappy in consequence.

'No, I won't,' I said.

'Anyone,' said Jenny, 'can be wrong once. But remember
that *on all other occasions* I have been right.'

Oddly enough, I have worried less about my health since
that time. When you really have been ill, you have a pretty

247

clear idea of what illness is like and you come to disregard a good many of the minor creaks and pinches. So it is with me, anyway.

We saw a fair amount of Emily who, during my stay in hospital, had sent me bunches of the largest, blackest, most expensive, most tasteless grapes I have been confronted with. 'Seems a pity to eat them,' one of the nurses said. It was, I agreed, a pity, and I didn't.

Emily's life these days seemed to me not unlike those grapes, on the outside smooth, rich and bloomy, under the skin green, mauve, washed out, watery and without flavour. But I may have been wrong. Anyway, I am sure it was the kind of existence which pleased her best.

To look at Jenny and me, you would not have supposed that Setter's life had ever touched ours. We spoke of him occasionally, but only as of an eccentric friend long lost to us. We mused on his oddities, on the basic absurdity of his self-struggles, of his failure, failure with himself and with others. What a waste of a life! When you came to think of it, what pusillanimity! Jenny was particularly scornful of that. We didn't touch on the Sammy side of it at all. We had pushed it down out of sight, in all its crapulous absurdity, its monstrous indecency. Anyway, we could no longer believe in it. '*People don't do such things,*' we assured each other, silently, speaking comfortingly soul to soul.

As the year went on, we stopped expecting to hear from Setter, or about him. He had simply walked away into the maze of the earth, and wasn't coming back.

Even that seemed to us miraculous: *could* a man, in this day and age, just walk off and disappear? But why not? There was nothing to stop him. Since the days of the identity card, no man was forced to register his address. 'He'll just come walking in, one of these days,' said Emily, 'of course he will.' But she looked uneasy.

248

## An Error of Judgement

One morning Jenny spotted an advertisement in *The Times*. A firm of solicitors requested Dr. William Setter to get in touch with them, since they had news to his advantage. She telephoned Emily, who admitted being behind it. 'I made them put it in.'

'But what *is* to his advantage?'

His sister, Emily said, had just died, leaving him a couple of hundred pounds and a wine cooler. 'It isn't much of an advantage, but one has to admit it's some. Anyway, I want to flush him from coverts.'

Jenny asked why.

'You can't let so much of your life disappear quite so lightly,' Emily said, with some stateliness. 'I *think* we shall hear from him now.'

But Setter was not to be flushed.

In the autumn Roger, who had been on holiday with friends on the Dalmatian coast, came back swearing he'd seen his father.

When Emily told me this, I said, 'Not in a sloop off Trieste.'

She looked uncomprehending. 'No. Just in a crowd. Roger gave him a yell, but the man went off and he lost sight of him. I don't expect it was Bill at all.'

'I don't expect it was, either,' I said.

This was one of those crisis years which, since the end of the war, have made people nervy and ruined their summer holidays. It is almost impossible, of course, to contemplate steadily and with full seriousness the mass murder of us all, and of course I don't; but I know that there must be people, old ones, edgy ones, neurotic ones, who are living out their lives in a kind of cosmic nightmare. It gets on my nerves sometimes, of course, as it does on the nerves of us all. Yet when I am in this kind of state I have to keep to it myself, since I am never quite sure that anyone else shares it. Perhaps there is something I miss, perhaps there was some significant line in somebody's speech or statement, or leader article, which, if I understood it, would give me quite a different perspective on the whole affair. After all, people don't *look* any different. The sun shines: girls in the parks wear sun-suits: a man throws a ball to a dog: people try on shoes. Yet I want to go up on a high mountain with a super megaphone and scream down at every statesman, general, politician, Oh, for Christ's sake, sit down and shut up! My own fears push me into infantile fantasies of this kind. Jenny says she often feels the same, has the same Messianic delusions — i.e., she would only have to buttonhole the leaders of the great powers, put the matter to them *simply* and in *human terms*, and they would say to her, opening wondering eyes like daisies dew-washed as dawn, 'Why, of course, Jenny! Now at last we see the point. How could we have been so blind? We shall put matters right at once and nobody will ever have to worry again.'

It seems to me remarkable, therefore, that in such a world, where millions of men might die by a conscious decision of men, human beings like Setter should be obsessed by killing in microcosm. I don't know if, in representing this aspect of mankind, he makes it look the more crazy or the more creditable. Not that he could really represent anyone but himself. 'Thou shalt not kill, so I will kill you in order to see that you don't,' is a principle not commonly left to the individual, but only to the law. His could be a sort of lynch-law, the dirtiest kind of law there is; but can one man lynch, without a mob?

Take the old Hiroshima excuse: 'We had to kill them to save our own boys.' What was Setter saying? 'I had to kill X (Sammy) to save a possible Y.' I don't like either of those arguments. But I am not persuaded that Setter was a bad man. I cannot forget the good time he gave Sammy in Paris, intending nothing more than to present him with happiness, because so little of his life was left.

A week or so ago, I woke in the night to find the bedside lamp on and Jenny sitting up in the sheets, looking thoughtfully down at me.

'What's the matter,' I said, 'can't you sleep?'

'I thought you were awake, as a matter of fact. You said something.'

'I wasn't awake. I was flat out.'

She apologised, but made no move to put out the light again. I looked up into her grave face, moist and pretty. Her hair was draggly and very soft; she was one of those women who are charming in bed and smell nice.

'What is it?'

'I want you to sit up too.'

I did. We sat together like, I thought, birds on a bough, looking about as intelligent as birds. My watch said half-past four.

She put her arm round me and I kissed her, feeling suddenly excited because, for the first time in God knows how long, I felt close to her. It was our word, 'close'. I hadn't used it lately, nor had she.

Then she told me solemnly that she was in love with me again. It had all come back. She had felt it happening for some little time, but had not dared to tell me until she was sure. It had been like a bad dream, our separation from each other, but it was over now. It made her ashamed to think how she had treated me: she thought she couldn't have been quite in her right mind. *She was in love!* With me! She gave me a brilliant, wonderful smile, full of honesty, full of happiness.

Well, I was glad and I told her so and we kissed again, and after a while turned out the light and lay snuggled together in the dark.

Of course, I didn't believe a word of it, because I do not think that love, once destroyed, ever returns. Affection may return, yes: but not love, not that particular unmanageable force which cannot be sought for in the first place, or wrenched back by any act of will once it is spent. I had managed to cut my losses, and pretty bitter ones they had been; they weren't going to be made good.

But I was glad for us both that Jenny meant what she had said, because if she went on believing she was in love with me it would be almost as good as if she really were so. It would make things easier for both of us, break down the remaining tensions, allow us to act, without self-consciousness, without stage-fright, at each other for the rest of our days. Really good acting becomes a kind of truth.

I was feeling pretty happy, really. I had a little brightly-coloured pre-dream, a rectangle of Mediterranean sea, yellow beach-umbrellas, orange roofs, a little boat with a red sail skipping across the bay. Jenny's breathing, for she had fallen asleep, was the breathing of the vivid and tender sea.

Since that night, things have gone well with us: it is as though some outside agency is at work to make things specially easy. Something is making things up to us, and so it damned well ought to.

For some reason, the garden-soil seems to be getting richer. Jenny is thinking of planting begonias next year. I tell her it will look far too like the factory, not a home from home but a works from works; she pays no attention. I suppose, after a time, I shan't notice them; after all, there are other things than begonias in this life.

THE END

PRINTED BY PURNELL AND SONS, LTD.
PAULTON (SOMERSET) AND LONDON

OXFORD

# MORE TWENTIETH-CENTURY CLASSICS

Details of a selection of Twentieth-Century Classics follow. A complete list of Oxford Paperbacks, including The World's Classics, OPUS, Past Masters, Oxford Authors, Oxford Shakespeare, and Oxford Paperback Reference, as well as Twentieth-Century Classics, is available from the General Publicity Department, Oxford University Press (JH), Walton Street, Oxford, OX2 6DP.

In the USA, complete lists are available from the Paperbacks Marketing Manager, Oxford University Press, 200 Madison Avenue, New York, NY 10016.

Oxford Paperbacks are available from all good bookshops. In case of difficulty, please order direct from Oxford University Press Bookshop, Freepost, 116 High Street, Oxford, OX1 4BR, enclosing full payment. Please add 10 per cent of published price for postage and packing.

# THE SMALL BACK ROOM

## Nigel Balchin

### Introduced by Benny Green

Sammy Rice is one of the 'back-room boys' of the Second World War. The small back room of the title may also be Sammy's own living quarters, where he tries to control a drinking habit, and lives with a woman he loves but won't marry for fear of imprisoning her in a life he sees being slowly eroded by the unreality of war.

As an account of the war experience, the book is realistic and unsettling, and as a study of a personality under stress, it reveals perennial truths. As Benny Green says, 'to the battle which Sammy Rice wages against himself no precise date can be attached. The struggle goes on.'

'His theme is of intense and irresistible interest.' *New Statesman*

# THE ROOT AND THE FLOWER

## L. H. Myers

### Introduced by Penelope Fitzgerald

Myers's great trilogy, is set in exotic sixteenth-century India and records a succession of dynastic struggles during the ruinous reign of Akbar the Great Mogul. It is an absorbing story of war, betrayal, intrigue, and political power, but Myers's ultimate interests lie with the spiritual strengths and weaknesses of his major characters. The book explores a multitude of discrepancies—for example between the vastness of the Indian plains and the intricacy of an ants' nest—and yet attempts subtly to balance them. Throughout the trilogy Myers persists in his aim to reconcile the near and the far. *The Root and the Flower* demonstrates both his determination and his elegance in doing so, and, it has been said, 'brought back the aspect of eternity to the English novel'.

# HIGH TABLE

*Joanna Cannan*

*Introduced by Anthony Quinton*

Theodore Fletcher is a bit of a misfit, but he *is* clever. So it hardly seems surprising that a boyhood devoted to study is followed by an academic career and, finally, by the Wardenship of an Oxford College. All seems secure and untroubled in his life, until a guilty secret from his past appears in the shape of a young man who might be his son. Joanna Cannan constructs her plot deftly and with considerable irony. No one writes better of academic life at Oxford.

'A plot of extraordinary delicacy, pathos, and irony.' *Observer*

# C

*Maurice Baring*

*Introduced by Emma Letley*

' "In this parcel," he said, "you will find a bundle of unsorted papers. You are not to open it till I die. They contain not the story but the materials for the story of C . . . I want you to write it as a novel, not as a biography, but write it you must." '

It is from C's personal effects, passed on by his dying friend, that C the novel is finally written; no ordinary novel, as Maurice Baring says, but one in which the truth of events and personalities is rigorously observed.

Throughout his short, unhappy life C is accustomed to hiding his true feelings. Belittled by his parents, misunderstood at Eton and Oxford, and out of place at the high society functions he is obliged to attend, C acquires a reputation for secrecy. It is only after his death that the details of his private life are discovered.

# IN ANOTHER COUNTRY

## John Bayley

### Introduced by A. N. Wilson

John Bayley's only novel explores the effect of 'the first cold winter of peace' on a group of British servicemen stationed in a small town on the Rhine. Some, like the ruthless Duncan Holt, use army life to further their own ends; while others, like the naïve Oliver Childers, must fight against their own personal defeat in the wake of national victory.

'now that you can't get "books from Boots" any more, and country lanes and democracy seem to be going the same way as "proper drains", there is every reason to savour an intelligence as extraordinary as John Bayley's, and a novel as good as this' A. N. Wilson

# TURBOTT WOLFE

## William Plomer

### Introduced by Laurens van der Post

When this novel first appeared in 1925 the wide critical appreciation it attracted in England was matched by the political controversy it caused in South Africa. It remains acutely relevant, and if, as Turbott Wolfe declares, 'Character is the determination to get one's own way', then history bears the marks of this book and testifies to the depth of its perception.

Plomer records the struggle of a few against the forces of prejudice and fear. The book is full of images of exploitation and atrocity. Yet it is also the love story of a man who finds beauty where others have seen only ugliness. The narrative, which never shrinks from witnessing the unforgivable, is also characterized by sensitivity and self-control, and in the end manages perhaps the most we are capable of: continuing bravery, the voice of individual affirmation.

# MR BELUNCLE

*V. S. Pritchett*

*Introduced by Walter Allen*

'At twelve o'clock Mr Beluncle's brown eyes looked up, moving together like a pair of love-birds—and who were they in love with but himself?'

The imposing figure of Mr Beluncle more than fills his world. Neither his home life in the London suburbs nor his failing furniture business can contain his fantasies. He speculates in imaginary businesses and prepares to move into smart new houses he cannot possibly afford. He spends profits he has not earned. His motto is 'Give Love'. Yet as Mr Beluncle's suits become more fashionable and expensive, his wife's dresses grow shabbier, his sons are morbid or foolish, and his mistress and business partner, Mrs Truslove, desperately tries to shake off her infatuation with him. Throughout Mr Beluncle steps grandly towards financial ruin. This is his novel, and by the grace and consummate art of V. S. Pritchett, a novel not only of laughter, but also of tears, and often both at once.


# THE ESSENTIAL G. K. CHESTERTON

*G. K. Chesterton*

## Introduced by P. J. Kavanagh

The extent to which G. K. Chesterton is still quoted by modern writers testifies to his outstanding importance in twentieth-century literature. In this selection from his work, P. J. Kavanagh fully explores the many sides to Chesterton's personality and writing. Chesterton the novelist is represented by a complete work, *The Man Who was Thursday,* and his poetic gift is displayed in a fine selection of verse. But the lion's share of the volume goes to Chesterton as essayist and journalist. Here we can enjoy his lively writings on the issues and debates of his day.

'Mr Kavanagh's selection is extremely rewarding.' John Gross, *Observer*

## BIRD ALONE

*Séan O'Faoláin*

### *Introduced by Benedict Kiely*

In late nineteenth-century Ireland Corney Crone grows up in a family marked by poverty, pride, and spoiled aspirations. The recurring theme in his own life is the Faustian one of solitude, present in the private dreams of his boyhood and the insistent independence of his manhood. In old age the note of loneliness is more dominant: he is the 'bird alone', reliving the experiences of his youth, above all the secret love for his childhood sweetheart, which began in innocence and happiness, and ended in tragedy and shame.

Everywhere the book shows a poetic mastery of its material and a deep understanding of human nature. Corney Crone's private joys and sufferings belong to a common humanity, and as we read, his experiences become ours.

## FACIAL JUSTICE

*L. P. Hartley*

### *Introduced by Peter Quennell*

The world is recovering from its third great conflict when Jael 97 is obliged to present herself to the Ministry of Facial Justice. She is too physically attractive to pass unnoticed in a society that denies not only beauty, but individuality of any kind. She must exchange her 'alpha' face for a 'beta' one. But Jael has a sense of pride that won't be extinguished and in this fine novel Hartley explores how she becomes both instigator and victim of a new conflict.

'That Hartley was a fine writer with a strong moral sense had already been confirmed by his *Eustace and Hilda* trilogy . . . I hesitated to prefer *Facial Justice* to the trilogy, but, on points of imagination and originality of theme, it seems to win.' Anthony Burgess

# NEVER COME BACK

*John Mair*

*Introduced by Julian Symons*

Desmond Thane, hero of *Never Come Back*, is a cynical, heartless, vain, cowardly smart-alec with a flair for seductive charm, an inexhaustible capacity for deceit, and a knack of bending pokers in half. He is also a very desperate man, who finds himself pursued by the agents of a shadowy political organization bent on turning wartime uncertainty to their own advantage. Unwittingly, he becomes the prime obstacle to the success of their operations.

John Mair was one of the most promising literary figures of the 1930s, and a man whose charisma is still remembered. When first published in 1941, *Never Come Back* was immediately recognized as worthy of his promise. George Orwell saw in it the beginnings of a new kind of thriller: a powerful, politically astute burlesque. This is the first reissue for over forty years.

'Don't on any account miss *Never Come Back*—lively, exciting, and intelligent.' Maurice Richardson, *Observer*

'vigour and imagination, and humour as well as nastiness: a drink with a kick in it' *Sunday Times*


# THE VIOLINS OF SAINT-JACQUES

*Patrick Leigh Fermor*

*Epilogue by Simon Winchester*

*The Violins of Saint-Jacques*, originally published in 1953, is set in the Caribbean on an island of tropical luxury, European decadence, and romantic passion, and its story captures both the delicacy of high society entanglements and the unforeseen drama of forces beyond human control. Throughout, the writing is as beautiful and haunting as the sound of the violins which rises from the water and conceals the story's mystery.

'Beautiful is the adjective which comes uppermost ... outstanding descriptive powers.' John Betjeman

## THE DEFENCE

*Vladimir Nabokov*

*With a Foreword by the author*

This novel, by one of the twentieth century's most accomplished novelists, has attracted widespread critical acclaim but not the popular attention it deserves. All Nabokov's characteristic power and grace are much in evidence in this sad but sympathetic story of a Russian Grandmaster of chess who comes to perceive life as a great game of chess being played against him.

'Nabokov treats the theme of obsessive genius in a light comic vein with superb results.' *Birmingham Post*

'Endlessly fertile, overflowing with an energy and intelligence that converts whatever it touches to literary gold.' *Observer*

'marvellously executed, with wit and precision and a shining newness of vocabulary' *New Statesman*

'The style is dense and allusive, the intelligence vast. *Lolita* was a best seller because of its theme—a perverseness which lubricious readers gloated over while missing the beauty and intricacy of the writing. *The Defence*, less regarded, is more metaphysical and more typical of Nabokov's large talent.' Anthony Burgess

## THE DEATH OF VIRGIL

*Hermann Broch*

*Translated by Jean Starr Untermeyer*

*Introduced by Bernard Levin*

Broch's magnificent novel describes the poet Virgil's last hours as he questions the nature of art, and mourns the death of a civilization.

'One of the most representative and advanced works of our time . . . an astonishing performance.' Thomas Mann

'Broch is the greatest novelist European literature has produced since Joyce.' George Steiner

'One of our century's great novels.' *Sunday Times*

# THE NOTEBOOK OF MALTE LAURIDS BRIGGE

*Rainer Maria Rilke*

*Translated by John Linton*

*Introduced by Stephen Spender*

*The Notebook of Malte Laurids Brigge,* first published in 1910, is one of Rilke's few prose works. It has as its eponymous hero a young Danish poet, living in poverty in Paris, and is closely based on Rilke's bohemian years in the city at the turn of the century. In Malte's *Notebook* present and past intertwine. He is fascinated by squalor and observes the poor and sick of Paris, victims of fate like himself. Sickness intensifies his imagination, and he recreates the horrors of childhood, probing the many faces of death. It was in this novel that Rilke developed the precise, visual style which is largely associated with his writing.


# THE DESIRE AND PURSUIT OF THE WHOLE

*Frederick Rolfe*

*Introduction by A. J. A. Symons*

*New preface by Philip Healy*

'The desire and pursuit of the whole is called love' Plato

Grahame Greene described Frederick Rolfe—better known under his *nom de plume* of 'Baron Corvo'—'a writer of genius'. *The Desire and Pursuit of the Whole* is one of Rolfe's most autobiographical novels and was written in Venice in 1909, a year of tremendous hardship when he came close to starvation. It is a masterpiece of invective—a bitter attack against almost all those around him—yet it also celebrates life and love. One of the first English novels to extol homosexuality, it was considered too subversive and libellous to publish until long after Rolfe's death, but is now ranked among the finest novels of the early twentieth century.

# BEFORE THE BOMBARDMENT

## Osbert Sitwell

### Introduced by Victoria Glendinning

Written in 1926, *Before the Bombardment* was Osbert Sitwell's first novel, and also his favourite. It studies change, both social and psychological, when a world of obsolete values come under the bombardment of a new and harsher era. Set in an out-of-season seaside hotel, it portrays the loneliness of the few remaining guests with a masterly satiric humour.

'It is a book which you will never forget; a book which nobody else could have written; a book which will frighten you, yet hold you with the richness of its beauty and its wit.' Beverley Nichols, *Sketch*

'Few novels that I have read during the past year have given me so much pleasure . . . a nearly flawless piece of satirical writing.' Ralph Straus, *Bystander*


# ACADEMIC YEAR

## D. J. Enright

### Introduced by Anthony Thwaite

Three expatriate Englishmen teaching in Egypt towards the end of King Farouk's splendid and shabby reign live through the academic year of this novel. Apostles of an alien culture, they stand somewhere between the refined English aesthetics of Shelley and T. S. Eliot and the chaotic squalor of the Alexandrian slums, trying to balance the unattainable against the irredeemable, the demands of scholarship against the dictates of reality, while making a modest living for themselves. Their consequent adventures and misadventures are either hilarious or tragic, and sometimes both. And, we suspect, as near the truth as makes no difference.

'This first novel is funny, extremely funny; it is an Alexandrian *Lucky Jim* with much more humanity and much less smart lacquer.' *Daily Telegraph*